Clarissa's Warning

Clarissa's Warning

Canary Islands Mysteries Book 2

Isobel Blackthorn

For J.F. Olivares

Contents

Buying a Dream

Everyone has their price. It is my father's favourite saying. He is a used-car salesman turned property developer. I am neither of those things. But when I read in a local newspaper that the owner of the house of my dreams was intent on demolition I took swift action. I tossed sanity into the Jetstream and, in a single if complicated move, threw my all into saving that house.

In truth, not a house, it was nothing that could be called a home, the building – not much more than sections of stone wall and roof – holding on through its own tenacity, little left to brace against a relentless wind. For the ruin was located not among the folds of green in my home county of Essex, nor in any other quarter of bucolic pasture, but on a flat and dusty plain in desert dry Fuerteventura, an island I had been visiting each year for my annual holiday.

I wasn't entirely devoid of common sense. My ruin was situated in the inland town of Tiscamanita, a safe distance from beach-crazed revellers yet not so far off the beaten track as to be isolated and remote. The island was desolate enough without secreting myself away in one of its many barren and empty valleys. In a well-established village, I would have everything I required for a comfortable life, secure in the knowledge that there were others nearby if I needed them. As a single woman used to living in a bustling English town, one had to think of these things.

The troubles began the moment I decided to act. The former owner of my beloved ruin, the gentleman poised with his wrecking ball, had not been difficult to identify. His name was mentioned in the same newspaper article, the Fuerteventura journalist at pains to detail some of the recent ownership history. The various genealogical details meant nothing to me. I could read Spanish well enough—I've been learning for years—but I had no understanding of Spanish nobility, and I lacked a deep knowledge of Fuerteventura's colonial history. In the age of information technology, when business deals could be conducted remotely with a few mouse clicks and the odd signature here and there, nothing might have been simpler than purchasing a property overseas. There were websites talking prospective buyers through all the legal requirements, pitfalls and traps. Were it not for the fact that the possessor of my coveted dream home resided somewhere in mainland Spain and had he not been bent on using the property for whatever development aspirations he may have held dear, the purchase would have sailed through to completion in a few months.

The first complication was locating the owner's address. Entering the name in a few online searches revealed his business interests. With those scrawled in my notebook, I hired a lawyer to make the initial contact and establish my credentials: I, Claire Bennett of Colchester, a humble bank teller by profession until my fortunes turned on the numbers of a lottery ticket and I found myself astonishingly well-off.

Possessing all that wealth had taken possession of me, given me the will to leap, to take a chance. The greater part of me remained shocked I had the courage to go through with it.

Much to my chagrin, the owner, Señor Mateo Cejas, responded to my inquiry with a cool and firm refusal. The ruin was not for sale. Well, I knew that. The local government, in a fit of guilt over letting so many old buildings fall into ruin, had deemed the dwelling of special interest and already made an offer and it was declined. A full account of the frustrations of various officials and the local community were felt by the writer of the newspaper article who shared their view.

I suspected Señor Cejas opposed the building's transformation into yet another island museum, the restoration of a traditional windmill in Tiscamanita already serving the purpose. Or perhaps he had in mind the construction of holiday lets on the substantial parcel of land. It was the sort of plan my father, Herb Bennett of Bennett and Vine, would have had in mind. Demolish and rebuild. Sell at a premium to investors keen to rent out to holidaymakers; developers couldn't lose. They were an inexorable breed, prepared to play a long game. No doubt Cejas would have waited until the walls collapsed to rubble then the government would have given in and granted a demolition permit. That Cejas may have had a deeper, more complex reason for wanting to erase the structure didn't enter my mind.

My father tried to talk me out of my plans. He took to phoning me in the evenings when he knew I was watching Kevin McCloud, and he would go on and on about how there were a million better uses for my winnings. I would hold the phone away from my ear and let him rant until he ran out of advice.

I was immutable. I had passed by that ruin numerous times on my drives down the island's backroads and grown fascinated by it. I stopped one time and took a photo. Over the years, I had taken an abundance of photos of the ruins littering the island, but I had that one blown up and framed and it hung above the fireplace in my living room. I would stare at it every day, the image becoming for me a focus of wishful thinking, fervent at times, a potent symbol of longing for a different sort of life to the one I was stuck with. Until I won the lottery, that was the nature of my desire.

One very large deposit into my bank account and I was no longer stuck where I was. I had freedom and that freedom entered my life like a lightning bolt, destabilising me to my core. Suddenly, I couldn't imagine doing anything else with my life. Out of all the old dwellings falling to ruins on the island—a combination of lack of interest, strict restoration regulations, apathy and the ease of building with concrete blocks—I had chosen to save that one, like a child with her nose pressed to a sweet-shop cabinet, her pointy finger tapping the glass.

The stubborn Señor Cejas had not come across the likes of Claire Bennett, a woman fixated on a dream, a woman prepared to offer far in excess of the already overly inflated amount offered by the government. Initially, I offered the four hundred thousand Euros they had. It was declined. Four-fifty. Declined. I upped the offer in increments of fifty thousand, the tone of my lawyer's letters to Cejas increasing in indignation, his letters to me in exasperation, until at last we agreed on a sum. Six hundred thousand Euros and I had my grand design.

By the time I received word my offer had been accepted, I had already relinquished my position as clerk at the bank. I resigned the moment I knew I was rich and would never have to work again if I was sensible with my money. It was with considerable relief that I walked out of my branch for the last time, saying goodbye to the only career I had ever known.

For twenty years I had endured that cloistered environment, dealing on a daily basis with deposits and withdrawals, mortgages and loans, and with those incapable of managing their finances, one way or another. I preferred the pre-Internet days when we had to write in passbooks. Even in 2018, there was always one for whom internet banking was unfathomable. Often, they were old, but not always. Or there were those who used telephone banking but couldn't recall their customer reference number or pin, or the answers to any of the security questions they themselves had created, or even the balance in any of their accounts. They would come into the branch to get their account reinstated after it had been suspended. They would rant about that little injustice as though the bank had forced their hands beneath the teller screen and guillotined their fingertips, then they would go on to take an age making a number of simple transactions and I would imagine a steel plate descending with force to cut them off from breathing their disgusting germs through the Perspex.

When that type of customer surveyed the bank staff, they inevitably chose me, kindly Claire, to dump a potent mix of outrage and desperation on, and I would look at them coolly and explain that internet banking was really very easy and it would put them in control of their own banking and they wouldn't need to come out in all weathers and wait in a long queue to do what would take all of two minutes seated comfortably in the warm and the dry with a nice mug of cocoa. Many a time a disgruntled customer argued they were keeping me in a job and I responded inwardly with, I wish you wouldn't, because I didn't want the job. In fact, I loathed it. I had applied twenty years before only because back then it was the late 1990s and Blair was in power after years of economic recession and jobs were hard to come by and finance seemed to be the new god and I, like many others, believed things would only get better. I was fresh out of school and banking was the place to be. But not in Colchester.

Banking was never my dream. The world of finance was all about numbers, whereas I had achieved a good grade in A level English, which I found fascinating, History, which I adored, and General Studies, the latter due to my quiz loving father insisting I went with him every Wednesday to the local pub's trivia night. He would sink a couple of pints of Directors and I would sit on a lemonade and a packet of pork scratchings and I acquired a sizeable array of seemingly irrelevant facts. Highly relevant, they turned out to be, when it came to sitting the General Studies A level, a course cleverly designed to weed out the riff raff from achieving enough high scoring A levels for entry into the most prestigious universities.

When it came time for me to choose a career, my dad shunned all notions of university, especially in the humanities and the arts, describing those courses as dead ends.

There was no mother to argue my case. She passed away in the summer of 1985, when I was seven. I did what any obedient daughter would do in the absence of alternatives, I secured a job at the local bank. On my last day, I handed in my uniforms and went home via the Indian takeaway and the off licence to celebrate.

My house, a humble abode set halfway down a row of drab and poky terraced houses on Lucas Road, sold in a fortnight. As the settlement of the sale and the purchase went through I felt as though I had rubbed Aladdin's lamp and was about to be transported to paradise on a magic carpet.

The only other person with a vested interest in my life is Aunt Clarissa. She is my mother, Ingrid's older sister, a retired psychologist with a predilection for all things occult. She played a vital role in my upbringing after Ingrid died. A robust, no-nonsense woman with an affection for deep colours and aromatic smells, Aunt Clarissa exposed me over the years to Ouija, tarot, palmistry, enneagrams and her mainstay, astrology. I took little interest in any of it, for the occult seemed to me to be built up on spurious associations and make believe. Yet I could not deny that through it, my aunt was uncannily accurate when it came to seeing beneath the surface of people to their deeper, darker motives. I ascribed this talent to her training as a psychologist, but she insisted her perceptions were entirely the result of the occult. Not being one to argue, I took a passive, accepting role in her company, humouring her for the sake of our relationship. When I let her know I had bought a property on Fuerteventura and was about to move to the island, she invited herself over for morning coffee.

I was getting a tray of white chocolate and raspberry muffins out of the oven when the doorbell rang.

'Smells marvellous,' she said as we dodged by packing boxes on our way through to the kitchen, where she perched on a stool.

She was a stout and big-boned woman with thick and wiry hair framing a keen yet welcoming face. Those perspicacious eyes of hers followed me about the room as I attended to the muffins. Then she rummaged in her bag and extracted a sheet of paper protected by a plastic sleeve.

Without wasting much time on pleasantries, she said she had punched my birth details into an online astrology site that calculated relocation charts. The idea being, she said, that the angles of a birth chart can be adjusted to the new location. Indeed, the whole of a person's natal chart can be superimposed on the globe in a series of straight and wavy lines, providing an enormous source of fun and intrigue for astrologers and holidaymakers alike. Clarissa had explained it to me once before. She was a big fan. I was sceptical.

As I poured the coffee and put muffins on plates, Clarissa said, 'I am not sure how to tell you this, but I thought I'd better warn you. In fact, seeing this,' she pointed at my relocated chart, 'I wish you'd told me before you went ahead and bought the place. Has it all gone through?'

'It has.'

'You wouldn't consider selling? No, I suppose not. Silly question.'

Repressing my irritation, I stared at her inquiringly.

'Well, you see, the thing is,' and she pointed at the lines and glyphs, 'relocating to Fuerteventura puts Neptune on your Nadir.'

'And?'

'Well, Neptune also squares your relocated Ascendant. As if that were not caution enough, you have Moon and Saturn both in the twelfth house, the house of sorrows.'

'I meant, what does it all *mean*?'

She lifted her gaze to the ceiling. 'Typical Leo Moon.'

'I'm sorry I have a Leo Moon. Please, tell me.'

'The Neptune placement will leave you open to deception on the home front, at the very least. It really is one of the most difficult placements when it comes to buying a home. Unless you are opening a spiritual retreat, I suppose.'

'Do you really see me doing that?'

'Hardly, but anything is possible.' A glazed look appeared in her face as she went on. 'You'll be open to psychic impressions. With your Moon in the twelfth, this tendency is strengthened. And with Saturn there as well, you'll endure much isolation, aloneness, and you will be exposed to much fear. Beware of hidden enemies.'

I didn't reply. I maintained a bland face as I held back a burst of cynical laughter. Seeing my ears were closed, she didn't pursue it.

As we ate and drank she brought me up to date on her own adventures and little bits of gossip about her friends.

When the muffins were reduced to a few crumbs on our plates, she returned to the topic of my chart. 'I'm sorry to be the harbinger of doom. It might not turn out that bad. Especially if you're careful. On the positive side, you'll learn a lot.'

'Well, that's a comfort.'

'Just be aware that people are not always as they seem.'

'I wasn't born yesterday.'

'Oh, now you're offended.'

I fiddled with my cup. 'I know you mean well, but it's just that everyone is against me. Even the owner, Cejas.'

'What did he say?'

'First he wouldn't sell until I upped the price.' I left out by how much. 'Then he wrote to me personally advising me to do what he had planned and demolish.'

'I wonder why,' she said slowly.

'To build holiday lets, I expect.'

I went and put my empty plate on the draining board and stood with my back to the room to finish my coffee. I felt defensive, ganged up on, my grand design scorned. It was isolating; when I really needed support, none was forthcoming. Seeing my face when I turned, Clarissa slid off her stool and gave me a hug.

'Astrology is not the be all and end all. There really is no telling how it will all unfold. There are always other factors. Be positive. You are following your dream. Not many get a chance to do that.'

Buoyed by her sympathy, I described my renovation plans. I soon became animated and enthusiastic, and she said she could see I was acting on a noble impulse.

'I'll visit when it's done.'

'Not before?'

'I cannot abide building sites. Too unsettling.'

After she left, I continued with the packing and reflected back over her words. Even if she had warned me in time, I would never have put off a major life decision on the basis of an astrological coincidence. Besides, I was acting on my deep appreciation of the island and my desire to save one of its grand houses from complete ruin. And I wouldn't be upping and moving were it not for the lottery win. I didn't dare ask Clarissa the astrological significance of that stroke of luck. I didn't want to know what the stars had to say. My bank balance said enough.

Arrival

One early morning in March, I was seated in the departure lounge at Gatwick airport, all smug and pleased to be leaving the murk that was British weather. Dressed as though for an appointment in plain trousers and a loose-fitting blouse, I was squashed beside a rotund man garbed in shorts and a large white T-shirt, and a fake-tanned and wiry woman smelling strongly of coconut oil. She was decked out in a tight skirt barely reaching her mid-thigh and a matching, bosom-revealing top. Both characters were stark reminders of the holiday destination I was heading for. They seemed to know each other, too, and held a conversation across me. I leaned back further in my seat to let them have it, each informing the other of their preferred island locale, the man heading for Gran Tarajal, the woman Morro Jable – both seaside towns in the south. They were the sorts of holidaymakers I had never minded being amongst on previous flights. This time, I felt set apart. With my newly acquired wealth, I had no need to travel economy, but the only upmarket flights to Fuerteventura involved changing planes in Madrid. Still, considering the conditions the budget airlines forced passengers to endure, that hassle might be worth it.

The departure lounge, an enclosure with a deceptively large feel upon first entry, had become claustrophobic as passengers filled all the available seating and crowded around the perimeter of the space. The door to the walkway was closed and there was a marked absence of staff. People were getting restless. The woman next to me on my right was fidgety and the armpits of the man on my left, if my olfactory system was serving me well, had started to hum.

The room breathed a sigh when a woman in a neat suit appeared, and behind her a clean-cut man. They each took their position behind a computer screen and stared blankly into the crowd. People stood up and a queue formed. The woman received a phone call, made eye contact with the person at the front of the queue and boarding began. I sat back. I was assured of my spot on the plane and I decided the least amount of time spent squashed into a narrow, vinyl-covered affair with no leg room the better.

The flow stalled when a woman in ludicrously high heels tried to carry through a shoulder bag the size of a large suitcase. An argument broke out, the woman insisting she take it aboard, the young man insisting it go in the hold. Then others piped up, irritated, and the whole fiasco had the makings of a pub brawl. I felt sorry for the staff. Any job that meant dealing with the public came with its down side.

When the departure area—it could hardly be called a lounge—had all but emptied, I stood and took my place at the end of the queue.

I was travelling with a lightweight canvas tote containing my purse, keys, iPod and wireless headphones along with various official documents permitting me to reside in Fuerteventura, safely ensconced in a thick plastic wallet: my future.

It was hard to know whether the aisle or the window seat was the preferable option. It was certainly not the middle seat, as the airline was determined to cram in as many passengers on the aircraft as was humanly possible, basing the calculation on the general proportions of a slender child of ten. I had plumped for the aisle, despite having to lean aside whenever anyone went by.

How the carrier could justify packing holidaymakers into their aircraft in such a fashion was a matter for considerable speculation but most were happy with the cheap fares and were prepared to put up with it.

I buckled up and extracted my headphones. A four-and a half hour flight meant I could listen to a fair slap of my Cocteau Twins' playlist.

I hadn't always enjoyed the Cocteau Twins. I had never heard of them when my mother had died. Aunt Clarissa told me in my early teens that Ingrid used to listen to the band on her Walkman. She let slip in a wistful moment that a refrain of their single, 'Pearly Dewdrops' Drops', was the last thing my mother heard before she slipped from her mortal coil. Her Walkman had stopped as Elizabeth Fraser was halfway through the first verse.

My mother, Ingrid Wilkinson, was a lot like Aunt Clarissa. Although she had been much more than a dabbler when it came to the mystical side of life. The sisters came from a long line of psychics, scryers and occultists. One of their great grandfathers was a member of the Hermetic Order of the Golden Dawn.

One of their grandmothers a Theosophist. The Wilkinson's were of good social stock, among them could be found bankers and wealthy businessmen. How did a woman of Ingrid's background come to marry a used-car salesman from Clapton-on-Sea? The answer lay in my father's exceptional looks and natural magnetism coupled with a compatibility chart indicating they were soul mates. Besides, they met in the flower power years when idealism formed an illusory mist in the minds of the susceptible and my mother believed him when he told her he was an actor. Which, in a fashion, he was.

Clarissa never took to my dad. In a candid moment, she expressed her view that men like Herb Bennett belonged behind bars for all the conning they did. She had never been one to mince her words and had always held the conviction that he had railroaded me into a mediocre career in banking when I was capable of much, much more.

Ingrid had been the dreamy one in the family. Born in 1950, her musical tastes moved from The Beatles' White Album and trippy Grace Slick to the vocal acrobatics of the Cocteau Twins' Elizabeth Fraser via the likes of Tangerine Dream, favouring the electronic side of the 1980s' post-punk era. After her death, my dad was quick to clear out her things, but Aunt Clarissa stepped in to salvage mum's record collection, photos and a scrap book of musical memorabilia.

After discovering the close association between the band and my mother's passing, I wouldn't listen to the Cocteau Twins, even when my dream-pop loving friends at school were raving about the band's latest release. By then I had heard the track my mother had been enjoying at that fated moment and I rejected all the band's output on a point of principle, as though their music in its entirety had caused her demise. I went through my twenties and much of my thirties deaf as a post to the sounds emanating from the band. It took the thirtieth anniversary of my mother's passing to trigger an interest, thanks to a record store assistant who had chosen my entry to put on the offending track, 'Pearly Dewdrops' Drops'.

I stopped, and for the first time in my life actually listened, opening myself up and letting in the sound, and in seconds I was mesmerized. It was a kind of awakening. I used the birthday gift voucher given to me by my aunt and made up the rest to buy everything they had by the Cocteau Twins. Thirty years, and I was cured of my stubborn resistance and I felt closer to my mother than I had in all that time, as though she were with me, bobbing her head beside me, enthralled.

From that moment, the only band my mother and I both appreciated was the Cocteau Twins, and their music was the only way I felt connected to my mother.

The plane taxied then took off, and there I sat, content in my little world of sound, filled with anticipation. I had no idea what sort of life I was flying into.

Liz Fraser accompanied me all the way to Fuerteventura, the mellifluous tones of her voice on 'Aikea Guinea' soaring as the plane descended. We were coasting along the runway as the song ended and I turned off the iPod and returned the headphones to my tote.

I sat up straight with my bag on my lap, keen to disembark before the throng. The moment the plane came to a stop and others shifted and stood, I bolted to the nearest exit, fighting by men pulling cabin luggage from overhead compartments and women pointing their butts into the aisle as they attended to their bits and pieces on their seats.

The runway runs parallel to the ocean and the airport building runs with it. Designed to resemble a hanger, the building is elongated with an elegantly curved roof, walls of glass and lots of skylights. It is an open, light and airy space that gives an impression to the first-time visitor of a climate accustomed to endless sunshine.

Back among the throng, I collected my luggage—two suitcases of modest proportions—and checked in at the car hire booth.

Freedom greeted me as I crossed to the car park. I located my car sheltered under its own corrugated iron awning and I was away on that bright and sunny day in March, heading north on the highway to the capital, Puerto del Rosario, where I had booked an apartment for a month.

Everything appeared as it always had, but I felt markedly different, as though behind me the airport were folding itself up like a deck chair and carrying itself off into storage.

The drive was pleasant enough, the ocean coming into view, and then the capital, a distant sprawl of white cutting into the dry and rugged plain. To my left, on the high side of the highway, I passed a sprawl of unimaginative, cheek-by-jowl dwellings—developers, residents and holidaymakers alike enamoured with the ocean view and the beach, a short distance away. Although the trek with thongs and a towel was made ludicrously difficult by the obstructive presence of the highway. It seemed to me development on the island was in dire need of strict regulation and town planning. Otherwise every square inch of land would be given over to greed and the result would assault the senses.

I was familiar with Puerto del Rosario, enough to know the best areas to stay in. I chose to rent in the capital as the shops, banks, industrial areas, car yards and trades were all close to hand.

My apartment was in a side street off Avenida Juan de Bethencort, named after the Norman knight who had first conquered the islands. A supermarket was a few blocks away and the port itself was about a fifteen-minute stroll; downhill there meant uphill back so I would choose my moment. Calle Barcelona was one of the more established streets, but development in the city had been sporadic, and even here vacant blocks still waited to be filled.

The streets are narrow, the traffic one way, the pavements lacking room for street planting. Buildings are mostly two-storey. The combination hems in the citzenry, somewhat like the streets of Colchester. In all, there are too few trees, a paucity of green, although the council has taken the trouble to squeeze in some foliage here and there, demonstrating an awareness of the need for shade in such a hot and dry climate.

Taking in the city streets, I made a mental note to set to work establishing a proper garden on my property, a garden filled with natives and palm trees, whatever was hardy and drought and wind tolerant.

On impulse, I stocked up at a supermarket I passed, and arrived at my apartment in the middle of the afternoon, pulling up in the designated car space out front. The woman next door was expecting me.

Dolores must have seen me pull up for she came out and greeted me in the street, proffering my keys. Her Spanish was rapid and her accent thick but over the years of visiting the island I had come to anticipate the hurried flow, the nasal tone, the lack of fully enunciated consonants. A brief exchange and Dolores left me to ferry inside my suitcases and groceries.

The apartment was on the ground floor and comprised an open plan living room with a small kitchen tucked in a corner, a double bedroom and bathroom. The furnishings were basic and clean. Once the perishables were in the fridge, I sat back on the couch and put my feet up on the coffee table. I was about to take possession of my stately old ruin. The sense of triumph made me swell to twice my size.

I had no idea what lay ahead of me, other than what I had learned from Kevin McCloud. I had no idea what I would do with my life on the island either, now I was a lady of leisure, but I felt confident some activity would present itself. All that mattered to me was I had arrived and I was brimming with anticipation.

Gazing at the bare white walls of the apartment soon invoked a listless feeling and I was eager to drive to Tiscamanita. I downed a glass of orange juice and made a sandwich of the local cheese and ham and headed out the door.

Tiscamanita

There are five routes to Tiscamanita and I have taken all of them. The fastest involves heading due west from Puerto del Rosario and cutting a path through Casillas del Ángel before veering southward and on through Antigua. The road cuts a straight path across the flat and denuded coastal plain, making a crow's flight to the mountains that rise in the near distance. Away from the arterial road that connects the northern fishing village turned resort town of Corralejo, down to Puerto del Rosario and then on south to Morre Jable, Fuerteventura takes on its true nature, a vast empty expanse of treeless land, farmed in places, decorated with low mountain ranges that define the landscape and give it its beauty. Pleased to leave the city behind me, I was drawn by those barren ranges, their moulded shapes and delicate hues.

Most holidaymakers come for the beaches. Fuerteventura is an island of beaches. To appreciate the interior the beholder needs the artist's palette, an eye able to detect the soft tones of ochre and gold and sienna and pale umber, the hints of pink and copper and bronze. If the beholder thinks of all that as brown, they have no place being on the island. Unless the eye catches the nuances, the heart the fragility of the desert environment, then the observer will only see lifeless plains flanked by lifeless mountains, the sort of land many would conjure in parts of North Africa and the Middle East and deem fit for nothing. The ever-changing subtle colours was one of the features of the island that first captivated me. The traditional architecture a close second. After three holidays, my friends started to ask why I chose not to go somewhere else, after all there was the whole world to see, and I defended my decision by saying I was guaranteed heat and sunshine and, to satisfy their prejudices, gorgeous beaches.

Tiscamanita is a small farming village situated a little south of the island's epicentre, on a sloping plain surrounded by an array of interestingly shaped peaks. The views are three-sixty and splendid. The village itself is not much to speak of. Some effort has been taken with the main square and a few shops struggle on, the hinterland consisting of farmhouses dotted here and there, interspersed with patches of land and half-built houses sitting beside crumbling dry-stone walls or the remains of the walls of some ancient dwelling, evidence that folk still try to make a go of things while many have failed. It's always been a harsh place to be. The odd field is cultivated where once all were. For the most part Tiscamanita has abandoned the traditional way of life and who could blame the farmer for wanting things easier? How does anyone farm land that receives eight inches of rain a year at best? It is brutal.

Yet Tiscamanita was once wealthy by island standards, made rich on the belly juice of a beetle. The little sap sucker drank from the prickly pear and its insides turned a rich red hue, and when crushed, the beetle juice seeped into flesh and fabric making bright red stains that no doubt proved hard to remove. Those discoveries resulted in the late eighteenth century cochineal industry, and the poor farmers were faced with the uncomfortable task of cultivating fields of cactus, which they then had to fight their way through to pick off the beetles. The only positive on the farming side of things was the harvesters remained upright. On the other hand, I was about to discover that the bane of any farmer's life can be found in the bending. There was a lot of money in cochineal, and the bourgeoisie land owners had known it. Lucky devils. They were not the ones who got their hands pricked. Looking around as I drove through the town, evidence of the prickly pear was everywhere, but it didn't look like anyone was farming it, even for jam.

My heart swelled in my chest as I pulled up outside my property. I could scarcely believe I owned the whole half acre. The ruin had been built at the northern end of the block, leaving a sizeable patch of land stretching from the street to the dry-stone wall at the rear. Beyond, dominating the landscape to the northeast and rising up behind some low hills, a volcano sat with its gaping maw and russet flanks. Towards the south-east were the other volcanoes in the chain and due south, a range of serrated-edged peaks in the distance. The Betancuria massif rose to the east, with mountains dotted before it. After four decades cooped in Colchester, the effect on me was one of exhilaration. The wide expanse of arid land elevated my spirits and I dismissed as hocus pocus

Aunt Clarissa's worrisome predictions. I took comfort, too, knowing I had a neighbour to either side and one across the street, although there was no sign that anyone was at home in any of those houses.

I walked over to the ruin. The structure was set back from the street and built with much uniformity. The main façade comprised eight boarded-up cavities where once were windows. The cavities were evenly spaced, four above and four below. On the lower level, one of the central cavities was wider than the others and would have contained the front door. In places, the render was crumbling. Some areas were exposed stone. The side walls were uninteresting, containing two bricked-up window cavities on the upper level. At the rear were three small outbuildings, one in good repair although minus its roof.

By rights I needed permission in the form of a key to get into the main building, not that there was a door to open, but I knew a way inside at the rear where there was a gap in a poorly boarded up doorway. I came across the gap on my last visit to the island, on the day I took my prized photo that I had blown up and framed, the photo that had hung in my living room like a lure.

I squeezed through the gap and entered a short passage that led to an internal patio, taking in the interior of the building that I had only seen in online images emailed to me by my lawyer when Señor Cejas was bent on putting me off the purchase. Dilapidation scarcely described the state of disrepair. Some of the interior walls were freestanding. Much of the roof was missing. Stairs to the upper level did not exist, and the balcony that would have run along three of the walls of the internal patio was missing save for a section cantilevered in the western wall and supported by two skinny posts. I didn't dare walk beneath it. I could hear Kevin McCloud's voiceover telling his viewers that, yet again, the owner had bitten off far more than she was able to chew and the cost and time blow outs would be enormous.

Not if I could help it.

I picked my way around. There was evidence of paintwork in some of the rooms, harkening back to more glorious times. Many of the walls had been painted a yellow ochre. A simple frieze decorated the top of some of the walls, straight lines of cobalt blue and black and stencilled flowers in the corners. Different, more earthy colours had been employed in a similar design of straight line borders and simple stencil work in other parts of the house.

There appeared to be four large living areas, a dining room and kitchen, and what was probably a laundry or bathroom. There was no way of accessing the upper level but I imagined a similar arrangement of grand rooms and estimated at least six bedrooms. In one of the downstairs rooms the floorboards had been pulled up, revealing the subfloor of bearers and joists.

The whole arrangement of rooms faced the internal patio, which had been divided into two by a partition wall. The wall had a large hole in its centre as though someone hadn't wanted the wall there and bashed through it, and evidence that it was a later addition could be seen in the way it cut off a portion of architrave, and dissected the existing balcony in the west wall.

I stood beside the hole in the partition in what would have been the centre of the patio and absorbed the atmosphere. The wind blew through every crevice of the ruin, moaning and whistling. Other than the wind there was no sound. I couldn't hear a dog bark or a vehicle engine or any other evidence of life beyond the walls. Despite the wind, there were pockets of stillness and the ruin exuded a timeless quality. Embedded in its dilapidated state remained faint echoes of its history, overlaid with sorrow, as though the very stones and ancient timbers mourned their former selves, when they were united as one, strong and proud and true.

The house was rumoured to be two hundred and fifty years old, built by a wealthy family from Tenerife enjoying the riches of their wine exports and later sold to a family of lawyers. I pictured what it may have been, the grandeur of the carved wood and the vaulted ceilings, the balconies, the patio filled with plants and elegant outdoor seating.

I imagined men and women in period dress, all straight backed and God-abiding, going about their daily business in hushed voices. They would have had servants too, to cook and clean. The lady of the house would tend her plants and go to mass. The gentleman would read a book or a newspaper and take trips away on camel-back or donkey to attend to business. They would discuss their concerns over the weather, public health, the harvest, matters of politics and trade. Perhaps they received visitors, the priest, overnight guests. And there would have been children and extended family members. Aunts and uncles and cousins. A surviving grandparent or two.

Outside the walls, the wind would have blown and picked up the dust. The interior of Fuerteventura endures many a sweltering day in summer, and with no trees to shade the rocky land, ambient temperatures rise to infernal heights. I couldn't imagine any of my dainty well-bred family venturing out unless they had to. Not in summer. Instead, they would have taken full advantage of their cloistered life within, enjoying the cool of the internal patio.

A faint odour of animal urine wafting on a breeze brought me back to the present. A dog? Or a cat? The light was fading and I thought it wise to make my way back to my apartment before nightfall. On impulse, I thought to take with me a small piece of my new country estate to mark the occasion. I picked a craggy stone out of the partition wall. It was the size of my hand and the colour of orange ochre and rough to the touch. As I walked away a sudden gust of wind blew through the hole in the wall. It was a preternaturally cold wind for the climate. Goose pimples broke out on my skin. I thought nothing of it.

The Builder

Back in my apartment, I gave my rocky memento pride of place on the living room's single shelf, between the television and a white, urn-shaped vase, arranging the rock in various positions until I was satisfied it displayed its best face.

Around dinner time, I threw together a cheese omelette and salad. After eating, I soaked in the ambience of the modern, rectangular space, with its clean, streamlined feel.

I felt somewhat stunned. There I sat, having left the only career I had ever known, sold the only house I had ever owned and moved to an island where I had no family or friends, to embark on a major restoration project. Had I taken on too much? It was not a thought I was prepared to give shrift. I was tired from the travelling, that was all, and fatigue was colouring my thoughts. I needed an early night.

I was asleep by nine despite the unfamiliar noises in my new neighbourhood.

The following day I was up, showered and out the door by seven-thirty. Back in Colchester, I had asked the Fuerteventura lawyer in charge of my conveyancing if she knew of a reliable builder. She put me in contact with Mario, who I promptly emailed. We arranged to meet on site that day at nine. I was there at eight, wandering around my land in the morning cool, marking my territory with my footsteps, toying with the idea of buying a campervan instead of a car and parking up in my would-be garden for the duration of the build. I could only imagine what the locals would think of a strange English woman emerging each day from her home on wheels.

Was anyone watching me through the windows of any of the houses I could see? Were they judging me? For there I stood, dressed in beige capris and a loose white blouse, my mane of copper hair held in place with the assistance of a large headscarf, my fair skin and blue eyes unsuited to the terrain, my bank teller shape, larger at the haunches and soft about the belly, a far cry from the wiry musculature needed to till the land. But Claire Bennett of Colchester was no longer a bank clerk. Claire Bennett planned on getting fit, and there was plenty for me to do.

I thought I would begin by creating a garden bed in the corner of the property furthest from the restoration work. Plant some trees and shrubs. Or at least start tidying up the place. There were stones all over the ground and the dry-stone walls at the rear of the block were in disrepair.

A dusty old van pulled up a little after nine. There was a long pause before the driver's side door swung open and a solid, deeply tanned man with short black hair got out. I waved. He looked over and approached. I could see he was a builder at a glance. He had that air of authority as he observed the ruin and he carried a large, battered notebook under one arm.

'Mario,' I said, the moment he was close. I held out my hand.

He didn't match my smile but he gave my hand a firm shake.

'Claire.'

His gaze slid to the ruin. As we walked over, I drew my knowledge of the Spanish language to the forefront of my mind, ready to reel off the building terms I had learned by rote in preparation. But Mario was not the talkative type and he wasn't the least bit interested in my opinion. His eyes were everywhere, making quick assessments of this and that and scribbling in his notebook. Even before we had entered through the crack in the boarded-up window, he was making noises that suggested a negative take on the project.

Inside, his attitude was even worse. Before long, he was shaking his head and sighing and making soft tutting noises. In all, his demeanour began to irritate and I had it in mind to find another builder, for there had to be dozens on the island with the skills to work on a restoration.

After he had poked about in all the downstairs rooms and gazed long and hard at the rafters and beams and what was left of the roof, we stopped in the patio beside the hole in the wall, the only area of the entire structure that felt safe to stand in for any length of time. The building may have been standing for centuries, but there was no telling when something might slip and a whole section tumble on our heads.

'This is a partition wall,' he said, patting the crumbling render and looking at where the wall met the rest of the structure.

'I want it gone, obviously.'

'It is bracing the two walls, there and there,' he said, pointing ahead and behind him.

'It does need to come down.'

'Okay, but we start with that room there.' He gestured at the living room in the north-west corner, the room in the best repair.

'Any reason?'

'We can finish it faster. There is not so much to do.' His eyes bore into me beneath thick, arched eyebrows. 'This will cost a lot of money.'

'I am well aware of that.'

And I have a lot of money, I thought. I didn't say it. I didn't want to give him the impression I could afford more than a basic restoration in case he saw me as an excuse for extravagance.

Despite an urge to look away, I held his gaze.

'When can you start?'

He exhaled and leafed through his notebook, which seemed to double as his diary. The wind gusted and one of the timbers groaned. He looked around in response and we both waited for another groan. It was not forthcoming, but that single sound caused him to close his notebook and say, 'Why don't you demolish and put up something nice and modern?'

I was instantly defensive.

'I love this house,' I said, infusing into my voice a measure of indignation.

He ignored my reaction, or was indifferent to it.

'A new build will be cheaper and faster.' He grew in enthusiasm as he spoke. 'We can re-use the stone. Make it a feature. You will have a very nice house.'

'I don't want a very nice, modern house. Look, Mario, I was told you were the best builder to restore this ruin. Will you do it? Otherwise I will need to find someone else.'

'Of course, I can do it. I just want to be sure it is what you want. I thought I would make an alternative suggestion. This is a lot, I mean a *lot* of work and it will be very expensive. But if you are sure.' He paused as though to allow me time to reconsider. I made no comment.

'Do you want to use it for something?' he inquired.

'I just want to restore it to how it was.'

He puffed out his cheeks as he exhaled. Then he said, 'Do you have architect plans?'

'No, but I want it restored, not changed.'

'You will want some changes, believe me.'

If you say so. Although he was probably right.

'What happens next?'

'I can draw up the plans for you and submit them to council for approval. Then I must find local materials. You cannot use new materials in an old building like this. And I must make a team. You need everyone here, for the roof, the carpentry, the masonry, and then the plumbing and electricity. That is a lot of men.'

'How long will all that take?'

'Three months?'

'Three months!'

'That's fast. I can draw up the plans for you straight away. I have a friend in council who can make the approval process go faster. But I will need a deposit.'

With the situation suddenly looking positive, I said, 'Tell me how much and I will transfer the amount.'

'Okay.'

'You'll get to work on the plans as soon as I pay you?'

'Yes, yes.'

He looked at me expectantly. He seemed keen to leave. I led him outside through the gap in the boarded-up doorway, careful not to snag or soil my nice clothes.

We stood together for a moment. He held out his hand and I was about to take it, but at the sight of the outbuildings I had an idea.

I gave him my winning smile and said, 'Mario, surely you can get started sooner. I mean, isn't there work you can be doing before the council gets involved?'

He looked at me blankly.

'Maybe you can make a start out here,' I said gesturing at the outbuildings.

He seemed resistant. 'Usually the owner wants the house complete before working on the outbuildings.'

'Usually the owner has run out of money by then. I know how it goes. But in my case, that won't happen.' I wondered if I had revealed too much but his manner didn't change.

I went over to the largest outbuilding, the one with no roof. Mario followed. The building consisted of thick stone walls, an opening where a door would have been, and a small high rectangle in the adjacent wall serving as a window. The floor space looked about fifteen feet by twelve, large enough for a studio or workshop of some kind. A pile of stones in the centre was evidence of some sort of interior wall.

'For keeping in the goats,' he said, kicking a pebble and created a puff of dust.

'With a roof, a floor and some render, I could use it for storage.'

'You will have a lot of space in there,' he said, pointing back at the house and then eyeing me with puzzlement.

Did he have to be so resistant?

'You could use it, too,' I said. 'You might want to store tools or bags of cement, maybe.'

'True.'

'When can you start?'

'On this?' He shrugged.

'Tomorrow?'

He laughed. 'I will message you.'

'I want it done straight away, if at all possible,' I said to his back as he walked away.

Watching him get in his van and drive off, I couldn't say I liked Mario. He was evasive, non-comital and a touch inscrutable and I fully expected never to see him again. Aunt Clarissa's warning flashed into my mind and I dismissed it without consideration. I would give Mario a few days to prove himself, and then look for another builder if need be.

Paco

I couldn't steal myself away from the block. The sun had a sting to it and I was growing hungry and thirsty, but I wanted to do something on my property, make a small difference to mark the occasion. Thinking I would tidy up, I went back to the outbuilding and picked up the rocks scattered around in the dirt, creating a small pile of them outside. I soon tired. My gloveless hands burned and my back was stiffening from the effort. I hadn't dressed for hard labour and I didn't want to dirty my capris.

I needed gloves, a wheelbarrow, gardening tools and a strategy for re-using all that rock littering my block. I was about to head off back to Puerto del Rosario to a hardware store when I noticed a man standing on the other side of the road, gazing my way. Already, the project had aroused interest, I thought, feeling pleased if a little intruded upon. A neighbour perhaps? Or a nosy holidaymaker? Curious, I walked over.

He crossed the road and we met on the pavement.

'Lovely morning for it,' I said with a cheery grin.

He didn't return my warmth. Hearing I was English, he said in a low and thickly accented voice, 'What are you doing on this land? It is private.'

'The land *is* private,' I said. 'I own it.'

He shook his head. 'You cannot. It belongs to the Cejas family.'

'Not any more. They sold it.'

'That's impossible. Not even the government could make them sell.'

'The government were not offering enough.'

He eyed me appraisingly, perhaps a little taken aback, as though I didn't appear to him the type to be rich.

'You're English. And you buy this?' He tilted his head at the ruin. 'What for? A hotel?'

'I bought it to live in it.'

Who the hell does he think he is, treating me with such disdain?

We both looked back at the ruin, all forlorn and dilapidated, its windows and door cavities boarded up, the render crumbling off what walls still stood. I took the opportunity to steal a glance at this abrupt and somewhat rude man who was taking an extreme and perhaps possessive interest in my house. He was tall, over six foot, slim and fit. He had long black hair, tied back in a ponytail, framing a well-proportioned face, with an intelligent turn to the mouth and a fervent glint in his deep-set eyes. The swarthy complexion indicated a Southern European lineage. A local? I placed him in his late-thirties. A satchel—grubby, worn and bulging—hung from his left shoulder.

'A big house, no?' he said in his stilted English. 'You have a husband? Children? A large family?'

I found his prying intrusive.

'Only me.'

'Wow!'

I could detect the judgement in that simple word even in Spanish and he wasn't referring to my marital status. I was awash with guilt, guilt that didn't belong to me, but to expats in general. There were too few affordable dwellings for the locals, while foreigners bought up the housing stock at exorbitant prices and lived out a paradisiacal existence on land that really wasn't theirs. In essence, the trend was a form of colonisation and it was a common complaint in the Spanish social media groups I was in. The key difference in my case, was not many foreigners bought ruins. No matter where you lived, they were notoriously expensive to restore. Not to mention time consuming. Standing before the tall and mysterious stranger I was made to feel as though I had committed the ultimate cultural transgression. I had no right of ownership. Worse, I sensed he might have thought I was appropriating local history. I should have bought an apartment in Corralejo like everyone else of my sort and left the hinterland well alone, my notion that I was doing the island a public service, dashed.

My second day on the island as a resident and something sour pervaded my being. I hadn't realised how much I wanted my choice to restore a ruin and save it from demolition sanctioned, not until that very moment when it wasn't. I couldn't help seeing the absurdity in the situation too. For what ordinary local could ever afford the expense of the purchase, let alone the building work. Such projects had become the terrain of the rich and the government. This man before me should be thanking, not condemning me.

The wind picked up, catching the ends of my headscarf and using them to slap my face. I brushed the fabric away and shifted my stance. With my back to the building, I gazed up at the stranger and some part of me, call it self-preservation, compelled me to heal the rift forming between us. I did not want animosity from a man I suspected would pop round at whim.

'I'm Claire.' I held out my hand.

He hesitated, took it and said, 'Paco.'

'Pleased to meet you, Paco. Do you live in the village?'

'Tiscamanita? No.'

He didn't supply an alternative. I had no idea how to progress the conversation or how to close it. An awkward moment passed between us. The wind showed no sign of abating. Despite wisps of his own hair whipping across his face, Paco was untroubled by it.

'You have an interest in this house?' I asked, stating the obvious.

He patted his satchel. 'I'm a photographer.' He announced his profession, or hobby, as though it, of itself, were sufficient explanation.

'Then you'll be pleased to know I plan to return the building to its former glory.'

'Ha!' he said with as much sarcasm as it was possible to pack into that short word. 'And then sell it and make a fortune.'

The man, Paco, was driving me crazy with his antagonistic remarks. I did my best not to give him the benefit of seeing my chagrin, keeping my voice cool and firm. 'To live in it, like I said. You've been inside?'

'Many times.'

I thought about offering him another tour but wasn't sure how he would interpret that. In a final effort at assuaging the irascible photographer I said, 'Then perhaps you'd help me. I have been visiting the island every year and I have driven by this ruin many times. But I don't know its history. I'd like to learn everything there is to know. Maybe I'll write it all down and produce a booklet as a keepsake. That way, whatever I, we, discover will be preserved.'

I had no idea where the idea came from, I hadn't kept so much as a child-hood diary in all of my forty years, but his face lit with interest and I felt I had committed myself, through an uncommonly loose tongue, to a project I didn't have the capacity or the inclination to pursue. It was a moment of desperation to appease, but why I felt I needed to go to such considerable lengths to gain Paco's approval, I couldn't fathom. Perhaps some intuitive part of me knew he would play a significant role in the months ahead, or maybe deep down I had decided I needed an ally and since he had a keen interest in my ruin, he fitted the bill. Whatever the motive, I assured him he was welcome to visit any time he wanted and observe the progress.

Reassured, he headed off and left me to tramp about my block, quelling a mix of trepidation and frustration, and an equally strong desire to get on and make an impression on the garden.

Moving Rocks

Not long after Paco left, I set off for Puerto del Rosario, heading to the hardware store on the town outskirts. There, I bought a shovel and spade, a garden fork and trowel, four pairs of heavy-duty gardening gloves, a watering can and a small wheelbarrow. I had to fold down the back seats to get the wheelbarrow in the car. Mindful of the dirt those tools would bring into the boot, I went back and bought a sheet of thick plastic. I dearly wanted to get back to Tiscamanita but it was nearing lunchtime and my stomach was eating itself.

I drove to my apartment and made a ham and cheese baguette, and poured and large glass of juice. I ate and drank so fast I belched on the last mouthful. Then I changed into a loose t-shirt and shorts and a pair of canvas plimsolls and I was back on my block within a couple of hours.

That afternoon, with gloved hands and a wheelbarrow I managed to clear out all the rocks in the outbuilding, making a heap about ten strides away. I added to the heap with other rocks lying around. I was pleased with the result. The area around the outbuildings looked much tidier. I'd left my mark and it felt like progress.

In the days that followed, I went up to the block and spent a few hours braving the sun and the wind to scour the land clearing rocks, determined to cover every square foot of it. I heaped the rocks into cairns that grew and grew in size until they were visible from a distance.

Now and then I would fully straighten and stretch my back, and take a moment to absorb the curves of the volcano that rose up behind the nearby hills, it's gaping maw evidence of the fiery lava it had spewed long ago, evidence too of the powerful geography of the Canary Islands. It was odd that on Fuerteventura, an island with few volcanoes compared to its sister, Lanzarote, I should have chosen to have one dominating the view from my back yard. The volcano was the first in a chain of four that had spewed lava and ash eastwards, towards the coast. Standing by one of my rock piles, beholding the majesty of that natural killer, I wondered if I had been drawn as much by the setting as the ruin itself.

A week of back-breaking labour out in the sun and I gained a tan and lost some kilos, the waistbands of my trousers noticeably looser. The exposure out on my bare land had put paid to the campervan idea. I contacted the owner of the apartment and booked myself an additional month. Not the most luxurious accommodation, I could have afforded anywhere, but I was still Claire Bennett of Colchester and frugal suited me to my core.

In the evenings, I blocked out the noise of the neighbours with my headphones, and lost myself in the music of the Cocteau Twins. Sometimes, I would think of my mother and wonder what she would have made of the island. I imagined she would have been as enchanted as me. She would have seen the beauty and the subtlety in the stark desert vistas. They would have reminded her of the Persia and Arabia of yesteryear, of Morocco, of desert lands and ancient mysteries, of Sufis and Dervishes with their mystical ways. She would have walked down the streets of Tiscamanita imagining she was on her way to a souk. Clarissa said Ingrid had that sort of imagination. She would be walking down a street lost in another world, a world of her imagining. She had been a danger to herself, Clarissa said. When they were growing up, many times Clarissa had to tell my mother to stop at the kerb as she made to step out across a street. It was a quality she never lost.

On Fuerteventura, Ingrid would have enjoyed the beaches, too. Clarissa told me once Ingrid loved to be beside the sea. I have no recollection of us visiting, but apparently, we went on outings to Clacton-on-Sea. We would build sand castles and enjoy the amusements on the pier and eat sticks of sugary rock. It must have been when I was very small.

Mario contacted me on the Wednesday of that week of hard labour and we talked through the project. He sounded more amenable on the phone and I thought perhaps he had been having a off day when we had met on the block to discuss my proposal. Hearing him bend to my wishes, I softened and paid the deposit. We discussed my ideas and I sent him photos of my hand-drawn sketches. I begged him to draw up the plans as soon as he possibly could and he told me I was fortunate he was having a day off to look after one of his children who was off school. The next day, he sent me screenshots of his drafts. Not wanting to quibble and slow the pace, I agreed to his small alterations and suggestions. He then drew up the final plans which he submitted to council before close of day that Friday.

After that, in the evenings when I tired of listening to music, I poured over my electronic copy of the house plans.

The design was formal. The living room on the north-western corner was a room of about twelve by fifteen feet, accessed via the vestibule that led to the double doors facing the street. Entry to the adjoining room, once the dining room, was from the patio and those two rooms were interconnected. There was a window in the living room, facing west like the front door. The other room was windowless, there being no downstairs window in the north-facing wall. Sensible, as that was the direction of the prevailing wind. On the northeast corner was the kitchen, a room fifteen by eighteen feet. There was no door through to the dining room. Like most rooms in the building, access was via the patio. The two kitchen windows overlooked the volcano. Imagining rinsing a glass at the sink, I began to see through the building's magnificence to the joy of living amid stunning views.

There was a laundry centred in the east wall beside the rear exit. A bathroom would take up the south-eastern corner. A room identical to the dining room would be a study or library, and on the south-western corner would be a large L-shaped living room. Both rooms had windows facing the garden and the corner room also had windows facing the street.

The entire building was forty-five feet wide and forty-eight feet long, with walls three-feet thick. Upstairs mirrored downstairs in the dimensions of the rooms, and would comprise six bedrooms and two bathrooms, and an area of flat roof for a terrace above the laundry. I chose the best room for my bedroom, the one above the kitchen, with a magnificent view of the volcano.

The internal patio was about twenty-seven by twenty-one feet, large enough to contain the wide balcony that would run along three of the walls, and the aljibe beneath the ground in its centre. The plan was both grand and simple and eminently liveable, a nobleman's home with every thought given to a kind of sub-tropical comfort.

After picturing myself in each room, I studied other restorations online and visualised how my home would be. My mind was buzzing with ideas for linens for drapes, fabric patterns for furnishings and rugs, kitchen designs, lamps and light shades, even and bathroom fittings. Mario warned me I would need to consider every single detail in each of the rooms and it was a good idea to start browsing. The only difficulty I faced was needing to restrict my searches to the island. It was too easy to slip onto websites where the goods were only available in the UK. I didn't want to ship furniture over. I was drawn to vintage styles and the antique furniture traditional to the islands and limited my searches accordingly.

While we waited for council approval, Mario pulled together a small team of labourers to tackle the largest outbuilding, which Mario was calling a barn.

On the first day of the build, I did an early shop at the supermarket and spent the morning tidying up the apartment and washing my clothes that had formed a small mountain on my bedroom floor. Listless, I sorted through my suitcase. Buried at the bottom was the framed photo of my ruin that I had brought with me on impulse; a symbol of the reason for my being there. The rest of my possessions would be arriving by ship.

Wanting the photo on display on the one shelf in the entire apartment, I put it between the television and the vase, relocating the rock I had taken from the partition wall to the other end of the shelf, placing it in front of a short row of books held in place by carved-wood bookends. The books included a Spanish-English dictionary and another in Spanish-German, a guide to Fuerteventura in English, an Agatha Christie in Spanish, two romances in what appeared to be Dutch, a hardcover on German Expressionism and a Stephen King in French. I imagined each had been left behind, intentionally or otherwise, by a previous guest. The rock blended nicely with the arrangement. A rock of no particular beauty or significance other than it came from that wall, and already I had imbued it with meaning; the first rock removed from a wall that had for too long divided that ruin, cleaving it into two separate dwellings.

I was about to restore that house to its original unified whole. Thinking about how the partition detracted from the building's integrity, that wall seemed to me a transgression and the sooner it was gone, the better.

I picked up the rock and turned it over in my hand. It had six distinct faces in amongst the little craters and outgrowths. I traced a finger over the surface, felt the weight of it—about half a pound—and returned it to the shelf, sitting it down on its largest flattest surface, pointing a prominent bulge to the front. That way the rock took on the shape of a broad and flattened head and I could pick out eyes, a nose and lips from all the indentations and protuberances, as I used to as a child with my mother's floral-patterned curtains.

Done with domesticities, I deposited in a thin canvas bag what had become my customary ham and cheese baguette, along with two oranges and a litre of water, and set off for Tiscamanita. I doubted the workmen would want me there but I needed to witness the occasion.

In the narrow streets of Puerto del Rosario, I hadn't noticed the dust haze, but out in open country, there it was, reducing visibility, the mountains no longer distinct, the horizon behind me fuzzy. The temperature was rising steadily as the air blew in from the east. It was a calima, a Saharan dust storm. I had no idea how long it would last or how intense it would be, but when I pulled up outside my property in front of a row of cars and vans and opened the car door, my English self was brutalised by weather conditions that made sense of any apparel that covered the body head to toe, including, no particularly the face. I had endured my share of calimas and they varied in intensity, but that day conditions were especially bad and, I thought, unseasonal.

The other vehicles were facing the other way to me. The men must have all come up from the south. I didn't know whether to leave my window open a crack to let out the heat or keep it closed to keep out the dust. I left it shut and snatched my lunch bag off the backseat.

Signs of the build were everywhere, in tools and wheelbarrows, voices, and sharp repetitive dings of hammer on chisel. Timber was stacked near the rock pile I had created beside the barn. Although it was a rock pile no longer. My neat and tidy arrangement had been flattened, the rocks scattered. I quelled my dismay, all my hard labour for nothing.

Mario and I had agreed on a pitched roof. In the searing heat and the dust and the wind, four men—I counted four—were at work repairing and capping the stone walls in preparation. I was ignored, but one of the men must have said something to Mario, because he looked around and seeing me standing by the side wall of the house, he came over.

'You did all this?' he said, not bothering with even a hello, waving a disparaging hand at my rock pile.

'I wanted to help.'

'Help? You have made an easy job hard. Those rocks inside the barn had fallen off the walls. They would have been better left where they were and not mixed up with all the other rocks. Now the men are having to hunt for each rock, thanks to your pile.'

'I had no idea,' I said defensively, succumbing to a sudden rush of humiliation. I did my best to repress it. How dare he address me with such impatience, such rudeness!

'Please, Claire,' he said in a sudden change of manner, 'you must leave the work to us.' He reached for my hand and pressed it between both of his, a gesture that was as much conciliatory as it was patronising and I snatched my hand away. The turnaround had me wondering at the truth of Clarissa's metaphysical warning. I had no idea where I stood with this man. Yet I knew he was right; I needed to leave well alone. They were the experts, me, the owner, clearly the ignoramus.

'Are they already capping the wall?' I said, anxious to display my scant technical knowledge and progress the conversation past that juncture.

'There was not much to be done to some sections.'

I took a step forward. He stepped to his left and stood squarely before me, blocking my path. I craned to see past him. He emitted a humourless laugh as he stepped aside but he had made it clear in the most blatant manner he didn't want me approaching the men. He was advancing far beyond what I would have considered appropriate behaviour, even if he was mucking around. Besides, his eyes and his words were serious. He would brook no interference from me.

'Mario,' I said, smiling to soften the tension. 'This is an important day for me. I will leave the men to work, but first I would like to take some photographs, if that's okay.'

I didn't wait for a reply. I marched by him, phone to the ready.

The men all looked over at once, stared briefly at the crazy Englishwoman lining up a shot with her phone, then continued working. As I neared the barn I overheard their chatter. They assumed I understood no Spanish or that the wind would carry away their voices. Both were true to some extent, I had to strain to hear and interpret their thick accents.

'Who is she?'

'The owner,' said a man in a white shirt. 'Mario says she wants to restore the main house.'

There was a ripple of dark laughter. I pretended not to notice.

'I'm not working on that,' a short man in a dirty fawn shirt gestured behind him.

'Me neither.'

'Glad to hear it. You would be mad to,' said a third man.

'Mario will have to bring in men from Lanzarote.'

'He'll find workers here,' the white-shirted man said. He seemed to have authority over the others.

'You think so? Foreigners maybe. No local will work on it.'

'True. They'd have to be crazy.' He spat on the ground.

I took three discrete photos and walked away. My mind raced. Whatever did they mean? Had I heard them correctly? I began to doubt I had.

Mario exited the opening in the boarded-up doorway. I put away my phone and joined him.

'Any news on the house plans?'

'In one week?' He laughed. I didn't laugh with him. 'When this is done, we will start.'

'Those men just said they won't work on the house.'

'Take no notice of them. There are plenty of men I can use.'

So, I did hear them right.

'But they are saying no local will either. I don't understand. What is wrong with my house?'

'Relax. It is just superstition and local gossip.'

He walked away before I could inquire further. I was left nonplussed. Superstition meant ghosts, paranormal activity, a curse powerful enough to stop rational, hardworking men from earning a good wage on a major project. Something had to be very wrong with my ruin to cause that reaction. Perhaps it explained why no one had restored it before, why Cejas wanted it demolished. He had wished me good luck. It sounded like I was going to need it. Aunt Clarissa's warning sprang to mind again but I shooed it away. The relocation chart she had created pertained to the whole of the island, not just my block.

I hung around for a few moments longer to take a slug of my water. The baguette, tucked in my thin canvas bag all this time and steadily getting warmer was, I decided, inedible. If I wanted packed lunches, I needed to invest in a cooler bag. The men kept glancing over at me. Realising my presence was slowing the pace, I went back to my car.

Opening the door on a furnace and scalding my hands on the steering wheel that had taken the brunt of the sun, I realised why all the other vehicles were facing the other way. I had a lot of acclimatising ahead of me.

I turned on the radio for the drive back to Puerto del Rosario to drown out my scrambled thoughts. Above all, I refused to heed the voice within that was busy assessing the inaugural day of the build as portentous. The coincidence of the calima hadn't helped. The trouble was, those workmen knew something I didn't and while Mario fobbed off their fears, part of me couldn't. It was the part of me formed by Ingrid and Clarissa, one at odds with my rational bank-teller self. I chose not believe in ghosts or the supernatural or in Clarissa's scrying, but those men clearly did and I remained unsettled by it.

The car indicated an outdoor temperature of thirty-five degrees and there was a lot of day left for the temperature to rise further. In the past, locals would have stayed indoors, closed all the shutters on the windows and rode out the easterly, ready to sweep up the dust once the wind turned. I had washing drying outside, a bathroom window open, and the sooner I followed in those sensible traditions the better.

I pulled up outside the apartment with my equanimity partially restored. It remained that way for a full two minutes. Then, I entered the apartment and saw that the rock I had so carefully positioned on the shelf in front of the books, was lying on the floor.

How the hell did it end up there?

I raced for explanations to soothe my alarmed mind. Had it fallen? No, it couldn't have. How was that even possible? It was resting on its natural base from which it could not have toppled. The floor tiles were not chipped, and had it fallen or even been dropped, surely there would have been a chip. Had someone been in my apartment? Dolores? The owner? An intruder? Why would any of them put that rock on the floor? Yet that had to be the answer. Maybe they had come with a child who saw the rock and picked it up and examined it. Yes, that is what had happened.

I looked around for other evidence that someone had been inside while I was out, but there was none. Clarissa's omen shot to the forefront of my mind, but she had said nothing about ghosts and I refused to put store in a poltergeist. Preferring to avoid a recurrence, I put the rock in a kitchen cupboard, well-hidden at the back behind a stack of plates.

It took a cold beer and a bowl of ice cream to settle my thoughts. Then I brought in the washing and closed the bathroom window and set about saving on my hard drive the photos I had taken of my outbuilding.

Later, I wrote my first entry in my notebook, pleased to at last be using the pretty, folio sized hard cover I had found in a local bookstore. I called my first entry, Day One. It was not an easy entry to scribe. I had wanted the day to be joyous and celebratory and I had come away with a trough full of negativity. My build sat beneath a cloud of doom. I described the calima, Mario, the men, the good progress and even my faux pas with the rock piles. I saw no need to mention the partition-wall rock in my living room.

Betancuria

The calima lasted another three days. I remained indoors for the duration, reading the Agatha Christie in Spanish translation that had been left on the single shelf, and when I tired of that I listened to music through my headphones. I steered clear of the Cocteau Twins, choosing Fela Kuti and Angelique Kidgo, upbeat music with a happy, exhilarating vibe, from artists with roots not too far from the Canary Islands. A boyfriend – Simon, I think it was – had put me onto them one time.

When the Kidgo album came to an end, I sent my father and aunt each a short email informing them the building works had begun. Neither replied, at least not soon enough. I found myself checking my inbox intermittently, craving human interaction, even at an electronic distance. Alone in my tiny apartment as I rode out the dust storm, listening to the laughter and clatter of my neighbours through sound-porous walls, I stared into my immediate future wondering how I would fare for much longer with no friends and little meaningful human contact. But I wasn't about to let a spot of isolation bother me. The answer was simple. I would keep busy. My friendless state wouldn't last forever. I had always been good at the self-pep talk. Perhaps it is an attribute that comes with the single life.

On the Friday of that week, I drove to Tiscamanita and parked outside my property on the opposite side of the road, with a direct sightline to the barn. Binoculars would have been handy, but I could see at a distance that the timbers had begun to go up on the roof and the doorway had a new lintel. Four men meant fast progress. The barn was small and in much less disrepair than the main house. It was a pleasing sight but I didn't hang about. The moment one of the men spotted me in my car, I turned on the ignition and drove off.

Keen to learn more about the history of the house, I pulled up in the main street of Tiscamanita near a small café that had 'local' stamped all over it. Before I went in, I stood on the pavement and surveyed the surrounds, realising as I did that in all the time I had driven through the village, I had never bothered to stop and visit the shops and cafés.

The businesses in the village centre comprised a bakery, a butcher, a small grocery store, a hairdresser, two cafés and a restaurant all huddled around the church and plaza. Enough to service the local population and nothing more. With a population of about five hundred, you couldn't expect much by way of facilities. Yet the village was doing little to appeal to the passing holidaymaker. The potential was there; the village was cut in two by the Antigua-Tuineje road and home to a restored windmill, Los Molinos, that had been turned into one of the island's numerous museums. Although, the windmill was situated on the edge of the village and holidaymakers would no doubt be on their way to the next tourist site. It would probably take a lot to make them stop awhile, much more than a bit of village titivation.

Sadly, Tiscamanita had an atmosphere of decline. Shop premises were vacant. Many of the farms abandoned. There was not enough to attract people, nothing around to keep people. Most of the foreigners favoured the coast and who could blame them, and the locals who remained probably enjoyed their quiet lifestyle while their offspring left in search of work and excitement.

It was with a sense of unease that I approached the café, wondering how I would be received, this blow-in from Colchester, a cashed-up new resident keen to establish herself amongst the locals. At least I was able to communicate in the language. Surely that would invoke a positive response.

I had chosen to live in Tiscamanita in part because situated there I could disassociate myself from the rest of my cohort, the Brits, or at least, so I thought. Standing on the pavement observing the quietude, my assumptions seemed unrealistic. I didn't know a thing about the village or its people, save for what I could see with my own eyes and a few paragraphs I had come across online. I was, and I suspected would be for a long long time, an outsider.

I entered the café, foregoing the outdoor seating in favour of a table by the window. It was too early for lunchtime trade. Two men in work gear ambled in not long after I sat down. They made their purchases and went on their way, leaving me the only patron. I scanned the menu written on three small boards hanging on the wall behind the counter. There was to be no table service. I got up and approached the woman standing by the tapas bar and ordered a coffee. Thinking to please her with my custom I also ordered a slice of the tortilla on display. She seemed pleasant enough: dumpy, middle aged and proud. I guessed she was the owner.

I resumed my seat and when she came over with my order, I gave her my warm bank-teller smile and asked if the café was hers. When she nodded warily, I let my smile broaden and, holding her gaze I said, 'Then we are neighbours.'

The woman appeared taken aback, no doubt thinking, not another English migrant buying up the real estate. She opened her mouth to speak and changed her mind.

Seeing she was about to walk away, I shifted round in my seat. 'I've bought the Cejas house. In Calle Cabrera.'

A curious look came into the woman's face, part wonder, part hesitation, part fear.

'Casa Baraso?' she said slowly. 'I heard someone had bought that. It was you?'

'Casa Baraso? Was that the original owner?'

The property had been in the Cejas family for many generations and I had presumed they were the original owners. I had not come across a Baraso.

'Señor Baraso never owned the house,' she said, taking a small step closer. 'He lived there for many years. He was a government official from Tenerife.'

I thought back to that article I had read, the one that had piqued my interest in purchasing the house. I felt certain there had been no mention of a Baraso. Perhaps it was local knowledge, or I simply hadn't taken in the information. I wondered how I would go about investigating the man. A library? A historical society? I should start by quizzing the café owner.

I opened my mouth to speak when two women entered and greeted the owner in loud voices. They all headed to the counter together and I had clearly lost my chance. I attended to my omelette, enjoying the faint garlicky flavour, and sipped my coffee, which was average. As I ate I could feel the eyes of the women on my back. They had lowered their voices but I knew they were talking about the house. I heard 'Cejas' and 'Baraso' clear as a bell. I wanted to ask more questions, especially about Señor Baraso, and I also wanted to ask the café owner if she knew the reason for my labourers' refusal to be involved in the restoration, but confronting three local women at once felt daunting. Small village gossip and the knowledge that I was being judged had already caused me to retreat somewhat. It was a defence. Whenever I felt threatened, I retreated into the clam shell I had created as a child to protect myself from hurt. Right then it was a shrinking back that served to reinforce a sense that my new life would not be as easy a ride as I had thought.

I finished my tortilla and coffee and waited for the two women to either sit down or leave—they left—before approaching the counter to pay. I tried to catch the woman's eye, but she showed no interest in talking to me. I thanked her and as I was leaving I told her the tortilla was delicious, which clearly pleased her but she remained impassive.

After the interior gloom the sudden brightness of the day, glaring off the café's whitewashed walls, stung my eyes. A a cool reception in the café, and despite the oven heat that blasted me when I opened the car door, I was relieved to get going.

With the men on the building site preventing my presence on my property and the whole day to fill, I decided on a whim to drive to Betancuria, the island's original capital, taking the southern route via Pájara to enjoy the sweeping bends up through the mountains. I would behave like a holidaymaker, I thought, and take my time. I even stopped at the designated lookout to admire the view of the mountains.

Betancuria nestles in a small basin of a valley, surrounded on all sides by low mountains with their smooth, almost sensual curves, the massif undulating like a scrunched and ruffled blanket. Elevated, and situated on the western coast, the old town tends to be cooler than the rest of the island. That day, it certainly felt more refined to me, too, with its narrow streets zigzagging up the valley slopes, flanked by charmingly restored buildings. There was a sense of opulence to the village centre, the island's showpiece. Manicured and immaculate, attention had been paid to every detail.

The island's conqueror, Jean Bétancourt, had chosen Betancuria to be the capital not for its ambience, but for the protection it afforded from piratical attack. Its sheltered position did not prevent the town from being razed by pirates in 1593, an event that fascinated even as the violence of it repelled me.

I pulled up in the main street, lucky to find a place to park outside the church. Fuerteventura, I thought wryly as I got out of my car, was known not only for its beaches. Although it had taken a good few visits before I stumbled on the island's art.

La Iglesia Santa María de Betancuria is undoubtedly the finest example, a church that dominates the old capital. It is a magnificent edifice by all accounts. Baroque in style, it has arched windows set high in its brilliant white walls, a stout tower and stone quoining. The church shouts to all around. There is no escaping the faith that ruled here.

The structure is cut into the hillside. A large paved plaza, containing several stone seats and an arrangement of formal plantings, provides holidaymakers and locals a chance to soak in the atmosphere. Entry to the church is through carved wooden doors set in a rounded arch capped with an intricately carved pediment. I passed by a family who were preparing to head off to the gift shop and made my way into the cool.

The church interior exudes majestic religiosity, with its vaulted ceilings and impressive altarpieces made all the more striking beside the stark white of the walls.

Ignoring a few holidaymakers milling about, I went into the sacristy to stare up at the coffering. I had visited this church every holiday since the day I wandered inside to see what all the fuss was about, after overhearing two women enthusing.

The sacristy ceiling was enough to cause a crick neck in even the most cynical of observers. Each square contains a uniform pattern of rosettes and foliage painted in rich tones of gold and red and green.

When my neck felt stiff and sore, I studied the paintings. Then, I returned to the nave and sat at the end of a pew, my gaze fixed on one of the smaller altarpieces, rendered in the same rich colours. A statue of the Immaculate Virgin Mary stood in its own recess flanked by pilasters. My eye was drawn first here, then there, by all the intricate details. Such a piece of art was surely enough to lure even the non-religious into the church. You almost felt an impulse to worship.

I had never understood that impulse. Neither side of my family were devotees of any faith. My father is a materialist to his core, and my mother's side are dyed-in-the-wool occultists. Little wonder that to me, religion was brainwash, designed to force obedience in return for vague and unsatisfactory explanations of human suffering and spurious promises of an afterlife. Too often religion was used to control and oppress. When the Canary Islands were conquered, natives were forced to relinquish their own belief system and adopt Catholicism. If they didn't, they would die. For centuries thereafter, churches were built and congregations went to mass and took communion and learned to do what they were told. Stifling. The best that could be said was it left a legacy of fine old art.

People wandered in and out. In no hurry to move, I remained seated, absorbing the results of so much wealth and power. An inner peace infused me, but it was to be a peace short-lived. For it occurred to me in an unwelcome surge that I had bought into the island's colonial history. For I had fallen for a nobleman's house, not one owned by a humble farmer. Did that mean I had delusions of grandeur? Me, Claire Bennett, a humble bank teller from Colchester, the owner of a mansion by island standards. The realisation made me feel uncomfortable in my own skin. What did I imagine I was going to do in such a grand house once it was restored? That photographer, Paco, was right. I needed a husband, children, people to fill six bedrooms. Perhaps I should rent out rooms or otherwise turn a profit from it, but nothing of the sort held any appeal. I wanted my home all to myself, although sitting in that big old church, the prospect suddenly seemed absurd. It was as though I had been pierced by a pin that deflated my hot air balloon of fantastical, grand-design desire.

Shaken, I left the church and sat in the plaza, watching the sightseers ambling back and forth. I had been on the island two weeks. I had had little chance to enjoy my wealth, although the sense of freedom it gave was liberating. I was consumed with anticipation over the build. For yet again I knew I had not addressed one fundamental and ghastly question: Had I done the right thing moving to Tiscamanita? Shouldn't I have bought a villa on the coast?

Aunt Clarissa leaped into my mind, reminding me for the umpteenth time of all those astrological lines criss-crossing Fuerteventura. This time, I paused for thought. What was it she had said about Neptune and the twelfth house? Whatever it was, I doubted the relevance and my rational self waded in with an answer. There are times when bridges are burned and there is no going back. I had six-hundred-thousand-euros invested in that ruin and I was not about to buckle. Besides, I had no past to go back to. The only way was forwards. It might not prove an easy progression, but it was one that had to be made.

After a while my pep talk worked and my positive mind-set returned. On the hunt for a good place for lunch, I left the church and went for a walk down first one, then another of the narrow, paved streets.

I chose an eatery near the cultural centre, drawn by the old wine barrels serving as tables outside. Finding the restaurant full, I sat at a table by the door and ordered the menu of the day and a bottle of beer. I soaked in the din, the clatter, the delicious cooking smells. What better reason did I need to be here?

A vegetable soup came first and I tucked in, not realising I was famished until that first mouthful of rich stock enlivened my taste buds.

I was scraping the last of the soup from my bowl when a figure entered the bar. I looked up to find Paco staring at me. How odd.

'We meet again,' he said, hovering behind the vacant chair.

I raised a smile. 'Are you keeping well?'

He gestured at the table and, seeing my nod of encouragement, he pulled out the chair and sat down.

'How goes the restoration?'

'I'm having a barn renovated first. The men were working on it today when I drove by. I think it's going well.'

'I saw them too. Why are they not fixing the house?'

'You went by my property?' I said, feeling intruded upon, almost spied on, even as I knew that feeling was silly.

'I often take a detour,' he said, as though driving by my ruin was a daily occurrence. 'I'm a photographer.'

'You told me.' I held his gaze, expecting more.

'I like to monitor the old houses, make sure nothing bad happens to them.'

I was not convinced but his explanation would have to do. There didn't seem anything to say in response.

'What brings you up here?' he asked.

'What brings *you* up here?'

'I'm visiting a friend.'

'And I'm enjoying being a holidaymaker for a day.'

He smiled. It was a warm smile and I returned it with one of my own. The awkwardness between us eased. Paco hailed a waiter and ordered a beer.

'Why are you especially interested in my house?' I said, hoping for an honest answer.

This time, he was forthcoming, no, more than forthcoming; his eyes were ablaze and his face filled with wonder. 'A woman, an Englishwoman visited there many years ago. It is she who I am fascinated with.'

'Who was she?'

'Her name is Olivia Stone. You may have heard of her.'

'No, I do not believe I have encountered any Olivia Stone.'

'Then you must buy her books,' he said, leaning forward in his seat.

'She was a writer?'

'Of travel diaries. She wrote a very famous book about the islands.'

'I can't say I've come across it.'

'In the 1880s. A long time ago to you, perhaps. She came to Fuerteventura and stayed in a number of houses in the villages. Yours was one of them.'

'Wow, I'm impressed,' I said, not quite believing a single word he was saying.

'You should be impressed. She was a very special lady.'

I wanted to find out more about the mysterious woman, but my main course arrived along with Paco's beer, and after the waiter had cleared away my soup bowl, I beheld a generous sized dish of goat stew with whole potatoes and a garnish of parsley. The aroma made me salivate. I hesitated.

'Eat. Eat,' he said, gesturing at my food.

Chewing the first mouthful, I decided it was the most delicious goat stew I had ever tasted. Paco sipped his beer and watched.

'Are you not hungry?' I asked between mouthfuls, uncomfortable under his gaze.

'I've just eaten.'

Something caught his eye and he swung around and stood up, waving at a woman appearing through a side entrance.

'Until another time,' he said as he walked away.

I swallowed and raised my fork by way of goodbye, watching him leave and feeling his absence.

Back in Puerto del Rosario I swung by the local bookstore but they did not have a copy of anything by Olivia Stone. The assistant hadn't even heard of her.

I returned to my apartment and looked up the author online. It took several searches before I found it. *Tenerife and Its Six Satellites: Volume II* was available from several international bookstores. It was a peculiar feeling punching in my details and giving my current address.

Tears

It was Saturday. After writing a brief note in my notebook on the progress of the barn, as seen from my car window, I spent the morning creating a spreadsheet. I devised budgets for fixtures and fittings, the kitchen and bathroom suites, and furniture. Immersed in numbers and itemising each aspect of the interior gave me a sense of control and put me at ease after the turbulence of the day before. I needed to restore a sense of normalcy and crunching numbers was the best way I could think of to do it.

During my online travels to various homewares and hardware stores, I had downloaded brochures and price lists and taken screenshots of others to give me an idea. My Essex roots cautioned me against cost blowouts. I would adopt a style that allowed for the occasional piece of stunning furniture yet wouldn't diminish my bank balance. I decided against antique in favour of rustic and locally made wherever possible. I would have plenty of time to collect what I wanted.

Even with my frugal approach I was amazed at the size of the final figure. One curtain rod might only be ten euros but multiply that by the number of windows and costs soon start to run into the hundreds, even thousands. Power points and light switches were even worse. I had to keep reminding myself I could afford it. Adjusting to being a multi-millionaire after watching the pennies for decades was not easy. My banking background didn't help either. I automatically looked for savings.

Before I closed my laptop, I entered 'Olivia Stone travel author' in the search engine to see what came up other than her Canary Islands' book. I soon discovered she was the wife of a barrister, John Matthias Stone, and her book was presented to Queen Victoria. She was well-connected then, a society lady perhaps, and she was the author of an earlier work, *Norway in June*. She lived in an era of curiosity and exploration. She must have been one of those robust British women given to travelling to far-flung climbs. I could picture her, a rational dresser, big-boned with hefty thighs and a strident, forthright look about her.

I clicked on a few more websites and finding little more, my interest waned. I would wait and read the book for myself. I had enough going on without getting side-tracked researching a woman who may or may not have stayed in my house for a night or two.

I lunched on yet another ham and cheese baguette, this time with slices of tomato. I really ought to broaden my culinary habits, I told myself, as crumbs scattered across the counter.

Builders do not work weekends. With the afternoon ahead of me, I filled my water bottle and grabbed my car keys thinking I would check on progress. The drive had already become second nature and I was outside my block in half an hour without noticing how I got there.

No other car was parked in the street. Having yet to meet a neighbour, I was starting to wonder if all of the surrounding properties were empty. Otherwise, why had no one put in an appearance? Surely, they would be dying of curiosity by now?

The first change I noticed onsite was the complete absence of my rock pile near the barn. That, and all the roof timbers were on. On closer inspection, the walls had been capped with mortar and a top plate, and two evenly spaced beams spanned the width of the building. I couldn't be sure as I had no idea how long a job like this would take, but it appeared the men were working at breakneck speed. Adding to the pace of the works, when Mario had emailed me his full quote for the barn, he explained that the timber was left over from another job which was why it had arrived on site so fast. Not that it appeared I had been given any sort of discount. The hip roof would be clad in the traditional curved clay roof tiles which had also arrived. Presumably Mario had a stock of them ready to hand as well.

Mario might have thought me crazy to insist work started on that small barn, but once it was weather tight and lockable, I could use it for storage. My possessions would be arriving from the UK in about two months and, meagre as they were, I still had nowhere to store them at my tiny apartment.

I approached the main house with trepidation. I hadn't been inside since that time with Mario. Whenever I thought of the state of the ruin I felt anxious. I had a gnawing feeling the walls would fall before the council approved the plans.

The gap in the boarded-up doorway was bigger; a bottom section of the plywood had been snapped off. I ducked through and, keen not to stand in rooms with any overhead timbers, hurried through to the patio.

Nothing had changed. Not even the weeds had grown. I stood facing the direction of the street and observed the remaining section of the balcony, a balcony that would have provided access to the upper rooms, and I noticed how the partition wall cut the balcony in two, to prevent anyone upstairs from walking around the internal perimeter of the building. On the side where I stood, the timber was weathered and there looked to be evidence of borers.

Gingerly, I walked around, studying the walls more closely than before. Where the plaster had come away, the construction method was evident. The cornerstones were carved basalt blocks, the rest of the wall made up of large rocks wedged in place, much smaller stones and pebbles filling the gaps. Vertical cracks ran down the lengths of both gable ends at the northern section of the ruin, confirming my fear that if something wasn't done soon, the whole structure would collapse.

As though to reinforce my thought one of the timbers groaned in a room on my right. I heard a scuttle, and the flapping of wings as a bird flew down to investigate my presence.

On my last visit, I hadn't ventured through the hole in the wall. I bent and stepped through, noticing as I did a curious drop in temperature, as though the southern side of the building received less sun and attracted more wind. Yet the opposite was true.

The southern internal wall was in a dreadful state of repair. There was little roof left, no second level flooring and portions of the internal walls had fallen. Others were crumbling. The patio had been all but stripped of its balcony. Out of the two portions of the ruin, the south side was the most dilapidated and forlorn. Unlike the northern half, which groaned and threatened collapse, the southern had already done so. There was not much left to tumble.

Wanting to at least feel the thrill of ownership and gain a realistic sense of what I had taken on, I found a flat patch of rubble-free ground near the partition and sat down, cross-legged. I adjusted the buckle of a sandal that was digging into the ankle of my other foot. Then I straightened my blouse.

As soon as I was comfortable and still, a strange, trance-like mood overcame me. I was not one for meditating but I had taken relaxation classes once and I experienced the same heady tranquillity.

Instead of reflecting on the present circumstances of the ruin, I was drawn back to its past. I felt as though I was paying my respects to the previous owners, to all that had ever happened there. I found myself imagining the home's former glory. I pictured a pond and perhaps a fountain in the patio centre, and beneath the balcony stands of plants positioned in the corners and beside every post. I imagined doors opening onto a salon or a dining room, the stairs ascending. I sensed the stillness, and I could almost hear the acoustics.

Then I heard Elizabeth Fraser's voice reverberating around the walls, the music of the Cocteau Twins filling the atmosphere with ethereal beauty, a sense of godliness in sound, my ruin the equivalent of a cathedral. I was filled with a strong sense of well-being mixed with euphoria. Any doubts I had over the enormity of the project absented themselves and I was entirely mesmerised.

My trance deepened and it was then I saw my mother tiptoeing down the stairs in a long white dress. I was shocked to see her in this alien setting, shocked I was even able to picture her in this fashion. Yet there I gazed, at her locks of honey hair flowing, her face so serene, her eyes alight with wonder. Fascinated and transfixed, I watched as her hand slid down the banister.

She wasn't real. As her feet touched the paving of the patio, I lost her and in her absence an upsurge of grief overwhelmed me. Through the lens of my anguish, I saw the restoration as a homage to the mother I scarcely knew.

Tears tumbled from my eyes and streaked down my cheeks. My throat ached. I shuddered under a weight pressing down on my chest. Soon I was gasping for air, bending over where I sat, my hands clawing at the weeds around me, ripping out stems and leaves, reaching out and yanking at roots.

The emotion faded as fast as it had come and I was left feeling empty and stunned. The anguish, more the intensity of it, had been unexpected. I hadn't cried over my mother's death since the funeral and I only cried then because everyone else was. I had no idea I held within me unexpressed grief. For thirty years I had gone through life accommodating her absence, missing her, wondering what my life might have been like with her in it, but never once grieving for her as though I had been hollowed out.

Perhaps it was a mistake to listen to the Cocteau Twins so much. My imagination was becoming overactive. I had inadvertently invoked an opening deep within and I was disconcerted by it. I didn't want the restoration to carry a stamp of personal religiosity. I was not restoring the ruin to create a memorial to my mother. I wanted a home to live in.

I got to my feet and breathed deeply and wiped my eyes with the back of my hands. Somewhere in my handbag I had a tissue.

Eager for a sense of space around me, I ducked through the hole in the partition and headed back outside. This time I didn't dare take a rock home with me.

Puerto del Rosario

I awoke late the next day. It was Sunday and the neighbourhood was quiet. I opened the bedroom blind to find cloud obliterating the normally garish sunlight.

The cloud thickened and by lunchtime it was raining, not heavily, but enough to keep me indoors. My mood mirrored the weather and I succumbed to an attack of the doldrums. I skulked around the apartment like a caged animal, picturing my lonely life in a restored ruin, mistress of troubled memories. I was bored, tender and disturbed by turns. My grief had been unleashed and looked set to tramp about inside me with a will of its own. My doubts returned. I was taking on too much. I had no right to restore that ruin and should never have bought it. What would I do with myself when I had? I would be doomed to rattle around in my great big house and go slowly mad from loneliness, haunted by my own mother. I began to question what I was even doing on the island. I couldn't bring myself to listen to the Cocteau Twins for fear of stirring up my grief even more, so I played the Gorrilaz hoping they would cheer me up.

They didn't.

My miserable and fragmented state was so out of character, I didn't recognise myself. Eventually, I applied my listless mind to studying Spanish, looking up to watch raindrops trickle down the kitchen window pane as though they were my own tears.

Only once did I open the kitchen cupboard to make sure the rock was still there tucked at the back behind the plates. It was.

Monday the weather had returned to its normal fine and sunny self. I took advantage of the fresh, dry air and, with my notebook in my bag, headed out on foot to see if I could discover from public records something of the history of my house.

I strode down Avenida Juan de Bethencourt until it fed into Calle León y Castille. Both roads enjoyed a central reservation planted with established trees, including palm trees. Puerto del Rosario's efforts at beautification centred in the harbourside locale. My spirits lifted a little in the beholding. It was the tourist in me coming to the fore. I wanted everywhere on the island to look like Betancuria, although Puerto del Rosario was never meant to be a holidaymaker destination. An old fishing port once known as Puerto de Cabras (Goats Port), the capital was the island's commercial and municipal hub and that was it.

I have always found it a shame not more of the villages and towns of Fuerteventura have retained their quaintness. Yet pockets of olde worlde charm can be found, in La Oliva, Tuineje and Pájara, towns I have visited on numerous occasions to enjoy an amble in their sheltered, tree-filled plazas, and a nice lunch.

The ordinary and uninspiring surroundings of the city gave way to grandeur on the next block where the municipal council, a stately building, formal in design, faced the equally stately looking town hall. Both faced the same plaza that was dominated, not by government authority, but by an old church: Parroquia de Nuestra Señora de Rosario.

The plaza was elegantly laid out and paved, but lacked shade.

As if to complete the symbols of power, new and old, all that officialdom was accompanied by a number of banks. I found it striking that power and influence and money should all be huddled together like that, showing off their stature. Yet, why wouldn't they? It was more surprising that in all the time I worked for a bank branch in Colchester, I never once questioned or even acknowledged the same sort of clustering. Acutely aware of my own wealth, I had become self-conscious and therefore more conscious of the wealth around me, yet I would remain an outsider when it came to that level of privilege. I would never have power or influence. I didn't even want it. I would remain humble Claire Bennett forevermore. Unlike whoever built my ruin, who certainly had power, or influence, or both.

Wandering around the perimeter of the plaza, I found an even greater irony. Should a citizen commit a transgression, the police department was tacked on behind the town hall and I noticed the courthouse up behind the church. Every aspect of institutional power, then, was concentrated in that small area. It was probably happenstance, I thought, making excuses, and I supposed it would be convenient for the staff. And for me. If I was to discover the truth about the previous owners of my house, it would be amongst those edifices.

I went first to the town hall but was shunted to the municipal council where the titles of all the island's properties were held. The assistant at the enquiries desk greeted me in English. I explained my request and produced my identification and details of my property purchase. The assistant, an impassive, middle-aged man, walked away.

I had a long wait in that cool and austere interior. Behind me, a queue formed. I felt inclined to step aside, but no other assistant appeared so I stayed where I was.

The man returned with a folder, muttering something about lawyers and questioning to himself why mine hadn't shown me the details. I responded, in my best Spanish, telling him it was because I hadn't asked. His manner changed instantly and he turned a document around for me to read, pointing to the relevant details with a pen.

The newspaper article was accurate, he said.

I sensed restlessness in the queue but the assistant appeared in no hurry and since he clearly wasn't about to trust me with the file, I read as fast as I was able.

The original owner was a Don Gonzalez, a wealthy man who owned a vineyard in Tenerife. He built the house in 1770. What he hoped to gain by living in Tiscamanita, heaven only knew. Perhaps he was an absentee owner of that Tenerife vineyard, a don who resided in Spain and, being a beach-loving type, he chose Fuerteventura for his holiday home. In *Tiscamanita*? Oh, well. Perhaps he saw potential in cochineal. I read on. In 1870, his descendants, for whatever reason, sold the premises to the Cejas family. Upon the death of Señor Juan Cejas in 1895, the property fell into the hands of his daughter, a Doña Antonia Cejas and his nephew, Santiago Cejas. That must have been when the wall went up.

The article told me nothing more. I scribbled down all the details, thanked the assistant and took my notes to the municipal library, a short walk down Calle Primero de Mayo.

The library is housed in a modern building facing a cultural centre and concert hall, in what serves as Puerto del Rosario's artistic hub. Despite the separation of culture from institutional power, I like the compartmentalising of the little city in this fashion. It makes practical sense. On that day of my quest, I especially liked that I could walk to all I needed.

Inside, the library was light and airy, and on the upper level much use had been made of tubular railing painted primary-school yellow. I went straight to the information desk with my query and was directed by a helpful assistant in clearly enunciated English to a selection of local history books. I thanked her in Spanish and we exchanged glances and laughed softly together. She was young, perhaps no more than twenty-five, and her attitude was accommodating and, I thought, refreshingly cosmopolitan.

I went and pulled every book on local history from the shelf and stacked them on a table nearby. I trawled the indexes on the hunt for Don Gonzales and Señor Cejas. I found no mention of Gonzalez. He couldn't have made any sort of impression here or involved himself in local politics or culture. The house may have been an indulgence, a folly, even a way of sinking his wealth into rock and mortar. Maybe he was a reclusive type and wanted to hide. Or the records detailing him were lost. I did find a short paragraph on Cejas in a book on the history of Tuineje.

From what I could glean, the Cejas family were a distant and lesser arm of one of Spain's noble dynasties, and had derived much wealth from the cochineal beetle. Remembering the owner of the café in Tiscamanita referring to my house as Casa Baraso, I went back through all the indexes. I could find no mention of anyone with that surname. Having no idea when he lived in the house, I looked no further.

I hadn't discovered much, but browsing those volumes aroused my interest in the history of Fuerteventura, so I decided to hang around and have an explore.

I picked up a book entitled *Arte, Sociedad y Poder: Casa del Coroneles* which had been published in 2009 by the Canary Islands government. My Spanish would be stretched to the hilt in the comprehending, but after my recent observations of how power liked to cluster together and look after itself, I thought it appropriate I took some time to understand the history. I felt guilty that in all my years of holidaying, I had never once taken the trouble to really know the place. Owning a ruin had changed that and was fast putting paid to my ignorance.

The book concerned the reign of colonels that began in the early eighteenth century. The rule was dynastic, all the colonels coming from the same family, the Cabrera Bethéncourts. Primarily, the volume concerned a grand house in

La Oliva, Casa de los Coroneles, once the home of the much-feared Colonel Augustín de Cabrera Bethéncourt Dumpierrez. A preamble in the book provided a short history of life in Fuerteventura during the eighteenth and nineteenth centuries, which included the first hundred-year background story to my house.

From what I could glean, both the local bourgeoisie and the Spanish nobility held onto their wealth through intermarrying and bequeathing all to the first bon son, as the aristocracy the world over tended to do. Initially the rich, the Señores, lived up around Betancuria where the soil was fertile. That, I already knew. For two hundred years after its conquest, the island population was organised into militias under the command of the Lord's elected captain. Then, in 1708 under the Borbon dynasty, the age of the colonels began, and for the next one hundred and sixty-two years, up until the year Cejas bought my ruin in 1870, judicial and military power lay in the hands of a single colonel answerable only to the Spanish King. No other local authority or lord had any sway. So much power concentrated in one man, and since his overlord was the Spanish King who was far, far away, the colonel could do whatever he wanted. The church was no help. The bishops were in cahoots.

There had been seven colonels in all, and my house was built during the rule of the most famous, the brutal and greedy Augustín Cabrera who took up the post in 1766 when he was just twenty-three and he ruled for forty-four years. He was also at various times during his term as colonel: alderman, judge and chief constable of the court of the Inquisition. He became rich through taking out lawsuits against landowners who lacked the means to defend themselves, in order to take possession of their properties. He sounded like an absolute tyrant.

I had often tried to imagine what life might have been like for the locals before tourism took hold. I had visited many of the museums and pictured the subsistence farming life, primitive and simple, and inventive. I saw the windmills, marvelled over kitchen items and farm utensils and the water filters. The simple peasantry. Their goats. I saw old photos of oxen ploughing the fields and camels loaded with hay, and the curious domed grain stores the farmers built. Then there were the churches, one in every village, indicating a population devoted to Catholicism. I knew that religion had crushed the native's indigenous faith. I knew the island had been sparsely populated and I knew that the island's primary exports had been orchilla and barilla and much later, cochineal, along with grains when it rained enough for a surplus. I also knew Fuerteventura was looked down upon as the poor relation by its superior island neighbours, especially Tenerife. In all, I had built up a romantic image of peasantry battling the elements and it had aroused in me a desire to champion the underdog.

I also knew about the famous Winter house down in Cofete on the island's mountainous southern tip, home of a German engineer with close connections to Spain and Fuerteventura. Everyone who came to the island ended up knowing about Casa Winter. Gustav Winter had the house built in the late 1930s in a remote and inaccessible part of the island, and the house went on to be the source of much speculation and conspiracy theories associated with the Nazis. I had not visited Cofete, as I had no interest in wild beaches pounded by the Atlantic and there was nothing down there other than the mountainous terrain ending, on the western coast, in a long cliff.

Before I had entered the municipal library, I had felt armed with all I needed to know about the island. There didn't seem much to it. After all, how could there be, the place was that small. I had no idea I was holding onto a one-sided and partial understanding. What I had never taken the trouble to entertain before I bought my ruin was the domination of the peasantry by Spanish nobility and a local bourgeoisie. It was as though a veil was lifting. First Betancuria and now here. I wasn't sure what to make of any of it, other than it made me uncomfortable and, worse, uneasy.

I put down the book. Not given to wandering around stately homes, I had yet to visit the Casa de los Coroneles, but I decided I must, if only to see what sort of life the rich had led, while the poor battled it out with the elements. I would take a trip out to La Oliva sometime.

Claire Bennett from Colchester might be about to do the island a good turn in restoring one of the old homes of the local bourgeoisie, and I still felt it was important to do so, but I sensed I would be elevating the history of the oppressors, something that had been nagging at me since I sat in the church in Betancuria. For while that colonel and his cronies had gotten fat, misery confronted many a peasant farmer faced with drought and disease. It seemed bizarre that such opulence as was evident in the churches and stately homes could be derived from a land so difficult to live off.

I filled a couple of pages of my notebook with general information and took photos of old photographs and left the library with my head full of facts. After stopping for lunch at a local café, I trudged back to my apartment. The walk was uphill all the way.

Olivia Stone

My inquiries at the government office and the library had provided a taste of the history of my ruin but I was no closer to finding out about Señor Baraso, or why the locals referred to my house as Casa Baraso. The Olivia Stone wouldn't arrive any time soon and it felt like my investigations in Puerto del Rosario had come to a halt. I spent the rest of the week browsing through furniture stores, kitchen and bathroom showrooms, and car yards—I needed to purchase my own vehicle and lose the rental—whiling away the time. I replied to an email from my father with a brief update and sent a longer email to Aunt Clarissa, tailored to suit. By the following Saturday I had had my fill of hanging around Puerto del Rosario.

As the sunlight warmed the street and the air in the city heated up, I packed my gardening tools in the car boot and took myself off to a garden centre in Tefía which, according to their website, carried a wide range of drought and wind tolerant plants.

Tefía is situated on an elevated plain towards the island's remote north-eastern edge. The plain is windswept, stark and too exposed for comfort. The mountains at that northern end of the island are as moulded and as rugged as everywhere else. The tones pale, chalkier-looking in the gullies. In all, the locale is a backwater, if an island as small as Fuerteventura could have such a thing.

I exited the village and found the garden centre, accessed via a short stretch of dirt road. I parked facing north to avoid the worst of the sun on the windscreen, left the window open a crack, and crunched my across the gravel and on inside.

It was soothing browsing rows of plants. I enjoyed the green. A quiet contentment filled me as I wandered up and down. I found plant shopping infinitely preferable to the sterile environment of furniture and hardware stores. Although I faced the same problem. I had no idea what to buy.

Cacti and palms seemed the obvious choices but I fancied a different sort of look. I had been told the municipal council would provide up to forty free plants a year to every householder in an effort to green up the island, but I was yet to tap into that scheme. I settled on three drago trees, five aloe vera plants, ten tubes of a hardy-looking clumping grass and a few pots of a succulent ground cover. Not particularly adventurous choices, but they were all labelled hardy and drought and wind tolerant and they would need to be. I was planting up the far back corner of my block, well away from the build. It was an exposed spot and whatever I put there might well get forgotten.

The drive from Tefía to Tiscamanita took me back through the flat plain fringed by mountains, a plain that seemed to go on forever, although I was soon facing the Betancuria massif and heading down through Antigua. Half an hour and I was mounting the kerb outside my house, pleased I had cleared the block of rocks.

I parked a sensible distance from the area I planned to garden, pushing open the car door on a blast of wind. Eleven o'clock, and the sun had a bite to it. I reached in for my cotton scarf to wrap around my head. No doubt I looked strange, my head and neck covered in a scarf, my eyes behind dark glasses. I really needed one of those large hats the women used to wear.

With plant pots at my feet, my hands in gardening gloves, my garden fork and spade leaning against my wheelbarrow, I felt as far from bank-teller Claire as it was possible to be. My garden in Colchester—north-facing and grim—had consisted of a small paved rectangle decorated with a few straggly pot plants. A hanging basket beside the south-facing front door I maintained for show. Now, garbed in loose pants and a long-sleeved shirt, my head and neck shrouded in a scarf I wasn't sure who I was, this woman standing alone on an acre of land overlooking a volcano, about to dig holes and plant a garden.

Mistress of a ruin?

I looked back at the sad structure, and at my barn with its newly tiled roof. Standing on my own land, poised to dig my first hole and pop in a plant, I felt empowered and deflated all at once. I was alone. I had no one with whom to share any of my experiences. No mother, a father who took no interest—not that he would have been anything other than a bother, with endless reproaches and told-you-so looks—and no Aunt Clarissa, although she would have been at a loss in this wild, inhospitable environment. She favoured her creature comforts, did my dear old aunt. Besides, she was too old to help. As for my friends at the bank, they had started emailing me enthusiastically and were lining up to visit. I began to view the lot of them as freeloaders after a cheap holiday and I made a mental note to distance myself from each and every one of them. Which left a hole inside of me. I had been on the island one month and in that time I had made no friends on the island. Not one.

I shook off my maudlin thoughts, reminding myself that when visitors did come, I wanted to show them something I was proud of. I set to, choosing a spot a good six feet from the dry-stone wall and commenced digging.

The soil was dry, the progress slow. The only positives the paucity of weeds and the presence of a layer of volcanic gravel, which I shunted aside as I prepared a hole. How deep did the hole need to be? How wide? I knew that the plant must not sit proud of the soil that surrounds it, but what about the ground beneath? Didn't that need to be loose too? Or could I let the roots tough things out down there? Ten fork stabs later and finding the digging too hard, I compromised.

I planted a drago and stepped back to admire my efforts. The little plant looked lonely so I persevered with another hole about three yards from the first. The ground proved softer. Determination took hold and I got into a rhythm. When the third drago was in the ground I downed tools and went to the small supermarket for snacks and a drink, both for me and my plants, coming away with five ten-litre water containers.

Having to ferry water in that fashion seemed ridiculous and I could have done with a garden tap, but that idea belonged in England where plumbing was everywhere and it rained. Out here, water was precious. Each house has its own underground water tank. Thinking about how often those plants would need a drink, I decided I had better go easy on the gardening or I would feel like a water bearer.

I kept digging and planting, taking short breaks to slug water or eat potato crisps and fruit, grateful the smaller plants needed smaller holes. I put the grasses along the front edge of my triangular garden bed, and the aloe veras I spaced out beside the walls. I staggered the ground covers in between the dragos. It was three o'clock when I finished. By then, the sun was ferocious. I was beginning to feel faint and desperate for shade.

I stood back for a moment. Before I set about watering in the plants I whipped off my scarf and doused my hair and face in the bottled water, putting the scarf back on to catch the drips and trap the wet cool.

With the gardening finished I left my tools and wandered around the block, observing the house next door, all enclosed behind a dense prickly pear hedge, and the one on the north side, with its long and high wall behind which I heard no sign of life, not a whisper or a cry or a barking dog. The old farmhouse across the street was clearly another ruin behind its weathered facade, and further up, the front windows of another farmhouse were shuttered. No one drove by as the street led nowhere other than to more ruins. I couldn't have chosen a lonelier spot. When I reached my restored barn, I opened the new and unpainted door and peered inside but there was nothing to see other than the crisscross of beams of the roof and the new window set high in the back wall. The cement floor was yet to be laid.

I was about to return to my car to pack up when a dusty old four-wheel drive slowed and stopped outside my block. I recognised the car as Paco's.

Seeing me, he strode over, adjusting the strap of his battered-looking satchel. I wasn't sure how to greet him having only met him twice, but he decided for me by leaning down and offering me his cheek.

'Good progress,' he said, nodding at the barn.

We strolled past the ruin and I showed him around. He looked inside and up at the roof.

'When do they start on the house?' he asked.

'I don't know.'

I wasn't sure what else to say. I didn't want to go into an explanation of council permits. 'I ordered the Olivia Stone book,' I said, eager, perhaps a little too eager to keep the conversation going.

'You can probably get a pdf online.'

'I prefer paper. Besides, there's no rush.'

'Maybe not. She visited Tiscamanita.'

'You told me.'

'I did?' He appeared puzzled, as though he couldn't fully recall our conversation in Betancuria. To cover his embarrassment he added, 'She stayed in Don Marcial Velázquez Curbelo's house.'

'And he was?'

'The older brother of the man whose street we're in.'

His gaze slid to the view behind me, of my little garden. Seizing on his interest, I led the way. As we walked over I said, 'Calle Manuel Velázquez Cabrera,' I enunciated every syllable. 'Who was he?' I asked with sudden interest.

'A lawyer who championed the causes of Fuerteventura and Lanzarote.'

'Impressive.'

'His brother, Marcial, was a cultured and literary man who impressed Olivia Stone with his wit and intelligence. She probably read his newspaper.'

'He produced a newspaper?'

'El Eco de Tiscamanita.'

'How marvellous! Is it still going?'

'Hardly.' His tone was not disparaging, although perhaps a little mocking. He was difficult to read. We stopped near my tools.

'Wow, you have been a busy woman!'

'It's a start,' I said with modesty.

'Why here in this corner?'

'It's safe from the build.'

'Ah, yes, of course.'

I should have let the conversation end there, but I was curious about this Olivia Stone woman.

'You think she could read Spanish then?'

'Definitely. Maybe. A little.' He sounded vague.

Not wanting the topic of conversation to fizzle before it got fully underway, I said with much enthusiasm, 'She sounds like a remarkable woman.'

'She was a lot more than that,' he said, his tone strangely serious. He turned his gaze back to my face. 'She disappeared, you know. There is no record of her death and no one heard of her after she published her book.'

'Surely, they did.' I didn't mean to sound dismissive. It was a habitual response I had picked up as a bank teller. I cautioned myself to lose the tendency quick smart. Keen to re-establish my earlier interest, I added, 'What else do you know about her?'

'She was born in Ireland and married an English barrister. They lived in London and moved in high social circles.' As I had suspected, he had turned cold on me again.

I grinned, hoping to win him over.

'Where did you acquire all this information?'

'From a biography published in a highly regarded magazine. It came with references.' He sounded proud. I sensed my smile had had the desired effect. He went on. 'The writer of the article suggests, and I believe, that she came to live here in the Canary Islands. There was a mention of a Stone, singular, arriving on the Wazzan in Tenerife in the November of 1895.'

'And you think it was her.'

'Has to be.'

'But people would have known about her then. People living on Tenerife.'

'Not if she came here.'

'To Fuerteventura?'

'To Tiscamanita.'

'But you have no evidence.' I paused. 'I'm sorry, I didn't mean to sound rude. Maybe you do have evidence. Do you?'

'The article says she named her house in Dover, 'Fuerteventura'.'

I paused. *Was that it?* All my efforts at placating the guy only to discover Paco really was nuts.

'But that does not mean she came to Tiscamanita,' I said gently, my impatience rising. 'Besides, what happened to her husband?'

'He re-married in 1900.'

'Then she died.'

'Or they got divorced.'

'People didn't get divorced back then.'

'Maybe she just took off.'

'And abandoned her marriage? Did she have children?'

'Three boys.'

'There you are then. She wouldn't have left them.'

'They would have been teenagers. And a right pack of ratbags if they were anything like their father.'

'You can't say that. You don't know him.'

'The article has a photo of him. I will bring it to you next time and show you. He looks like a pig of a man.'

'Even so, there would have been a scandal. A woman of her standing, it would have been all over the newspapers.'

The wind gusted, plastering my trousers and shirt to my skin. I turned my back on the brunt of it. An empty plant pot fell on its side and rolled a short distance, coming to rest beside the wheelbarrow.

Paco waited for the wind to calm down before continuing with his theory. 'All I know is the evidence stacks up. There is no death certificate, no death notice in any newspaper, nothing at all to record her death. And there is no record of a divorce either. Not according to the article, which was written by a scholar from the University of La Laguna.'

'Okay, so she disappeared. Maybe she came to Fuerteventura, but why Tiscmananita?'

'The answer is simple. Once you read her travel diary you will see. She enjoyed the company of Marcial very much.' He paused. 'Maybe they had an affair.'

Was he serious?

'Maybe they did,' I said, deciding to humour him.

He pointed past me and said in a low voice. 'Right there, under your roof.'

'But this was Señor Cejas' house.'

'Just because Cejas owned it doesn't mean he lived in it.' He looked at his watch. 'Fancy a beer? You look like you need one.'

I laughed. It was a relief to mark an end to the conversation with a social invitation. 'I just need to pack up.'

'I'll meet you in the café opposite the church in Antigua.'

'The one at the end of the plaza?'

'You know it?'

'Café Rosa. Yes, I do.'

He turned, hesitated, then put down his satchel to help me pack away my tools. Then I watched him walk back to his car, puzzling over this strange man with an even stranger obsession, who might possibly become my first friend on the island.

Antigua

I was sweaty and sticky and my face burned hot despite the scarf and sunglasses. And I was as excited as a child anticipating cake. I saw Antigua up ahead. Paco made a left at the road leading to the town hall. I followed. The café was on the right, just past the police station.

The area around the plaza benefited from a dense planting of stout Canary palms. We both managed to find a park in some shade and entered the café together, Paco choosing a table in the corner by the window.

Spanish pop music played in the background. A young couple in shorts and T-shirts came in, gave the café a quick scan and, seeing the interior empty save for us and the local men and families at the back tables, walked straight back out again having evidently changed their minds or not seen who they were looking for.

'Beer?' Paco asked.

'I'm famished,' I said, picking up the menu on the table.

'They do a good goat stew.'

The man behind the counter came over and greeted Paco. They chatted in rapid Spanish I was too tired to absorb. Paco slowed his speech and ordered a plate of the stew and two beers.

'Aren't you eating?'

The man hesitated and we both looked at Paco, who patted his belly and shook his head.

'On me,' I said. He maintained a resistant look. 'Please, it's no fun eating alone.' I didn't wait for his reply. 'Make that two,' I said, and scanning the tapas menu I added, 'and give me the tomatoes and the olives.'

I handed him my menu. He grinned, clearly amused I had taken control.

'Anything more?' He directed his question at Paco, who had shifted his gaze to the window.

There was an awkward pause.

'That's all thanks,' I said to cover it.

The man walked away.

'I didn't mean to embarrass you,' I said, leaning forward.

'I'm not embarrassed.'

I didn't believe him.

'You know the waiter?'

'That's Juan, my mother's cousin's son. This café is his.'

I never considered myself socially awkward but there was something about the way Paco chose to converse, how I chose to converse with him, that felt stilted. I suddenly had to ask myself what to say as a follow up remark to his last. 'Are you from Antigua?' I knew I was jumping to conclusions, that he probably wasn't.

'Triquivijate.'

Another small village on the way from Antigua to Puerto del Rosario. Unlike Tiscamanita, the village is set back off the main road and receives no through traffic. It was a sort-after area with new subdivisions and luxury homes.

'Do your family own a farm?' It was the obvious question.

'Did. We grew prickly pear like everyone else.'

'And now?'

He shrugged. 'My parents live in Puerto del Rosario. My mother works at Costco and my father in an auto repair shop.'

'What about you?'

'I work in a restaurant in Caleta de Fuste.'

A waiter, then? A waiter in a restaurant?

'Is that where you live as well?'

'Too many holidaymakers there for me. I rent a small flat in Puerto del Rosario, near the beach.'

Paco's relative, Juan, came over with the beers and tapas, along with a basket of bread, and we occupied ourselves stabbing quarters of tomato drizzled with olive oil, and munching olives. I glanced out the window at the quiet street, thinking it odd that, just as in the past there were two Fuerteventuras, the peasants and their feudal overlords, today there are also two, here and the one on the eastern coastline dedicated to tourism where locals are forced into low-paid menial jobs as they yearn to hold onto a quieter, less foreigner-dominated existence. I felt a ping of awkward shame in the thinking. Then people like me come along and invade the hinterland. The island had already been sacrificed to the tourist dollar and I had no idea the effect that would have long term, but I doubted it would be good. Especially if nobody bothered to restore the old buildings. With the loss of the original architecture comes a loss of culture, a loss of identity. Despite my ethnicity—I couldn't help who I was—I shared Paco's interest, his determination to preserve what was left. Even if my house was the former residence of a fat cat. I wondered if Paco would see it that way. What *did* he think of me? He must warm to me, or why invite me out. He clearly wasn't as lonely as I was.

I guzzled my beer. The bitter fizz quenched a thirst I didn't realise I had. My face burned and my shoulders were beginning to ache from the hard labour of the day. Paco had gone quiet again. A photographer working in a restaurant? He was undoubtedly passionate but I had no idea the standard of his creative output. It seemed the only personal topic left to discuss and I pounced on the chance to discover more about this new and reticent friend.

I tried to catch his gaze as I spoke. 'Are you able to sell or publish your photos?'

He swallowed what he was chewing and chased it with a mouthful of beer before he spoke.

'In newspapers and magazines, yes. I'm working on an exhibition.' He hesitated and then added with a touch of irony, 'The restaurant where I work sells my postcards.'

'I don't suppose it all puts much food on the table.' I instantly wished I hadn't said that. I had probably offended him. I saw in a sudden rush that the comments I made as Claire Bennett the bank teller were no longer appropriate now I was rich.

'It isn't about the money,' he said. 'I take photos to capture the beauty of this island. Every passing moment of it, night and day.'

'Do you photograph the other islands?'

'When I can afford to travel. I want to visit El Hierro. Have you been? No? It is small and dramatic, the top of the volcano rising up from the ocean. There are no beaches there. But the views are breath taking.'

'I am not good with heights.'

He studied my face. 'You get used to it.'

I wasn't sure I would. England was comparatively flat, and I had never been any good up a tall building, let alone a mountain top or the edge of a cliff. Even at the lookout on the Pájara-Betancuria Road I'd had to stand well back from the edge to take in the mountains and the ocean far below.

The goat stew came and the conversation slid away as we each took our fork and spoon and dove in. The meat was tender, the flavours robust, the sauce thick and filling. I dunked in what was left of the bread. Paco looked over at his cousin and in a moment more bread came, and two more beers.

'Do you miss home?' he said eventually.

I felt instantly uncomfortable. 'Here is home,' I replied, hoping I didn't seem churlish.

'No family in England?'

'A father and an aunt.'

'That is all?'

'Yes.'

'That is sad.'

'Not sad. Just how it is.'

'And your mother?' he asked pinning me with his gaze.

'She died when I was seven.'

'A tragedy,' he said, smiling at me with sympathy. 'You miss her.'

I felt too uncomfortable to respond. 'And you?' I said instead. 'Brothers? Sisters?'

'Three brothers living here, and one sister in Gran Canaria. She's married with three boys.'

'Are your brothers married?'

'All married. All with children.'

'And you?' As the words exited my mouth I froze inwardly and was disconcerted by my reaction.

'Me?' He laughed. 'I have no one.' He looked sad for a moment. I thought something must have happened. A tragedy of the heart. Thankfully he didn't inquire of my love life, which was non-existent. I had gone on dates, tried out a few boyfriends – Simon was the longest – but none were my type. Who was my type? No one had broken my heart and I was accustomed to the single-person lifestyle. I had never felt I needed a man to complete me.

We were soon done with the stew. Paco set down his cutlery, glanced at his watch and sat back in his seat. Sensing the end to our time together, I murmured the name that had been playing at the fringes of my mind through the whole meal.

'Baraso.'

'Sorry?'

'My house is known locally as Casa Baraso. A señor Baraso lived there apparently.'

'Yes, I know. Baraso lived there for some time until his death in 1862.'

'Who was he?'

'A friend of Don Gonzalez's great grandson. Don Pablo Baraso Medina Rodriguez Bethéncourt.'

'What a mouthful. A nobleman then.'

I took a serviette and searched my bag for a pen. Amused, Paco reached in his satchel and handed me his. He repeated the name as I wrote.

'He had a wife and four daughters,' he told me. 'They all died in a yellow fever epidemic.'

I kept writing.

'Thirty years or so before you say Olivia Stone lived there?'

'She would have had the house to herself.'

'Maybe. Maybe Cejas never lived there. But when Cejas died he left the house to two lots of family and they had that partition wall put in. That would have been in 1895, around the time you say Olivia Stone stayed there. And that daughter and nephew must have lived in the house. Otherwise, what would have been the point of the wall?'

He considered my analysis without comment. I went on, insistent. 'It would have been a horrendous domestic situation, don't you think? They clearly didn't want to co-habit and perhaps even despised each other. They ruined the house with that wall.'

I sat back in my seat and waited for his reply which was not immediately forthcoming.

'They probably didn't care,' he said eventually. 'They were mainlanders and they were rich. To them, it was just a stupid little house on a stupid little island.'

I was surprised at his bitterness.

'Even so,' I said, determined not to let the topic go, 'I doubt Olivia Stone would have condoned that arrangement for one second.'

'She must have. Or maybe that wall was put up after she left. We don't know when the wall was built.'

'But surely, she could have stayed in any house in the area, more or less?'

Was I starting to believe his crazy story? He may have proof, however scant, and by her own account she did visit Tiscamanita and make a friend of Marcial, but I had no idea where he lived, although it was certainly not my house.

'You need to understand that she disappeared,' Paco said, shifting forward and resting his elbows on the table, holding my gaze, his eyes filled with intrigue. 'Desconocida. My theory is she lived in your house as a recluse. If she'd stayed anywhere else, with Marcial for example, then everyone would have known. There would have been a record. In Casa Baraso, shut up with only a maid, the villagers would have had no idea she was there.'

I couldn't quash the irritation rising in me. Paco was jumping to conclusions like a card-carrying conspiracy theorist. Casa Baraso was *not* Casa Winter.

'They must have known,' I retorted. 'The maid would have gossiped. What are you saying? That she arrived in the night and never left the house?'

All he said was, 'Yes.'

'And no one came? No one saw? She never even appeared in an open window?'

Paco didn't answer. I handed him back his pen and he dropped it in his satchel.

I pictured the size of my house, the enclosed patio, and speculated that it was possible Olivia Stone hid there. Not likely, but possible. Although, not for long, not for years and years.

My thoughts halted. The workmen believed the house was cursed and a curse could mean only one thing – something terrible and tragic had happened there. Maybe Olivia Stone died there and her ghost was trapped for some reason. Not that I believed in ghosts, not for one second, but Aunt Clarissa said the spirits of the dead became trapped on the earthly plane due to their intense emotions. In her case guilt, probably, if she had abandoned her sons. No, the whole scenario was just plain silly.

Not wanting to embarrass Paco, when his cousin came to take our plates I followed him to the counter and waited by the till.

When I turned back to the table, Paco was standing and putting his satchel over his head. I succumbed to a twinge of disappointment and regret. Had I blown a chance of friendship over my quarrelsome comments?

'Thank you for the food,' he said when I joined him to leave.

'It was nothing.'

I offered him a smile. Relief washed through me as he reciprocated.

'Are you returning to Puerto del Rosario?'

I had no idea why he asked, other than to make casual conversation.

'I thought I would head back to the house.'

'Mind if I join you? I'd like to take some more photos.'

'Sure.'

We had left Tiscamanita strangers, and returned as friends of a sort. I wasn't sure what Paco thought of me, but he was the only person I had had lunch with on the island and I wasn't about to pass up the opportunity of developing our friendship further.

He parked behind me. Together we headed around the back of the ruin and squeezed through the boarded-up doorway. Paco took out his camera and lined up a shot and then another. I watched, quiet, trailing him around. Eventually, he stopped and we stood by the partition wall. Every time I entered the ruin, that wall felt like the safest place to be. Yet it also felt wrong, impacting the integrity of the house, preventing it from expressing its glory, its true self. When Paco returned his camera to his satchel, I turned to him and said, 'Most days I can't believe I have taken on this project.'

'It will take years to complete.'

I hoped not.

'But at least it's going to be saved,' I said, absent-mindedly picking up a loose rock in the partition wall.

As if in response, our conversation was cut short by a protracted screech and boom. My heart responded with a boom of its own.

A plume of dust indicated the location. We went and peered tentatively in through a doorway in the northern end to find a small section of an internal wall had collapsed.

Tuineje

Dawn made its presence felt through the blinds. Deciding there was no point remaining horizontal despite the early hour, I lumbered out of bed, stiff from yesterday. I had scarcely slept. At the forefront of my mind, stuck on replay, was an image of the wall falling. How much wall had I lost? I didn't know. It may only have been a square foot but in the darkness that square magnified tenfold until I was buried beneath a great pile of rocks and rubble.

I showered and dressed and ate a simple breakfast of fruit and toast. The moment it was decent to do so, I phoned Mario. I hoped he wasn't religious because it was Sunday.

He answered on the third ring. I tried to keep the tone of my voice measured as I explained the collapse, but by the end of my explanation I was frantic.

'We must talk to the council at once, Mario. This is urgent. The whole house might fall before they make up their minds to approve the restoration.'

'They've only had the plans three weeks.'

'Can't something be done?'

Mario told me to meet him at the council in Tuineje the next day at ten.

I was gripped by anxiety for the whole day. It was the longest twenty-four hours of my life. I flew around the apartment, tidying up and folding clothes and doing the dishes. I put on a load of washing and even mopped the floor in a vain attempt at self-distraction. I tried to read, and failed. After lunch, I went over my spreadsheet of costings but found that only made my anxiety worse. I went for a long walk down to the port and back, hoping to tire myself out. I listened to Blur, to Enya, even to Van Morrison, but my mind would not be still.

I awoke Monday on the break of dawn, determined to look smart for the appointment. I coiffed my hair and put on some light makeup, choosing a formal suit to wear. I propped a leather, document case – it was empty – under my arm and looked in the mirror. There was only one word to describe how I looked: official. I had turned back into my bank-teller self.

The quickest route to Tuineje was via Tiscamanita, a thirty-minute drive. I set off at a quarter past nine to allow plenty of time for contingencies, pulling up in the car park opposite the town hall in time to see Mario emerge from the side of the building. He must have parked around the back.

The town hall was a modern building painted terracotta red, with small and low windows evenly spaced along the two visible sides, and a second storey set back from the street. Situated on a corner, the front façade of the lower level comprised a concave arc. The entrance was tucked in the deepest part of the curve. Access was via a small concourse. The effect of the design was one of authority and officialdom on the one hand, and a welcoming openness on the other. Hope prickled as I crossed the road and made for the entrance doors, entering a spacious foyer. I saw Mario talking to a man behind the inquiries desk and joined him.

The man hesitated mid-sentence and glanced at me. I could tell by the reaction in his eyes that my garb had created the right impression.

'This is Claire Bennett,' Mario said, turning to welcome my presence.

'Claire,' the man proffered his hand. 'I'm Raul. I understand you are worried about your ruin falling down.' He gave me a sympathetic smile.

Not wanting to come across the stereotypical hysterical female, I thought better of telling him I could have been killed had I been standing in the wrong spot. 'The house is vulnerable,' I said, setting down my document case. 'Building needs to start right away.'

'Yes, we know. The previous owner wanted to demolish it.' He smiled. It was a wry smile. Were the council disappointed not to have made a successful purchase? Did they resent me? Or were they pleased someone, anyone was taking the trouble to fix up that ruin?

'I want to save the house,' said, 'but I am frightened we'll be too late.'

The man nodded and flicked through the pages of a file open before him. I spotted the house plans and the original versions of letters I had been sent.

'Your application is under consideration. These things take time. There is a process.' He shifted his gaze to Mario. 'You have explained this to her?'

'Can't things be expedited?' I enunciated the word, having learned it only that morning. 'Surely there has to be a way to make this happen faster? It's an emergency.'

Mario reinforced my remark with a brief, 'She's right.'

'Wait here,' Raul said, closing the file and heading off through a door with it under his arm.

Mario explained in a low whisper—not that there was anyone to over-hear—that he was hopeful something would be done to speed things up. Before long, an older man in a white shirt came striding out, file in hand.

'Mario, Claire,' he said, proffering his hand to us both. 'You understand, there is a normal process that must be followed.'

'We know.' Mario spoke for us both.

The man opened the file and flicked through the paperwork, stopping at the plans. He studied them as though it was the first time he had ever seen house plans, pouring over every single drawing. It had to be a pretence. Without look-ing up, he said, 'Since you are making no changes to the original structure of the building, I am happy to say that we can grant you interim approval to make the building safe.'

'That's fantastic,' I said.

The man lifted his gaze to my face. 'For a fee of two thousand euros.'

I nearly fell through the floor. Daylight robbery, as my father would say. What sort of fee was this? Authentic? Or the greasy palm kind? I was pinned by both men's gazes.

'Very well,' I said, 'How do I pay?'

The man left the file and walked away, and before long Raul returned to attend to the payment. We were exiting the town hall fifteen minutes later.

'Thank you, Mario.'

He kept walking, turning to say, 'I will order the scaffolding and find the men. We'll start work straight away. Don't worry, no more of your house will fall.'

I watched him head off round the side of the town hall.

On my way back to Puerto del Rosario, I stopped off at the café in Tisca-manita. I thought it an opportunity to verify Paco's claim that the whole Baraso family had died there of yellow fever. Opening the door, I was relieved to find the café empty and the same woman behind the counter. This time, I walked straight up to her and held out my hand.

'I'm Claire,' I said warmly. 'Since you will be my regular café, I thought it would be good to introduce myself.' Even as I spoke, I felt ridiculous announcing myself like that.

Hesitant, the woman took my hand.

'Has the work started?' she asked.

'Not yet, but it is about to.'

She gave me a doubtful look.

'Who is working on it? Nobody here will go near it. You were lucky to get that barn fixed up.'

Someone has been down my street then, since she knows about the barn.

'Mario doesn't seem to think there will be a problem.'

'Mario Ferrero? It is good you have him. He'll find workers for you. He speaks good English, and German as well. He'll find you foreigners.'

Despite her cool manner, she didn't seem averse to me. Maybe she didn't want to lose my custom.

'I'll have a white coffee and a slice of your tortilla,' I said, keen to steer the subject away from the house for a moment. I didn't want to barrel in with my inquiry, in case she thought me intrusive.

I took the table by the window and when she came over, I couldn't wait any longer. 'I hope you don't mind me asking, but I am trying to find out more about Señor Baraso.'

She was instantly cautious.

'Yes?' she said slowly.

'A friend told me he had a wife and four daughters.'

'That's correct.'

'And they all died in a yellow fever epidemic.'

'Who told you that?'

'Paco.'

'Paco?'

'He's a photographer from Triquivijate.'

'I know Paco.' She laughed. 'He thinks he knows everything.' She laughed again. It seemed a good-humoured laugh, but I sensed she was covering something.

I was about to probe further when a mother came in with a pram and two small children.

The woman glanced at the family. 'He knows the official version,' she said quickly. 'That is what everyone else will tell you, too.'

She hurried to the counter and soon there was chatter and laughter and no sign of it stopping and certainly no chance for me to ask what she meant by her last remark.

Progress

Mario was true to his word. A week later, he phoned to say the scaffolding had arrived on site. I took the opportunity to thank him, conveying my appreciation of his efforts. We chatted briefly about the weather and I assured him I would stay away and not interfere with the build. He told me I would be more than welcome to visit any time I wanted. There was no sign of the hostile and obstructive Mario I first encountered.

Our relationship had changed the day after we went to Tuineje to visit the council, when he sent me the invoice for the barn restoration and, seeing he had chosen to charge me half-price after all for the roof timbers he had acquired from another job, I paid the invoice without a quibble. He then phoned to thank me. On a sudden impulse, I offered him a handsome bonus in exchange for expediting the build and he said he would try to have the structure completed to lock up in six months. From that moment, our exchanges had gone from cautious ambivalence to cordiality and good humour.

For me, the arrival of the scaffolding meant the day was of tremendous significance. I slipped my phone in my bag, thinking to seize Mario's open invitation.

Earlier, I had been bent on distracting myself from anxieties over the build and the mysterious history of my once grand house; I had planned to drive down to Morro Jable on the island's southern tip and go for a swim in the calm waters, taking advantage of a time of year when the holidaymakers were fewer and it was possible to enjoy a patch of ocean all to myself. It was an hour and a half's drive, but well worth the effort; the beach down there was superb and the day forecast to be a hot one. Already dressed in a T-shirt and shorts, I dashed out to my car, threw my beach bag on the back seat and headed off, taking a detour to Tiscamanita. It was a route I had become so accustomed to, I didn't notice the scenery, except to acknowledge it was there.

Cars and small trucks were parked bumper to bumper outside my property and beyond, save for a space that served as a driveway for trucks. I was relieved to see the workmen had the good grace not to use my land as a parking lot as I came to a halt at the end of the row of vehicles. Killing the engine meant killing the air con. I opened the door on the heat and went over to survey the scene. I was keen for shade but finding none, I stood back beside a giant rock dump located where my much smaller rock pile had been.

Delight filled me as I took in the progress. The front and side walls were enclosed in scaffolding and the men were assembling the various lengths of metal tubing along the back. Seeing me standing around, Mario ended a conversation he was having with one of the workers and came over.

'The men are fast,' I said, shaking his hand. 'I'm not recognising any from the barn restoration.'

'Those men were no good. They refused to work on the house.'

I already knew why and I didn't want to hear it a second time.

'Where are these men from?' None of them looked Spanish, from what I could tell.

'They are from all over the island. Two are from Lanzarote. We have English, Scottish, Irish, German, Dutch, Belgian and Swede. They're good men. Hardworking and skilled.'

'And not superstitious,' I said with a laugh.

He laughed as well, but it wasn't a happy laugh. He glanced back at the build. One of the men was trying to get his attention.

'I have to get back.'

'Is it okay if I stay and watch for a while?'

'Sure. Just don't go inside. You stand out here, you understand? You don't have a hard hat.'

I did as I was told. Giving the activity a wide berth, I wandered around. On the northern side the men were ferrying up rocks for the repairs to the rear gable-end wall.

Other than that northern section, the roof was hipped which meant the walls ended flat. Where the roof was intact, men were re-pointing the wall. Roof tiles were being removed with great care in preparation for repairs to the roof timbers. Boarded-up windows were being braced, as were door cavities. Mario had explained some of the methods they would be employing, including inserting steel ties to stitch together the vertical cracks in the gable ends before filling the gaps with stones and lime mortar.

On the south side of the building, which was in the greatest state of disrepair, sections of wall would need to be almost entirely rebuilt. All the existing internal and external plaster would be preserved. Sections of the wall where the plaster had come away would be repointed for additional solidity. All the timber would be re-used and Mario planned to use timbers from a demolition on Gran Canaria. From what I could see, the primary focus was stabilising the existing structure. I had no idea how many men were working inside the building, but I counted fifteen men engaged in various activities around the exterior. I poked my head in the barn to find the concrete had been laid.

The masonry, the noise, the dust, the stolen glances at me in my T-shirt and shorts, and I soon realised my property was no place for me to be. Before I headed off, I strode over to my little garden of dragos and aloe vera. I had forgotten to bring them water but they were said to be hardy and showed no signs of distress. There was no growth evident either, but it was much too soon for that.

There was no growth in the land beyond my block's perimeter either. At one time it had been cultivated but was now fallow. The field sloped to the low, barren hills. The volcano and the distant mountains drew my eye. There were days I looked out at that arid landscape and wondered why I hadn't settled for somewhere lush and green. Somewhere close to Colchester, to my father and Aunt Clarissa. No words could explain the attraction of a landscape so dry, a landscape that had been drawing intrepid Brits for decades despite holding no immediately obvious, greener-grass appeal.

I turned back to the street and looked around. All the activity on site, and not one neighbour had come to watch. Back in Colchester, when I had romanticised the restoration, I pictured a small group of retired men, or a couple of grandmothers, stopping by for a gander, inviting me into their houses for updates, bestowing on me their gushes of gratitude, grasping my hand in theirs telling me how pleased they were that someone was at last caring for the house. Instead, not one person stopped by.

It was almost midday by the time I left the site, entering my furnace of a car to head down to Morro Jable with my bathers and towel. The drive was pleasant, the mountains rising up from the plain, some near, others far, always present, always bare, like giant statues watching.

Once through Costa Calma, the landscape changed to undulations of sandy desert, sprinkled with round lumps of spurge, clinging on, the terrain resembling pale skin suffering a terrible case of scabby pox. Ahead, slipping in and out of view, was the Jandia massif.

The drive was shorter than had I come from Puerto del Rosario; an hour and I was heading down the main drag of Morro Jable. On the high side were the hotels, some of seven storeys, concrete and glass monoliths testament to the holiday idyll that was Fuerteventura, each apartment looking out at that expanse of sapphire and all that golden sand on my left.

Morro Jable had been squashed between the ocean and the Jandia mountains at the heel end of a long and narrow foot of land some one or two miles wide. The town stretched inland into a deep and narrow valley, stopping where it became impossible to build. The mountains sheltered the town from the strong north-westers, making the climate much warmer than that of the island's north.

Before arriving at the town centre, I took a left and pulled up at the end of a short street beside a beach-side café that had outdoor seating sheltered beneath large umbrellas. Keen for a swim, I forewent the delicious garlicky smells emanating from the kitchen and marched across the sand to the shore. The tide was out. The sand was warm underfoot, and it went on and on for maybe a hundred metres, the widest stretch of sand on one of the longest beaches on the island; little wonder holidaymakers made their way south.

I dumped my bag, unfurled my towel and removed my T-shirt and shorts as I looked around. The southern end of the beach was framed by a low rocky cliff and at that end, the beach narrowed. In the other direction, the breadth of sand widened. In the near distance, a lighthouse stood at the head of the beach at the point where the land curved to the north. Beyond was more sand.

Feeling the sun scalding my skin, I wasted no time heading into the ocean.

The water was warm and calm. I swam to the lighthouse and back, enjoying the push of the small waves, the gentle rise and fall. I might not want to mingle with holidaymakers, but I sure was able to enjoy what they did, what they saved up for every year. It was paradise. I bobbed about in the water a while longer, swimming and treading water until my arms and legs were tired.

Back on the beach, I dried off, wrapped the towel around my waist and pulled on my T-shirt. I gathered the rest of my things and headed to the café, suddenly famished.

I chose a table overlooking the beach and ordered the paella and a bottle of sparkling water. Taking in the empty chair opposite, I thought of Paco and our meal in Antigua. What did he make of Morro Jable? Did he enjoy the beach? Swim? When we next met, I would ask.

As expected, the food came almost straight away, the paella already cooked and ready to serve. I ate quickly, watching those around me leave their tables and saunter off or approach and sit down. It was all convivial but I felt no sense of belonging. The effects of too much sun had given me a headache. I extracted my notebook and jotted down the progress of the build while things were still fresh in my mind. Then, I ordered an iced coffee and sat back in the shade of the umbrella, content to let the afternoon drift by.

On the way back to Puerto del Rosario I played my favourite Cocteau Twins' album, *Heaven or Las Vegas,* and enjoyed the waves of contentment that swept through me, affirming in my heart and mind that I had done the right thing moving to the island. For some peculiar reason, or perhaps not so peculiar, that music made me feel expansive, and being on the island had a similar effect. In me, if no one else, the two, the music and the land, fused into one whole state of transcendent wonder.

My euphoria dissipated, my buoyant mood barrelling out of me on the heels of choking fear, when I opened the door to my apartment and almost tripped over the rock.

A letter from Clarissa

I couldn't cross the threshold. I stood in the narrow strip of front yard with the busy street behind me, staring down at the offending rock centred on a tile on its largest face with its craggy rear end pointing at me. The positioning was precise, thought through, planned. The rock had not rolled out of a closed cupboard and bumped its way across the floor tiles from the kitchen to the front door. It wasn't possible.

Behind me, a group of teenagers walked by, chatting and laughing.

Summoning what little courage I had, I stepped inside and closed the door. Shutting out the street felt final, as though inside the apartment existed an alternate reality, one I wanted no part of. I rounded the rock with caution, half expecting the cold hard lump to rise up and hurl itself at my head with sudden force, cracking open my skull.

Nothing happened. I went through to the kitchen and found the cupboard door closed. All looked normal. Nothing else in the apartment had been relocated. I extracted the beach towel from my bag and draped it over the back of a chair and went around opening windows to let in the fresh air. Then I went around closing them again, not wanting to make entry easy for whoever had been in here.

I craved a shower to wash off the salt, but I would feel too exposed and vulnerable knowing someone had been in the flat and moved that rock. Someone who had easy access to the apartment. Another part of me remained spooked. That was the part of me that drew me to the front door, that had me pick up the rock and set it down beside the trunk of a dracaena at the far end of the tiny patch of garden.

Taking no chances, I locked the front door behind me and went straight to the shower before I changed my mind, peeling off my bathers and stepping into the tepid spray.

Having no intention of going out again, I stayed in my bathrobe and tramped about the kitchen pouring juice and making a snack, normal tasks at the end of what should have been a normal day, no, much more than a normal day, a day to celebrate, the renovations at last proceeding.

I was on my way back to the fridge with the carton of juice when I paused. Could those renovations have anything to do with that moving rock? It was an uncomfortable thought, something Aunt Clarissa would speculate on in one of her mystical moments. I was determined to adhere to my original hypothesis. Someone had been in my apartment and that someone was a practical joker who had set out to frighten me.

I wasn't about to let them win, whoever they were. I needed a powerful distraction. The bonks and muffled voices coming through from the apartments to either side of me afforded little comfort. I considered playing music, but I didn't want to listen to music through my laptop's tinny speaker and putting on headphones would isolate me. I needed people close, even if they were a wall apart, even if one of them might be creeping into my apartment when I was absent.

I opened my laptop to an email from Clarissa. Hope stirred. I thought perhaps she would change her mind and visit, but instead, after a string of reassuring platitudes—Rome wasn't built in a day, patience was never your strong suit—the dear old thing launched into a chatty blow-by-blow account of her recent ghost tour escapade.

She had gone to an abbey in Suffolk that hadn't been occupied since the 1950s and had narrowly escaped demolition. Clarissa ended her sentence with a string of exclamation marks. Like mine, was the implication. The abbey was now being restored—more exclamation marks—and the estate included stables, basements and a cellar. The tour guides came with the usual gear: thermal cameras, voice recorders and an EMF meter to detect electromagnetic fields. The guides used stereotypical divination and summoning techniques including dowsing rods, a séance and a crystal ball. 'I was up all night,' Clarissa wrote, 'and despite my best efforts, I didn't detect a thing.' Neither, by her account, had anyone else. Clarissa had to ask herself if it had been worth the money. Those tours weren't cheap. The tour guides had played their parts well enough but the participants—who were there for the thrills—created so much psychic interference they had scared away whatever ghosts might have been there.

I read her account with indifference. Clarissa went on a ghost tour every few months, ostensibly to check out the guide's authenticity and to see, or rather feel for herself if any supernatural entities lurked in any of those supposedly haunted houses. Mostly, she admitted, it was a gimmick, like a parlour game. Cheap thrills, although on reflection, not so cheap.

Clarissa went on to reiterate caution against invoking the lower astral plane. Those tour guides were putting themselves at risk, she said. The participants were mostly too thick skinned to be affected. The entire fad was bringing paranormal sensitivity into disrepute and charlatans abounded, just as they had back in the late 1800s, at the time of the Fox sisters' rappings which led to a burgeoning of interest in the occult, especially in Spiritualism which purported to provide loved ones with access to their dead.

I had heard it all before. Aunt Clarissa's version of a holiday was a ghost tour. Before I wrote a reply, I did a quick search of the Olivia Stone article Paco had mentioned and found it without much difficulty. Reading it through, I could see that Paco had been accurate in his references. Olivia Stone had, to the best of the author's knowledge, disappeared, and there was a '*Stone*' mentioned by a Tenerife newspaper as having arrived on the 'Wazzan' steamship in 1895. The article also stated that Olivia Stone's house near Dover was named *Fuerteventura*. It was strange that no death certificate had been found and there was no record of a divorce mentioned in the article. More's the point, there couldn't have been a death notice or obituary written, or at least not in a major newspaper, one the academic researcher would have found. Perhaps Paco's reasoning was not so fanciful after all.

The article contained a photograph of both Olivia Stone and her husband, John. I studied each in turn.

The photo of Olivia was nothing like the robust Rational Dresser I had imagined. She was a slender, refined looking woman in her thirties, intelligent, introspective, deep perhaps. Her hair, dark and wiry, was brushed back from her face. She had demur eyes and a small mouth. Her manner was not shy and neither was it feminine. She looked haunted, unhappy, possibly of delicate health. Her style of dress—a flowing mid-calf gown tasselled at the short-sleeved cuffs and hem, and matching cape—denoted a woman who was practical and independent and free thinking, not a woman given to makeup or jewellery. Her outfit appeared a touch oriental, and as though to reinforce the style she was seated by a large, decorated urn from which grew a tall plant with feathery foliage.

Her husband was just as Paco had described him, a forthright-looking man seated on some wooden steps, proud with his white, coat-hanger moustache. He was garbed in a suit and tie and matching hat, neither formal or casual. His manner exuded authority and dominance. Perhaps Paco was right; John Stone had been a tyrant and Olivia had fled.

Yet the notion that she had come to Fuerteventura, to Tiscamanita, to my very house, seemed farfetched.

I sat back and glanced around the apartment. As soon as I looked at the front door I pictured the rock sitting outside and my anxiety flooded back. Not wanting my mind to fixate there, I set about translating the entire Olivia Stone piece, including all the references, so that I could send the information to Clarissa who, I thought, would love a fresh genealogical quest. She was a member of an online ancestry site and if anyone were able to uncover the truth about Olivia Mary Stone, it would be my aunt.

For the most part, the article discussed the importance of her book and the genealogy of her husband, John Frederic Matthias Harris Stone.

Translating was painstaking work, and it took me the whole of that evening and part of the following day. In the short breaks I found myself taking in what was, after all, a chore, I followed my interest and searched through all the old newspaper articles I could find online pertaining to my subject. I discovered Olivia Stone's book had made quite a splash in the media and that she had returned to the islands in 1889 and again in 1891, to make revisions to the original work. One newspaper referred to the swarms of holidaymakers flitting to Tenerife after the publication of Olivia's book. And there was a short reference quoting how she regretted what she had started, the islands already transforming into a holiday destination, threatening to destroy local culture.

Ironic, then, that the woman whose words had triggered that influx rued the day she ever wrote them down.

I imagined her in my house, hiding from the world, from her beastly husband, missing her sons—they would have been teenagers by then—and receiving Marcial, her only visitor. Were they lovers? Which room had they used for their trysts? There would have been no partition then; Olivia would have enjoyed the whole patio. She would have sipped tea and read her favourite novels and when night fell, she would have stepped outside to admire the stars. It was surprisingly easy to picture her in my house. As though she belonged there, hidden away. I wondered what had really happened to her. More than anything, I looked forward to reading her book.

The Building Site

It was with trepidation that I opened the front door to my apartment the following morning to find the rock was where I had left it. Relieved, I stepped out in the early morning cool and knocked on Dolores' door. She was surprised to see me and took a moment to recognise my face. I asked her if she had been in my house, or if she had seen or knew of anyone who had. I didn't mention the rock but I said I thought I had had an intruder, twice. She said she had no spare key and she had not seen anyone enter. She told me to contact the agent, who would ask the owner, who lived in Gran Canaria. She looked bemused, shook her head and mentioned the police. I thanked her for her trouble and asked her to keep an eye out. She said she would and I thanked her and returned to my apartment, giving the rock a sideways glance on my way inside.

I didn't want to appear to Mario, to the tradesmen, and especially to myself one of those fussing owners in a home renovation show, anxious for progress by the half hour, preoccupied with details large and small, but I couldn't face staying in the apartment and my body couldn't take another day at the beach.

My compulsion to be on site was endorsed by Mario, who phoned as I was getting ready to leave for Tiscamanita. He wanted me to swing by the hardware store in Puerto del Rosario and pick up ten bags of lime that the delivery guy failed to load on the truck.

I was happy to oblige, pulling up at the store having swung by a bakery for sweet treats for the men, hoping the offering would endear me to them.

I discovered ten bags of lime was sufficient weight to lower the back of my small rental, and I had to slip the gearstick into third on the inclines. The whole journey to Tiscamanita I had to reassure myself that 250 kilos was equivalent of two obese passengers in the back seat. I vowed to buy a robust vehicle at the earliest opportunity. When I arrived at the building site, I didn't dare mount the kerb.

Seeing me pull up, Mario hailed a guy to fetch a wheelbarrow and I stood by watching the back of my car rise in increments as he went back and forth.

I closed the boot and fetched the selection of pastries from the passenger seat and wandered over to where Mario had headed. He was talking to a tall guy in a singlet and baseball cap, on back to front. I instantly summed him up as cocksure.

Seeing me, Mario stopped talking and beckoned me closer.

'Claire, let me introduce Helmud. He's site manager.' The man made to offer his hand, glanced down at his dirt-encrusted skin and laughed. He was tall, blond and sinewy. His eyes exuded a kindly, warm-hearted nature and I was forced to revise my initial assessment. Beside him, Mario appeared serious and weighed-down with worries.

'We're planning a strategy,' he said. 'You might want to listen.'

'The north side of the building is almost intact,' Helmud said to me. 'I propose continuing to restore the rooms in that section, top and bottom, and re-build the walls on the south side before we pull down the partition wall.'

'I don't have a problem with that,' I said.

'It means no water,' said Mario. 'The aljibe is below the patio and the wall cuts right across it.'

'Why would anyone build the wall right there, then? It seems crazy.'

'Access was on the south side,' Helmud said, ignoring my remark. 'But the aljibe is old and needs to be repaired and cleaned before it can be used.'

'We can't get down there, Claire. It isn't safe with that wall sitting above. The weight of the stone is immense.'

'Fair enough,' I said. I didn't understand why they were making a deal of the aljibe, except that it would be my water supply, the dwelling rendered uninhabitable without it, at least by modern standards. Or perhaps they were thinking of my little garden.

'You won't have access to the upper level except via a ladder, not for a long time,' Helmud explained. 'But you will have two finished rooms downstairs that will be completely self-contained.'

'You wanted a room for storage,' Mario said. 'It would be ideal.' He turned to Helmud, 'She was intending to use the little barn.' They exchanged smiles before Mario said, addressing me, 'We've taken over that space.'

I looked over my shoulder at the barn. Following my gaze Helmud told me one end was crammed full of recycled windows and doors, leaving just enough space for the generator.

'How soon will those downstairs rooms be ready?' I asked.

'A few weeks. There won't be power, and the walls will need painting,' Helmud said.

'But the rooms will be usable for storage,' added Mario.

It meant somewhere for my possessions when they arrived from England and I could start buying furniture. Premature perhaps, but it would give me something to do.

I thanked the men and handed Mario the bag of pastries. 'For the workers,' I said, 'To show my appreciation. I hope there are enough.'

'Thank you. They'll like that. I'll hand them around later.'

I went and poked my head inside the back doorway – no longer boarded up – and took a few steps inside to find the scaffolding erected around the internal perimeter and an army of men tackling every corner of the build. It was a pleasing sight and I could see my offer to Mario of a bonus if he could get the building to lock-up in six months had stimulated a frenzy of activity. Seeing all those men, I knew there would not be enough pastries to go around.

The stone masons on the south side were engaged in the painstaking work of re-using the fallen stones to repair the walls. The outer wall was being tackled to a degree, but the main focus was around a front section of wall that had portions freestanding at the upper level. On the north side, the vertical cracks were slowly disappearing, the tiles were all off the roof and repairs to the roof timbers looked underway. New timbers were going into the subfloor where needed, and four men were navigating into place a heavy beam spanning the width between the exterior and interior walls. Downstairs, in the kitchen two men were building stone piers to underpin the subfloor. In all, the restoration was well underway.

Outside, beyond the scaffolding, more materials were being brought on site. There were stacks of timbers for bearers, joists, floorboards and lintels, along with two cement mixers and power tools of all descriptions, including an array of saws, powered by the generator.

Every man wore a tool belt. Amid the hammering, sawing, barrowing and the whine of power tools, there was much talk in a variety of languages, and I wondered if the men were working in their various national groups.

Forgetting my promise to take care on the building site, I went back inside to examine progress on the two, soon-to-be-usable rooms. I soon heard a shout and looked up. Helmud was standing on the scaffolding. He tapped his hard hat and pointed at my head. I gave him a coy, apologetic look and left.

Watching progress at a safe distance, I pictured that moment when I would move in and a sense of satisfaction filled me. All thoughts of mysterious curses and moving rock artefacts had faded away. A fleeting memory of how I had sat in the patio and cried over my mother threatened to invade my equanimity and I shooed it off.

Seeing me still standing around at a loose end, Mario approached and said, 'Tonight, you have some homework. I want you to confirm where you want all the lights, light switches and power points.' He ignored my groan. 'Especially in those two soon-to-be-finished rooms. I can arrange the electrician to rough in that section and then we can start plastering.'

My offer of a bonus aside, I wanted to ask why he was keen to have the build proceed at a breakneck pace. Did he have a backlog of other projects? Or was he in financial straits? He was too anxious, more on edge than ever, and I kept catching him looking at the structure with something like fear in his face. I dearly wanted to know the source.

My question was answered at least in part by the haze developing on the eastern horizon. Another calima was on its way.

I headed back to Puerto del Rosario with the dust haze edging closer. The cooling trade winds were abating, the air temperature rising and in hours Fuerteventura would be blanketed in Saharan dust. I had been told in the past a calima was a rare event in May but in recent years the dust storms had become more frequent, more intense and lasted a lot longer. Perhaps this one would pass over in a day. I wondered how I would cope on calima days in my new home with its patio open to the elements, when opening a door to the outside meant inviting in the dust.

I swung by the supermarket for more groceries and it was midday when I carried my shopping to the front door of my apartment. On my way inside, I shot a glance at the narrow garden. The rock was still exactly where I had placed it.

After lunching on slices of chorizo, tomato and local cheese, I laid the house plans on the table and, room by room, confirmed where I wanted the power points and light switches. At first it was easy. A light switch at each end of the vestibule and a light in the centre of its ceiling. After that, each room became harder, the bathrooms and kitchen worst of all. I had to preconceive the arrangement of furnishings for every room in the house. The entire process made worse by the awareness that I could have power wherever I wanted, no expense spared. It would have been much simpler were I only able to afford a single power point in each room. The process took the whole afternoon and I was exhausted by the end of it.

The dust haze cleared quickly and by the following morning the sky was clear. Mario would be wanting the house plans, but before I went to Tiscamanita I wanted to return to the garden centre in Tefía. Even though more gardening would result in more watering, it meant I had an excuse to be on site.

Keen to make an early start, straight after eating a breakfast of cold tortilla and toasted baguette, I filled the ten-litre water containers and loaded them into the boot along with my gardening tools and headed off.

At the garden centre, I bought three more drago trees and five more aloe vera plants, along with twenty tubes of various kinds of succulents. A cautious selection, but a voice in my head urged me to err on the side of uniformity.

Not wanting to start a precedent, I parked in the street and ferried my tools and plants to my little corner of the garden under the watchful gaze of the workmen.

The building work going on behind me as I laboured made me feel strange and self-conscious. I spent the afternoon tilling the ground and digging holes and watering in plants, extending twofold the existing garden bed, all the while striving to ignore the activities on the build. Whenever I stood and straightened my back I glanced over and observed the men at work on the southern wall, pleased to see progress being made, even if the going was slow. Rebuilding stone walls was a mammoth job when they were almost three feet thick. That amounted to a lot of stone. Whenever my gaze was returned by a curious worker taking a short break, I turned and bent down again and continued planting. At lunchtime, I went to the little supermarket for snacks. I didn't interact with the men other than to hand Mario the plans when he turned up for a short while.

The separation between Claire, the owner gardener, and that army of builders, along with the perception that I was not as welcome as Mario might believe, reinforced a growing sense of isolation. That creeping loneliness returned and grew larger inside me as the afternoon wore on.

I kept my eye out for Paco, who I hoped would call in, but he didn't appear. I regretted not asking for his phone number. It would have been nice to have a coffee or lunch with the only friend I had on the island, even if he was a little crazy with his Olivia Stone obsession.

When all the plants were in the ground and watered, I packed up my gardening gear and loaded the boot of my car, keeping my gaze down as the workmen drifted off the site and drove away in their dusty vans. It was clear I would need to find other ways of keeping occupied while the building was in progress, or I would have the entire property planted up.

As I pulled away from the kerb I thought I might try my hand at fixing the fallen sections of the dry-stone wall at the rear. Although I would only do that on weekends for fear I would be a laughing stock. Better still, I could pay an expert and find a more fitting occupation. Otherwise, boredom and impatience would send me doolally no matter how fast the progress of the build.

The following day, I bought a car, more than a car, a workhorse, a robust four-wheel drive to make ferrying water and bags of lime and tools and the wheelbarrow easier. Relinquishing the rental felt symbolic of my permanence on the island. To reinforce my status, I registered with a local doctor and dentist and enrolled in an upper-intermediate language course starting in early September. To further fill my days, I vowed to make a point of visiting markets and attending festivals, whatever was going on. I must participate, I told myself, if I was to feel I belonged and create a life for myself beyond the build.

The Curse

Three weeks into the restoration, Mario phoned to ask me to swing by the builders supplies yard, on the pretext that another delivery was short on the load. I discovered the truth when I arrived on site with more bags of lime.

Seeing my car pull up, he hurried over and told me through my open window before I even had a chance to turn off the engine and pop the boot, that there was trouble amongst the men. One of the stone masons, Cliff, had left his tool belt hidden in a section of wall the previous night, only visible from up high on the scaffolding. When he turned up for work that morning he found his tool belt on the ground, leaning against the partition wall as though propped there on purpose.

With the ignition keys in one hand and my bag in the other, I studied Mario's face, noting the fear in his eyes. He stood back from the car, head bowed, pinching the bridge of his nose.

'Cliff's accusing the others,' he said. 'They all deny it, of course.'

'A practical joke?'

'Probably kids. There's a lot of unemployment among the young. Maybe a school kid. You could ask the neighbours.' He looked at me imploringly.

'What neighbours?'

'Isn't there someone next door?'

'I've never seen anyone.'

'Strange.'

'But I'll ask in the café. The owner seems to know everything going on around here.'

'At least nothing was broken and nothing is missing,' he said, making to walk away.

'Just relocated,' I said as my skin broke out in goose bumps.

He stopped and turned back. 'That's right. *Moved*.'

From tucked away in the cavity of a wall two levels of scaffolding up, to resting on the ground against that partition wall, the incident was too similar to the rock that had moved in my apartment, twice. I wasn't about to tell Mario about that rock, but I wondered if something else, something of the same nature hadn't already happened to him and he was as reluctant as I to share.

I began to think I understood the reason behind Mario's haste. His was not a race against time to secure a bonus, or because he had a backlog of other jobs; he was trying to beat the supposed curse with speed. Mario knew that every day that passed without an occurrence of anything strange and inexplicable was a blessing. For he, too, believed in the curse of Casa Baraso, or was at least wary.

I scrambled to rationalise. Clearly someone was unhappy with the restoration, and wanted to intimidate me and cause disharmony among the workers. That someone had access to my apartment. It had been the conveyancer who had put me onto the estate agent, who I had yet to contact about the matter. Were they in cahoots? Or was all this the meddling of Cejas?

I left Mario to organise the bags of lime and went over to where the men were huddled. Some were returning to their various spots on the build, leaving the stone mason still arguing with his mate. They were both tall and deeply tanned. The man I assumed to be Cliff was the older of the two. He had a larger, heftier frame, and he was sporting a goatee beard and a small paunch. The younger man had bleached blond hair and striking blue eyes. As I grew nearer they lowered their voices.

'Hey, Cliff,' I said, putting on my bank teller's face, the one I used on belligerent customers. 'Mario has filled me in. We think it was kids okay, just kids coming on site after dark. I'm going to ask around, see if there are any known trouble makers in town.'

The older man, Cliff, hesitated, and I watched as his ire diffused.

I went on. 'Thankfully nothing was taken or damaged. It seems whoever did this had no intention of causing anything but mischief. I suggest we all put the matter behind us and get on with our jobs, if that's okay. The weather is only going to get hotter.'

I had no idea what the temperature had to do with the progress of the build but I needed to round off my little speech with something. It did the trick. Cliff thanked me in a thick Yorkshire accent for the pastries I had brought the other day and headed off up the scaffolding. The other guy followed.

I had a quick look around before telling Mario I thought Cliff would settle down; and then I headed back to Puerto del Rosario, fighting off my own misgivings.

Two days later, Mario texted me again for more bags of lime. The request had become a euphemism for trouble and I almost didn't bother swinging by the builder's yard. I pulled up to find Cliff yelling and waving his arms about, and Mario placating. I hurried out of the car and marched over.

The men gathered round went quiet. Even my presence settled things down without me needing to speak.

'It's happened again,' Mario said addressing me, his face more worried than before.

'Same as last time?'

'Pretty much.'

'Take your tools home, Cliff. For Christ's sake,' one of the guys said.

'Yeah, no one should be leaving their tools here.'

'I didn't think anyone would be so stupid as to do it again,' Cliff muttered, eyeing the others with suspicion.

I stepped forward and put my hands on my hips. 'I told you, it's probably kids.'

'Probably?' Cliff paused. 'You don't know for sure. Have you asked around like you said you would?' He paused, eying me critically. I looked away. 'No, I didn't think so.'

'I was planning on doing that today. In fact, I'm on my way there right now. If I hadn't been called on site to help diffuse your temper, I would already have the information you require.'

The men were as shocked as I at the manner in which I spoke those words. All those years working at the bank having to be polite and restrained no matter what idiot was standing on the other side of the Perspex, and a new freedom surged forth. At the back of my mind was the need to persuade all the guys to keep working on the build. Even if I found out nothing about a wayward teenager, I considered inventing one, just to keep the men from getting spooked.

Thinking we had reached a stalemate, I handed Mario my car keys and told him the bags of lime he wanted were in the boot. With one final glare at the men, I marched off up the street.

The front door to my neighbour's house was right on the pavement, midway along a whitewashed wall. I knocked and waited. Nothing, not even a rustle or a squeak. I knocked harder. Still no reply or any movement inside. I continued on past a vacant field to the next house and hammered my knuckles on the door. No one came to the door. All I got for my trouble was a dog yapping somewhere inside. I crossed over and was about to try another house when I began to feel ridiculous and stopped in my tracks.

I was in two minds whether to approach the woman at the café with my query as it would only arouse local gossip, but I had promised Cliff. I spent the short walk conjuring a ruse to discover what I wanted to know without invoking too much suspicion.

As I went in I realised I first had to make a purchase. The woman ran a business, not a drop-in centre. Finding myself the only customer, I ordered a freshly squeezed orange juice and another slice of her tortilla. She probably thought me the most unadventurous woman when it came to food so I also had some of her fish in vinaigrette and I ordered a coffee as an afterthought. She was more than happy to fill my order.

I sat at my usual table by the window. The loud grind of the juicer, the comforting bonks and clangs and chinks, and I wanted to stay seated for an hour or more to unwind.

'You didn't tell me your name,' I said when she brought over my food and drink.

'Gloria,' she said matter-of-factly.

'That's a pretty name,' I said, hoping to coax her into opening up.

'Thank you.'

She smoothed down her apron and stood back. She waited, although she didn't seem in a chatty mood. I knew if any of her local customers came in she would be all rapid talk interspersed with convivial laughter.

'Gloria,' I said, keeping her there with her name. 'I was wondering, what do the young people do in the village? Once they finish school, I mean. Is there much work around?'

'They leave,' she said with a sigh. 'Especially the boys.'

'Where do they go?'

'Puerto del Rosario, but most go to Gran Canaria or Tenerife or the mainland.'

'That's sad.'

'It is.'

'I wondered why I haven't seen any young people about.'

She folded her arms across her chest and tilted her head to the side, watching me closely as she spoke. 'That's because there aren't many families living here anymore. And the nearest high school is in Gran Tarajal.'

'At least you don't get all the usual problems. Vandalism, graffiti, break ins.'

'We get none of that here.' Now she sounded proud.

'Which makes Tiscamanita the perfect village.' I grinned at her and she gave me a strange look as if to convey she found me slightly unhinged.

I let her walk away. It seemed unlikely that any teenager was prowling about. A homeless person, maybe. Or someone from Tuineje? That village was only a few kilometres down the road. Yet as I pondered my latest thoughts they seemed increasingly unlikely.

I would have liked to ask Paco, who was sure to have an answer, but I had no means of contacting him and he hadn't shown up at the block. I was beginning to believe I had been abandoned, and wondered what I had done to put him off. Catching myself in the midst of my thoughts, I realised I had formed an attachment to him.

I drank the juice, ate the fish and followed on with the tortilla. By the end I wasn't sure I had got the sequence right. When I knocked back the last of the coffee and it was all sloshing about in my belly, I felt I might be in for a spot of indigestion.

I didn't return to the building site, preferring to let Cliff stew. I went back to the apartment and cogitated over the thought that Cejas was meddling in the build. I had no way of proving it was him, but the more convinced I grew that he was behind the relocation of the rock and tools, the more resolved I became to take action.

A week later it happened again. Mario dispensed with his lime-bag ruse and texted me to say I had better get up there fast.

I was out the door in a flash. When I arrived, Mario rushed over like a schoolkid ratting to his teacher. He explained the wheelbarrows Cliff had leaned against a wall to drain and dry he found slung on the ground on their sides.

The men were gathered over by the barn. No one was working and an air of unease pervaded the group. In all likelihood, word of the curse had gone around and met with caution if not trepidation among the men.

'Could be a dog,' one of them was saying.

'Or the wind.'

'You need to secure the site,' a burly Scotsman said to Mario. 'If you don't, there's no telling what will happen next.'

The others agreed.

'Mario,' I said. 'I tried to ask the neighbours. There doesn't seem to be anyone living in any of these houses. I called in at the café and the owner said there are hardly any young people in the village and never any crime.'

'This wasn't a crime, though,' Mario said quickly.

'We had an intruder,' said the burly man. 'That's trespass.'

'You don't know that.'

'It's pretty obvious, don't you think?'

'Mario,' Cliff said with sudden conviction. 'I can't work here anymore. Someone's got a vendetta against me.'

'Please, don't go,' I said.

'I'm sorry, but that's three times something of mine has been moved. It hasn't happened to the others. Maybe if I go, the prankster will stop.'

As Cliff packed up his tools and left the site, the other men grew uneasy. Leaving Mario and I standing by the cement mixers, they all drifted back to their various jobs but the mood was subdued. Mario looked more worried than the rest of them put together.

'I tell you what,' I said once we were alone. 'Let's meet here tonight after dark and see if anyone turns up.'

'You think someone will?'

'Someone must be doing this, surely?' I said. 'In fact, I am almost certain I know what is going on.'

'If you say so.' He sounded doubtful. Again, I sensed he was holding something back.

'It wasn't a dog that moved Cliff's tool belt, that much I do know,' I said, my rational self coming to the fore.

'Even so.'

'I'll be here at nine,' I said with determination I hadn't realised I had until I said it. 'Please say you'll join me.'

'I'll try.'
He didn't sound keen.

The Night Watch

In June, the sun sets around nine, the light quickly fading. The villages below the Betancuria massif sink into the gloaming about an hour before, missing out on the glorious sunsets over the ocean that the west coast enjoys. Save for one or two notable exceptions there is not much along that west coast other than cliffs, rocky coves and caves, and the wild beaches of Cofete in the far south. Fuerteventura looks firmly at the sunrise, at Africa beyond the horizon, most inhabitants clustered in towns dotted along the eastern coast. Driving at night down the lonely backroads of Fuerteventura for the first time, with only the distant lights of the occasional farmhouse for company, brought home to me the seclusion of much of the island. Away from the inland villages with their houses shuttered against the darkness, beyond the reach of the streetlights, there was nothing, just the road curving across the empty plain and over the foothills of the mountains. In daylight the terrain was stark, at night it was bleak, the dark reinforcing the desolate landscape. It was with relief that I approached the familiarity of Tiscamanita.

I slowed and turned left and headed down my street. Initially, the way was lit by the electric street lanterns that were attached to each power pole, but two poles on, and the lights were blown and no one had thought to report the matter to the council and have them replaced. My house, beyond a small curve, was rendered in almost complete darkness.

There was no vehicle in sight. Mario was yet to arrive. I pulled up on the opposite side of the road and switched off the headlights, leaving the car to idle while I let my eyes adjust. I could make out the volcano, silhouetted against the starlit sky. There was no moon and I had no idea if there would be. That was something Aunt Clarissa would have known without a doubt, and I could have done with her company on my lonely night watch. I could have benefited from anyone's company and dearly hoped Mario would join me as agreed.

I thought about remaining where I was, then realised no one would approach if they saw the car, so I turned on the headlights and drove across the road, mounting the kerb, and taxiing over my land and parking around the back of the barn where I thought I would be safely out of sight. Thinking to make my exit easier, I backed in towards the wall, so that the car's nose was pointing at the volcano.

I killed the lights and the engine, confident I couldn't be seen. Although, situated where I was, Mario would have no idea I was there either. If I heard his car, any car, then I would send him a text. I thought for a second. There wouldn't be time to fumble about composing a text. I took out my phone and wrote a draft, ready to send. I set the phone down on the passenger seat within easy reach. There was nothing to do but sit back and stare into the void. Facing the wrong way with the barn obliterating my view, I was unable to see in either wing mirror if anyone was walking down the street or, worse, across my block. I was blind. The best I could do was open the window and keep an ear out for movement. No one could walk on my land without making crunching footfalls. They would also need a torch, and I would see any kind of light, even from my obscure post.

For how long did I plan to sit and wait like this? All night? There would come a point when it would be past a criminal's bedtime, surely? Besides, the relocation of a tool belt and the tipping over of a wheelbarrow or two—those were not the acts of criminals. There was a prankster at work, a kid, maybe with a mate.

I waited, letting a soft breeze stroke my face. About half an hour passed. Half an hour of crushing boredom. I couldn't read or play music. I just sat.

Another ten minutes and the waiting was all too much. I couldn't stay cooped in the car a moment longer. I grabbed my phone and eased myself out of the driver's seat as quietly as I could, not that I thought I would disturb anyone. There was no light on in the house next door which confirmed my suspicion that whoever lived there had gone away. I made a mental note to knock on the front door of the neighbour with the yapping dog and introduce myself before too much longer. Then again, they hadn't bothered to introduce themselves to me, so maybe not.

The night was windless. I used the light of the stars to pick my way around the side of the barn and on towards the house. Every footfall sounded to my ears like a crash of cymbals. I thought I was doing well until I stubbed my toe on something hard, and had to resort to using the torch on my phone.

Instinct made me pick up a rock.

There was no sign of life, other than me, and I felt acutely conscious of my own visibility now that the sharp beam of the phone lit my way.

I peered at the illuminated patches of ground, at the piles of timber and stones, and the upended wheelbarrows leaning against the wall where one of the remaining stone masons had left them. I shone the light up into the scaffolding. There was no one up there, not that I could see that far, and I wasn't about to climb a ladder and find out if anyone lurked up there. I stepped through the back doorway and pointed the phone at the interior. I felt like a prowler. The state of disrepair and the chaos of construction were overwhelming captured in the narrow beam of light. Every feature took on a ghoulish hyper-reality spotlighted against the dark.

I stuck fast to the northern half of the house, shining the light into the kitchen. There was no one in there.

I noticed a new lintel above the dining-room door. There was no one in that room either, or the adjoining room. Summoning courage, I crossed the patio and shone the light through the hole in the partition wall. There was nothing to see other than areas of new wall.

I had to gather my wits to step through the hole and check more closely on the downstairs rooms on the south side of the build.

I crept around, shining the torch in each room. Nothing.

Before I left I paused on the spot where I had cried over my mother. I still hadn't thought through what could possibly have caused that peculiar trance state culminating in that strange vision. I began to feel weird in the recollecting and quickly went back through the hole in the partition.

My curiosity sated, I re-assessed the wisdom of my night watch. It seemed I was entirely alone, but what was I to do there? Crouch down somewhere and wait? I was hardly going to tackle someone, and they would have the advantage of being able to back me into any corner of the build. Unease trickled through my veins. I was too vulnerable, too exposed. Where the hell was Mario? I felt a sudden compulsion for the safety of my car.

I was about to turn back when I heard movement behind me. I froze. The sound of soft footsteps, a rustle. I rushed over to the dining room and hid in the doorway. My breath caught in my throat. I killed the phone light and peered round.

The darkness was thick, but I made out a shape moving close to the ground. That was no human. I hit the torch button and directed the beam at the patio entrance. There, huddled with its tail between its leg, was a scrawny, terrified dog. We locked gazes. I raised the rock and made to throw it as I emitted a low growl. The dog hesitated, not ready to give up its position. I raised the rock higher and growled louder, taking a step forward. The pathetic thing let out a soft whimper and scampered away. I threw the rock after it to reinforce my point, and picked up another in case the beast came back. It was only a half-starved mongrel, but my heart was pounding like a jack hammer.

At least I knew one thing; the dog had mostly likely tipped over the wheelbarrows. I doubted it had found Cliff's tool bag and relocated it downstairs, twice, but I was beginning to wonder if Cliff had made up that story to scare the others. Or he was absentminded and had left his tool bag down on the patio floor. My theories did not account for the strange relocation of the rock in my apartment, but perhaps the two were not connected, but merely coincidental.

I headed back to my car, picking my way past the rubble and stacks of timber. About halfway, I again felt too exposed. After doing a scan for the dog, I killed the light and waited for my eyes to adjust. I heard another dog bark in the distance, then nothing, not a whisper. I looked up. The stars were bright in the sky. There was still no moon. Perhaps it was a new moon.

I took a few steps and a few more, and then I stopped. The barn was about ten paces ahead. Beside it, were two other outbuildings, once storerooms of some kind, both without roofs, their walls at waist height in places. I had no idea where that dog went but I pictured it crouched inside one of the buildings, ready to pounce. I gripped the rock, raised to the ready.

There was nothing for it but to keep going.

I took a few more paces, my footsteps crunching on the gravel. They were much too loud. Between footfalls I thought I heard movement, behind me again. I froze. Was the dog stalking me? Should I bolt?

In my side vision, I caught a flash of light. I turned. There it was again, a pin point of sharp red, darting up from inside the house, rising above the back wall and veering to the horizontal before fading away.

I couldn't move. Panic held me in its grasp. I stared into the blackness, my mind scrambling to make sense of what I had seen. A firework? It resembled a cigarette glow. Had someone thrown a cigarette? But there was no one in there. Besides, how can a cigarette tossed in the air suddenly veer off like that? Especially without the help of even a breath of wind. I began to doubt my perception. All I knew was if someone was in there and I had missed them, I had to move, fast.

I turned and was about to switch on my phone light when another pin point of light shone brightly, ahead of me this time, coming from inside the smallest outbuilding. The light was blue, and as I stared, transfixed, it headed straight for me. I opened my mouth, prepared to scream. But the dot of luminescence moved faster than any sound that could come out of me. It bounced off my chest and darted up into the night sky and zoomed off, zigzagging like a dizzy insect.

Perhaps that was what it was, an insect, but I was not convinced.

Terrified, I ran back to my car. My body shook. I fumbled for the door and bashed my hip on the steering wheel as I got in. I wound the window up and locked the doors. My hands scrambled with the seat belt and then with locating the ignition. I turned the key, threw the gearstick into first and drove off my block as fast as I dare. Whoever or whatever that was, I wasn't about to hang around for more.

No Place to Stay

After the terror on the building site, arriving back at the apartment didn't offer me the solace I needed. My only comfort was seeing the rock where I had put it in the narrow slip of garden.

Hoping to numb my senses, I downed two large glasses of red wine in quick succession. In a mildly soporific haze, I played 'Aikea Guinea', needing Elizabeth Fraser's voice to fill my head and block out the flashback images of darting lights. The trouble was, hearing her voice instantly reminded me of my mother, which had never troubled me before but now it did.

Sleep, when it came, was fitful and interspersed with long periods lying awake with my mind spinning like a whirligig. I was hot, too, which didn't help. And I was annoyed with myself for keeping the windows shut, for it meant I had to endure the warm and stuffy air, but I lacked the courage to throw them open, lest some rock-moving stranger crept in.

At the first sign of daylight, I got up, my skin sticky with sweat. I dove in the shower then nibbled on a muesli bar for breakfast. I felt no inclination to return to the build. I sent Mario a text asking after his whereabouts the night before and while I waited for a reply, I checked my emails.

There was nothing from my father. I hadn't heard from him in over a fortnight. I pictured him engaged in some high-powered property deal, the way he would pace the floor with his phone pressed to his ear, the alcohol he consumed too early in the day strong on his breath. I recalled the way he would disappear all Saturday to play golf, leaving me, in my early teens with the house to clean. I wondered sometimes if he had treated me as a replacement for his deceased wife. Someone to do his cooking and iron his shirts. On those Saturday chore-mornings, I only ever made a half-hearted effort. Clarissa did the rest. Until one occasion when she yelled at him for putting too much on his only daughter. After that, he hired a cleaner.

Did my mother really cook and clean? I had no image of her ever having done so. She struck me as the lackadaisical type, or perhaps not. Perhaps, being more ethereal and dreamy, she left things unfinished while she wandered off on some whim. Was that true or had I been told or left that impression? Who *was* she? The only connection we had was a love of the Cocteau Twins. When it came to remembering, my mother and the band were fused and there was little that got past that fusion, it loomed so large in my psyche. It had started to bother me that I couldn't access deeper, more intimate memories. Memories of ice-creams and sandcastles on the beach, of birthday cakes and blowing out candles, of presents at Christmas, of hugs and kisses and tears. Instead, all I had was a feeling, an inchoate longing for some sort of union with my deceased mother that was aroused in me whenever I heard Elizabeth Fraser sing, one that had creepily manifested in that vision of her by the partition.

Clarissa replied to my last email saying she was sorry she hadn't had time to look into Olivia Stone due to a string of medical appointments—nothing to worry over, just the dentist, an annual medical and an eye test. Blood pressure a little high, but there were pills for that.

Disappointed, I closed my laptop. I checked my phone but there was no reply from Mario. The sounds in the street and the adjoining apartments had become familiar – children readying for school, parents for work. I drew comfort from the sounds, the everyday just a wall away, but it seemed bizarre to be in the middle of all that normality, while in the apartment I was enshrouded in a dark mystery. The partition wall rock, Cliff's tools and wheelbarrows, the moving dot of light—maybe the villagers were right and Casa Baraso was cursed, haunted by spirits bound to the earth by tragedy. I considered inviting Clarissa's ghost-hunting pals for a bit of occult detection, but quickly dismissed the idea as farcical.

Besides, there was no need. I already had the answers. The lights were insects. The dog, scrawny as it was, knocked over the wheelbarrows, no doubt scavenging for crusts left by untidy workmen. Cliff was responsible for his own tool box, and the relocated rock I put down to Cejas. The curse of Casa Baraso indeed!

But my mind drifted, lured by a nagging unease. What of Olivia Stone? Had she really lived in my house? Died there? Was her ghost bent on spooking anyone who dared to alter the way things were with that house?

What am I thinking? I don't believe in ghosts!

I pictured Olivia Stone in her finery, all demure and introspective, and for a fleeting moment I saw my mother, Ingrid, in her stead. It was unsettling, two deceased women merging like that. What was happening to me, to my mind, to my uncommonly over-active imagination? Whatever it was, I didn't like it one bit.

Ingrid, Olivia, the Barasos, I was immersed by tragedy, mystery and death. Aunt Clarissa had not mentioned I would be plunged into matters of a preternatural order when she had mentioned all those planetary lines crisscrossing over Fuerteventura on my astrological global map. Secrets and deception, yes. Illusion perhaps. But not ghosts.

I reassessed the events and my rational explanations. The only factor puzzling me was the same kind of occurrence had taken place at two separate locations. Was that really coincidence? If a supernatural entity *was* at work—and I didn't want to entertain it, let alone believe it for one more second—then the spirit would need to be able to travel. In the back seat of my car? Ridiculous! Ghosts, as far as I was aware, did not travel. Still, I needed to be sure. I typed a quick email to Clarissa, seeking clarification.

I re-considered those lights. Admittedly, they were just plain weird. Insects? I had heard of insects shining lights, fireflies, lightning bugs. I wanted to believe they were insects but an internet search soon revealed no such insects were found on the island. Even so, there had to be a rational explanation. When I saw the first light I was prepared to believe it was a cigarette, although how anyone could make it move in the fashion it did was beyond me. The second light was blue, and it had come straight for me before zooming off into the night. It must have been some kind of trickery. Someone had been there. Just because I didn't see them, doesn't mean they were not present. There was a lot of the building and surrounds I hadn't checked. If not, if I had not been alone, then who was doing this? Who would want to go to all this trouble to scare me? How had they even known I would be there? Those were questions I could not answer.

What had haunted me all last night and left me feeling haggard, I managed to at least partially explain away. At least in theory. I tried to think of alternative theories and I considered seeking proof that I was right about any one of my hypotheses, but I didn't know where to start. I kept telling myself my explanations were reasonable and sensible, and I was planning on holding onto them with or without proof. They made me feel calmer and more in control.

I began to think about the day ahead and what I might do to fill it.

The ringtone of my phone exploded into my reverie. Startled, I read the screen. I didn't recognise the caller. When I answered, a woman spoke to me in rapid Spanish. She sounded nervous, apologetic. I asked her to slow down and start again.

The second time, as she explained herself, the horrible truth set in. It was the estate agent. The owners were giving me two weeks' notice to quit. They gave no reason other than the apartment would not be available after that. I asked if there was anything else on her books, but the woman said there was nothing, because it was June.

I had no idea how true her last remark would prove to be until I sat down and searched online for an alternative. July and August were peak holiday months but June was popular, too, as the weather was a touch cooler, and the island was booked solid. There was nothing to be had from Corralejo to Morro Jable. I searched every booking agent and several more obscure sites, some probably bogus. I thought of trying for a long-term rental but there was nothing to be had. I began to despair. I re-considered my campervan option, but even the idea of living in the confined space of a campervan made me feel exposed and claustrophobic all at once. When it came to my domestic arrangements, I needed space around me. Lots of it. The sense of uncluttered space was what had drawn me, deep down, to the island and to my ruin. I was not about to let myself be caged.

What would I do? Stay on another island? Go back to Britain? Neither held appeal, not least because one way or another, Mario benefited from having me around and I needed to keep an eye on the building site after hours.

My musings were interrupted by a knock at the front door. I leapt up from my seat to answer it. A postman handed me a parcel and asked me to sign for it. I closed the door and tore off the paper packaging. As anticipated, it was the Olivia Stone book, the second volume of her *Tenerife and its Six Satellites*. Happy to have my attention grabbed by this mysterious woman, I leafed through the front-end pages and studied the illustrations, before jumping straight to her account of Fuerteventura.

Fuerteventura of Old

Olivia Stone devoted the penultimate three chapters of her travel diary to Fuerteventura, amounting to about sixty pages, a small portion of the thick volume, most of which was given over to Gran Canaria. In the opening paragraph of the Fuerteventura section, she described her arrival in Corralejo and I was confronted with a very different Corralejo to the one I knew.

I had heard holidaymakers comment that the town wasn't what it was back in the 1980s, but Olivia Stone forced me to picture what the place would have been like a hundred years before that. Every resident of Corralejo, then a tiny 'cluster of huts', came to watch a sailing boat drop anchor in the harbour. 'Not a multitude', Olivia said. A smattering then, of bemused and curious villagers wondering who was aboard. Among the onlookers was Don Victor Acosta, who was to be Olivia and her husband John's host. He was there with two camels and a donkey. It turned out the Stones were to spend a lot of time riding camels on the island, for it appeared the main mode of transport, other than feet. Donkeys were mentioned, but no horses.

Two paragraphs in and I could see why Paco was enamoured with the woman and her book. The way she portrayed Corralejo and its people, the simple beauty of the calm waters of the bay, the volcanic islet of Lobos and the mountains of Lanzarote beyond, hers was a portrait locked in time, a primary source depicting a group of islands about to undergo a rapid transformation.

Olivia's observations were plainly and concisely stated and it was easy to race on through the text, but I noticed I needed to go back over vignettes and even single sentences a number of times to absorb the fullness of what was being said.

Olivia was acutely aware of the poverty she witnessed all around her. The villagers she encountered had nothing but the bare necessities and eked out a very simple existence. Living alongside them were the rich, for there appeared to be little if nothing in between, and it was with the rich that the Stone's stayed, having arranged by correspondence various hosts prior to their arrival.

The Stones, I thought, were well-connected. I gained the sense that they were residing with the local intellectual set after looking up a Don Gregorio Chil y Narajano, and discovering he was an academic from Gran Canaria with an interest in natural history and anthropology. He seems to have introduced the Stones to his connections on Fuerteventura.

It was obvious Olivia enjoyed her stay and was taken by the landscape. She referred to the wind that blew across the plains, to the mountains and the volcanoes and the views, to the churches and the methods of farming, including the beehive grain stacks I had seen photos of, and the sorts of implements I had seen in museums.

Her journey took her to La Oliva, then on to Puerto del Rosario, then known as Puerto Cabras. From there the couple headed inland again, to Antigua, and up to Betancuria, making the arduous journey down the massif to Pájara before turning north a fraction and arriving at Tiscamanita, where they stayed until they journeyed to Gran Tarajal to board their next vessel and leave the island.

I took particular interest in what the author had to say about my village. She used the word 'straggling', aptly describing the arrangement of farms arranged around the village centre. She observed the rich red soil, the cinders used for mulch, the depressions in the plain where water would pool and provide oases after rain, and the glimpses of the ocean caught between chains of rugged mountains. Her words were my reality, so little had changed in the landscape.

The year she arrived it hadn't rained on the island for seven years. People were starving. Many fled to the other islands and beyond. I wondered want the Spanish government had done to help, but I already had the answer, knowing their reputation: nothing.

That she spoke Spanish was no longer in doubt, for she mentioned the strain of concentrating for hours on the conversation of others. It was a mental strain I was all too familiar with.

They did indeed stay with Don Marcial Veláquez, as Paco had said, and enjoyed their time with Marcial, his mother and his sister. Olivia was impressed by Marcial's collection of books and his knowledge of politics, history and geography, and in the same brief sentence she revealed her own predilections and intellectual refinement. She described Marcial's house as one storey.

There was no mention of her even walking by my house, let alone going inside.

I flicked back through the pages. Earlier, when they had been staying in La Oliva, she mentioned passing a quaint grey building that was two stories in height and I realised she was most likely referring to the colonel's house – Casa de los Coroneles. By then, the age of the colonels was over.

As a whole, the Fuerteventura she described bore little resemblance to the island I knew and loved, except for the landscape. The old way of life was long gone. All that remained could only be found in the museums. For people like Paco, Olivia's travel diary was a eulogy and I could see why. I supposed a lot of the world was swallowed up, one way or another, and old cultures lost, deemed worthless or unimportant by developers, men like my father, who, when all was said and done, could not have cared less.

I read and re-read Olivia Stone's book and copied some descriptions in my notebook. Following up on Paco's claim that she had absconded to Tiscamanita, I hunted for clues that she was an unhappy woman trapped in a bad marriage, dipping into the chapters on Lanzarote and Gran Canaria, but there was no indication of the sort. Olivia rarely mentioned her husband, other than to acknowledge his presence.

It was with bitter irony that at the end of the day I returned to my search for accommodation and, finding the island chock-a-block, I imagined camping under the stars, or sleeping in my car, as I had heard others resorting to. Those who, like me, refused to be defeated. If Olivia Stone, a less than robust woman by her own account, could manage to ride a camel in the searing heat and blasting winds, I could manage a little discomfort, surely?

Another thought occurred to me. There were two rooms almost completed in my house. If I could manage to persuade Mario to make them habitable, I could stay there even without power or plumbing. At least it would be a proper roof over my head and it would be a lot better than sleeping in my car. Having someone on site at night would add security, too, not that I thought any was needed. I refused to give sway to the notion of a curse, or let Cejas, a dog or those bizarre darting lights put me off camping out in my own home. Besides, I would have to live there eventually.

I suspected it would have been something Olivia Stone might have done. Not willingly, but she would have put up with it.

Theories Tested

I phoned Mario the next morning, as early as I dare, and asked as politely and indifferently as I was able what caused him not to turn up at the property the other night. I thought we had agreed, I said. He sounded apologetic as he launched into a tedious explanation involving a prior engagement he had forgotten about, and how he had to rush out the door almost the moment he arrived home and left his phone on the kitchen bench by mistake. The scenario he painted sounded plausible but I did not believe one iota of it. Frustrated and a little let down, I cut in, swiftly changing the course of the conversation with, 'Have the workmen finished plastering those two rooms?'

There was a moment of silence in which he processed my question and answered in the affirmative.

'Good, because I am going to have to move on site.'

'What?! Why? You have an apartment!' Thankfully my phone was on speaker or I would have burst an eardrum.

'Sadly, the owner wants me out,' I said softly, not allowing his hysterical tone to influence my own. 'I cannot find an alternative.' I described my online efforts of the day before in a measured voice. 'I don't feel I have much choice. Other than to leave the island for the summer.'

'Okay, okay. No, don't do that,' he said, calming down. 'Progress will be much slower without you around. When do you need to move?'

'Two weeks.'

I heard him exhale.

'You won't like it.' He referred to the noise, the dust and the lack of privacy, power and water.

'There's a generator.'

'That's only for the cement mixers and power tools.'

'You mean, I can't use it?'

'No.'

'Why?'

'Because you would need to run it all night for a fridge and there'd be noise complaints.'

It was my turn to react and I all but gasped. Who was there in my street to complain about noise?

'And the men won't like it,' he added.

That, I could understand. There would at the very least be the matter of an extension cord running from the barn all the way into my rooms. As my mind scrambled to assimilate the lack of power, I told him I would find a way to deal with all the difficulties and I would keep looking for an alternative. Meanwhile, at least having me around at night would keep away intruders. He relented, but not before telling me I should paint the rooms first.

'Me?'

'My men are not painters. I can't get a painter in until all the work is finished. Painters always come in last.'

'Can't you make an exception?'

'I have my reputation to consider. The painters don't like it and neither do the others. Can you paint?'

Of course, I could paint. What self-respecting owner of a mid-terrace home in Colchester didn't know one end of a paintbrush from another? Although I had to admit privately that I had only tackled the bathroom in an Easter break, a small bedroom in another, and all I did was paint over what was already there. Still, I had watched enough DIY shows to know the dos and don'ts and when I was tackling the bedroom, Clarissa showed me how to use a roller without making paint spatters, how to spread the paint evenly and achieve a brushstroke-free finish, and how to feather and cut in. She said she had learned from a professional when she was having her extension built and her painter fell sick; she had needed the room completed in time for a party.

I consulted my Spanish-English dictionary and jotted down the essential language and went to the hardware store. I took the advice of a helpful assistant and bought three six-litre tins of white paint, a roller and tray, an extension pole, masking tape, a paint brush for cutting in, drop sheets, a small step ladder and a painter's platform. Loading up my Hyundai SUV workhorse, I realised I had nothing suitable to wear. I swung by a cheap clothing store for slacks and a loose t-shirt, using their changing room to swap outfits.

Seeing me arrive with my gear, some of the workmen smiled at me, others grinned, although some of those grins were probably jeers and inwardly the men were rolling eyes. Mario must have told them. I responded in kind, vowing to ignore them all and set to work.

On my way in, I found a carpenter hanging the dining room door. He ignored me as I passed by with an arm full of drop sheets and entered the living room via the vestibule. The walls were grey plaster. The window with its curved seats and wooden shutters, and a sturdy wooden door, matched the exposed beams of the ceiling. The floorboards were yet to be sanded. I ferried in the rest of my gear, feeling like an oddball and as far from a team member as it was possible to be.

As I was spreading out the drop sheets, Helmud entered the room. With a quick sweep of his eye, he took in the paraphernalia of the painter and proceeded to issue me with instructions. He told me how to use the roller without making spatters. He demonstrated how to hold a paint brush and how to cut in. I watched in silence, noticing a look of surprised approval at my purchase of a rat's tail brush. 'Good brand, this,' he said. I was then treated to instructions on the use of a step ladder and platform and how best to stir paint. I smiled into his face and thanked him for his tips. I didn't mention Clarissa or my own prior efforts. I didn't say that I had a steady hand and I was planning to do a good job. I knew he would be back to check on me, over and again. He was a man, I thought, and men like to explain things. Some men, most men, all men? I had no idea. Still, I was grateful for the extension cord and the light he brought in.

What Helmud did not tell me and I had to find out for myself was how taxing painting would be, up and down ladders, stirring, pouring and brushing and rolling on paint, all the while taking care not to let it spatter. Yet I couldn't stop; seeing the grey turn white was satisfying and the process rhythmic, almost hypnotic and compulsive, and much to my surprise I was enjoying the process.

The render absorbed most of the first coat. Cutting in was easy in the corners and there was no skirting board to deal with—Mario had advised me to paint almost to the floorboards—but around the beams was a lot more challenging. I didn't want paint smears on my timber. Taping up the edges of all those beams meant stretching tall with my arms above my head. Yet I refused to ask for help.

As anticipated, Helmud kept a watchful eye on my progress, poking his head in the door from time to time. Seeing me reaching up and painstakingly cut in along the edge of a beam, he told me not to worry too much as they would need to be sanded and then oiled. That was when I realised those beams had my name on them too. 'Oiling with what?' I asked. When I next got down off the ladder I put sandpaper and linseed oil on my shopping list saved in Notes in my phone.

Ten-foot ceilings meant a lot of paint. I managed two coats of the first room before I finished for the day. By then, my wrist was aching, I had a headache and I felt dizzy from the fumes.

The following morning, I awoke with a stiff neck and shoulders. Undeterred, I set off for the building site early, getting there before the men, already at work giving the second room its first coat before I heard the usual hammering and footsteps and talk. This time, I put on my headphones and played Stereophonics and stayed lost in a musical world oblivious to the cacophony going on all around me.

On the third day, Helmud showed me how to sand and oil the old timber beams and lintels. This time, his instructions were welcome. I taped up my fresh paintwork thinking maybe I should have approached the tasks in reverse order.

I didn't take to the sanding or the linseed smell, but I did enjoy watching the colour of the timber darken. As the day wore on, the strain on my shoulders and neck had me deciding I needed to locate a masseur.

The doors and window required the same treatment. At least all that sanding and oiling was at body height. I had to wait three days between coats and apply a top coat containing varnish to stop the timber turning dull.

Next, Helmud arranged a floor sander and a man to go with it. I used that day to buy furniture, arranging delivery on the day I needed to move in. In the meantime, it was down to me, on my hands and knees, to seal the floor.

Eyebrows raised when the delivery men turned up with a bed, a chest of drawers, a table and chairs, a free-standing two-door cupboard, and two small and comfy arm chairs. All of it practical and none of it antique. Thinking hard about my needs, I bought a two-ring camping stove and gas bottle, saucepans, crockery, cutlery and utensils, a carrier bag full of candles, a lighter and ten boxes of matches.

Working out how I would get by with no plumbing, I arranged the delivery of a second portaloo, as I had no intention of using the men's. I had it put on the other side of the nearest outbuilding. Theirs was over by the barn. Recalling a scene in one of those survival television shows, I cleared an area inside that outbuilding where the walls were above head height and laid a square of pavers to serve as a base for the large plastic bowl and bucket I would use as a makeshift shower. Helmud helped me put a large water container on a low platform made of a couple of planks and some concrete blocks.

The other device I bought off a German guy in Tetir, was a solar battery and two small panels that came with props that I could angle at the sun. He gave me a demonstration and I took some notes, and I rigged up the panels behind my portaloo, well away from the build. It meant carrying the battery back and forth but it would be worth it.

I was busy arranging my things in preparation for my first night when Paco appeared. I saw him through the living-room window, which I had left open to air the room. I rushed out to greet him, his appearance a welcome surprise.

I hadn't seen him since we had lunch in Antigua about two months before and had given up hope of ever seeing him again. As he took in the scaffolding and the frenetic pace of the build, he explained he had been to El Hierro and then gone on to La Gomera and La Palma, in fact all of the islands to take photos for a travel brochure and website.

'It was unexpected. I couldn't pass it up.'

'A terrific opportunity, by the sound of it,' I said, Paco rocketing up in my estimation. 'I wouldn't have passed it up either. Your employers in Caleta de Fuste didn't mind?'

His eyes filled with amusement. 'The owners of the restaurant are my mother's sister and her husband, and no, they were fine with it.'

It was with a twinge of envy that I marvelled at the close-knit family network he was part of and wondered if all the families on the island were the same.

I covered my reaction with, 'Make sure you show me when it all comes out.' Seeing the men down tools for a morning break and gather over by the barn, I added, 'Come in and have a look at what's been happening.'

He glanced at the men whose eyes had no doubt gravitated to the English woman and her friend. Under their scrutiny, Paco appeared uncomfortable. 'Are you sure?'

'It's my house, Paco. Not theirs. Come.'

He followed me into the building and we stopped in the patio to look around. I turned and waited. He had extracted his camera and was taking photos of every little detail on both sides of the partition, murmuring to himself. He crouched on his haunches for a better angle of whatever had caught his eye, and I observed the pull of his pants around his butt, the way his ponytail trailed down his back, the thickness of his forearms, my gaze lingering on the tanned skin, the masculine hair. I found myself admiring the masculinity of him altogether and quickly looked at something else.

'Paco,' I said, sensing we were losing time and heading for the vestibule.

As he entered my new living space his jaw dropped.

'This is incredible.'

'You like my efforts?' Pride swelled in my chest.

'You?'

'I painted the walls and oiled the beams and varnished the floor. All me.'

'Wow!' He eyed the furniture. 'You are living here?'

'I had to leave the apartment. They wanted me out.'

'Bastards. Did they give a reason?'

'No.'

'That's because they know they can get more money charging someone else a daily rate.'

'Really?'

'It's holiday season.'

I wasn't convinced although I had no alternative explanation. I didn't want to argue with him. There seemed nothing else to say, nothing either of us was prepared to say. A pressure built.

Then, in a moment of courage he said, 'I came to invite you to lunch.'

'It's a bit early,' I said much too quickly, cringing inwardly at my knee jerk lack of grace.

He looked disappointed and I wasn't surprised.

'Where are you thinking of going?' I smiled up at him to atone for my lack of consideration.

'Pájara.'

'I need a few minutes to get changed.'

I showed him to the door and closed the window, putting myself in near-total darkness. My eyes soon adjusted and I changed out of my scruffy pants and t-shirt and pumps in favour of a colourful beach dress and sandals. A quick brush of my voluminous hair and I was done.

When I exited my rooms, Paco was taking yet more photos and the men were making their way back up the scaffolding and to their various stations around the build. Gazes shot back and forth. Dressed as though for a date, I was pleased to hurry away.

The day was heating up and there wasn't much of a breeze. I walked with Paco to his car. It seemed natural to travel with him, even though I was fore-going the luxury of my brand-new Hyundai for his dusty old bomb. I hadn't been a passenger in a car since Aunt Clarissa drove me to the station one time when my Vauxhall was in for a service, and never on the island. For once, I could fully take in the scenery, the mountain chains, the skyline, the sweeping plains. It was over too soon, a ten-minute drive and we had arrived.

Pájara is one of my favourite inland towns. Situated at the southern end of the Betancuria massif, it has a quaint, historical vibe with a beautiful plaza in its centre filled with established trees and pretty hedgerows. The plaza is dom-inated by the modern town hall building and the old church, Nuestra Señora de la Regla, famous for its Aztec-style carvings. Paco parked in a side street and we strolled to a restaurant facing the plaza. Sitting by a window afforded a pleasant, side-on view of the church's façade.

I had visited the church on my last holiday. I much admired the Aztec feel of the stonework on the pediment above the entrance and, inside, the magnif-icent floor to ceiling altarpieces, intricately painted, predominantly in red and gold. The church was completed about seventy years before my house, and the vaulted ceilings were made of the same carved wood.

While my attention was drawn to the sightseers ambling about in the plaza, Paco studied his menu. Behind us, the café was filling. The atmosphere felt relaxed and convivial. The hiss of frying and the rich cooking smells I had come to expect aroused my appetite.

'What would you like?' he said, interrupting my reverie.

My eyes landed on the mixed tapas platter and I suggested we share it.

He looked back at the bar and a young woman came over and took our or-der, Paco adding two beers. We sat for a short while in companionable silence. He seemed preoccupied, or momentarily lost in thought. I considered confid-ing recent events, particularly the strange lights I had seen darting about, but decided against it. I didn't want spooky preoccupations to spoil our lunch. I wanted nothing more than to enjoy the local food surrounded by people, and especially to enjoy the company at my table.

When the food came he grew chatty, sharing stories from his childhood growing up on his family farm in Triquivijate, and of the large gatherings, the feasts and fiestas. I listened, attentive and fascinated, while envious of his large family network. He sounded especially fond of his mother. Hearing him praise her, I wished I could remember mine. I was saddened that I had managed to erase whatever recollections there might had been. I hadn't a clue what to do about it. Perhaps it was too late and nothing would ever be retrieved.

When we were done soaking up tapas juices with crusty bread, Paco fished out his camera and showed me the photos he had taken on his trip, the camera passing back and forth between us as he explained the sequences of shots. Those he had taken of El Hierro were impressive. The sense of elevation at the island's peak, and the great expanse of cliff that embraced a littoral where the land was cultivated and a town and some farmhouses were dotted about. 'Frontera,' he said, pointing out the town itself. What an exceptional place to find yourself, facing the Atlantic to the west with a great cliff rising up behind you. I wasn't sure I would feel comfortable with so much elemental power all around me. Paco had taken shots of the special wood at the mountain top and others of ribbons of houses hugging narrow lanes that wended down steep-sided ravines. Views typical of the other islands, as I discovered viewing his photos of La Gomera. When Paco described the journey he had made from the port to the west side of that island, the road clinging to steep mountainsides, the hairpin bends and plummeting views down into ravines and to the ocean, my palms broke out in a cold sweat.

His shots of La Palma were even more breath taking. He had taken dozens looking down from a purview above the clouds at the shimmering ocean far below.

'It's two-thousand five hundred metres at the peak,' he said.

'Is that the Canary Island's highest?'

'No. Mount Teide on Tenerife is.'

'How high's that?'

'Close to four thousand.'

I had never been to Tenerife. I tried to imagine being four kilometres up a mountain, and instantly preferred the low-level vistas of Fuerteventura. But it occurred to me as Paco described his trip that the islanders had no problem with altitude, and were quite prepared to terrace steep mountain slopes to make use of fertile soils, chasing whatever rainfall there was to be had. Where there was height there was water.

He handed me the camera again to view a photo of El Tablado, and I was gazing at a track meandering up through a hamlet and carefully farmed fields situated on what could only be described a razorback, because the land fell away dramatically to either side. The fields on the plateau were lush and green and the mountainsides all around forested, reinforcing my thinking about harvesting the rain. I couldn't see any way to access the locale other than by following the track up into the mountains.

'The plateau ends in a cliff,' he said, reinforcing my observation as he pointed at the next photo, this time of the end of the little plateau where a sheer drop looked down on forever.

I swiped forward anticipating more of the same and saw instead photos of my house. They were the ones he had just taken. I flicked through them and was about to hand back the camera when a photo of the partition wall caught my eye, or rather a dark shape seated in the hole. I thought for a moment the shape might have been that stray dog or, on closer inspection one of the workmen crouching down, but the dark figure was neither man or dog. It was something else, something inexplicable.

'What is it?' Paco said, holding out his hand for the camera.

I passed it back and he stared at the image. The expression on his face darkened.

'It's Olivia Stone,' he said slowly. His face wore a wry smile.

I wanted to tell him not to be ridiculous.

'Let me look again.'

The camera passed between us several times before he put it away in his satchel.

The figure did look human, hunched down beside the wall, but the shape of the clothes was vintage, the outline resembling a woman garbed in a long and sleeved dress, a hat with a wide brim tied closely around her face. Who was she and what was she doing there? Or was Paco right? Could Olivia Stone have lived in my house and taken to haunting it?

On impulse, I asked if we could exchange phone numbers. 'Saves you turning up and having a wasted journey,' I said, although that was hardly likely and hardly my motive. He remained my only friend and despite his apparent obsession with Olivia Stone I found I liked him more and more. He was attractive in a rugged, bohemian kind of way and I admired his passion for his islands. He had earned my esteem too, for his recent travel assignment. He really wasn't some loser serving beers in his family's restaurant. I had never seen him that way, but I imagined that was how my father would picture him, and even Aunt Clarissa, who had no time for wastrels.

He told me his number. I entered it in my phone and sent him a text, watching him save me to contacts. The act bound us somehow, even casually, and I felt reassured.

First Night

When Paco dropped me back at the building site, the workmen were packing up and leaving. Concerned something had gone awry, I said my goodbyes and rushed over, approaching one of the stone masons, who explained Helmud had given them the rest of the afternoon off to enjoy the festival in Tuineje. The mason looked at me with interest and wanted to know if I would be going, but I said I preferred settling into my new home. A look of amused incredulity appeared in his face. I ignored it.

As soon as I was alone I changed out of my dress and went and tried out the portaloo, which wasn't as bad an experience as I thought it might have been. I exited the plastic capsule and wandered around the block, soaking in the expanse of view and affirming I belonged there, on the island, in Tiscamanita and right there on my half acre of land. The locals would respect me in the end for restoring one of their great houses. I could become a patron of ruins. Not a saint, a real living patron rescuing abandoned dwellings, their saviour. I could start with the ones in my street. There were enough of them to absorb a decade or two of my time. It was a noble if fleeting thought.

I returned to my quarters for the wide-brimmed hat I purchased in Puerto del Rosario one time, securing the ties under my chin. With my head and neck and face shaded, I pottered about tending and watering my plants. I selected some large stones from a nearby rock pile to edge the garden bed. Then I made an effort at rebuilding a small section of the collapsed dry-stone wall, telling myself whoever had built the wall couldn't have done a good job since it had collapsed in so many places, and I couldn't possibly do a worse job, especially as I took a lot of care positioning my rocks so that they fitted into each other more or less. It was an assumption that kept me going and from which I drew some satisfaction. The work was slow and peaceful, and it was good to be outdoors feeling useful.

Now and then I lifted my gaze to the volcano and sat and stared. Whenever I raised my head, there it was, dominating the landscape and I asked myself who else I knew that had a volcano for a view. No one.

The robust sun was on the wane when I headed inside. After stepping over bits of timber too heavy to shift with my foot, I set about shoving all the moveable obstructions in the patio out of my way, keen for a clear path to the ablutions. Living on a building site, I was fast discovering, presented numerous hazards in the dark.

I had taken the living room as my bedroom. Access was via the vestibule. The window overlooking the street opened out beneath the scaffolding. I planned on keeping the window closed to seal off the room from dust. I had arranged the bed against the wall facing the door. Two bedside tables completed the furniture along that wall, along with a chair in the corner to sling my clothes. I had centred a chest of drawers in the length of wall behind the door. A suitcase, half-closed on the floor, contained clothes that needed to be hung. I had thought of buying a free-standing wardrobe but preferred to keep my things covered as much as possible. I had even taken up a local tradition and bought a large clear plastic cover to serve as a dust sheet for my bed, to throw on during the day when the men were at work.

The dining room was mostly empty, save for a table and chairs in its centre and a low, two-door cupboard beside a length of benchtop on trestles that I planned to use for a makeshift kitchen. Four large water bottles sat on the floor. The two small armchairs I purchased for comfort completed the furnishings.

There was no door separating the two rooms. I had asked Mario to leave the double doorway open, although standing in that cavernous space I could see that at night in bed I might feel exposed. Too late to change what I had decided in a moment of haste, and besides, when the rooms were filled and used for what they were designed, the opening would be desirable. Even so, I made a mental note to think through every future decision carefully, approaching it from all angles. When it comes to a build, decisions are hard if not impossible to undo.

The sun had yet to set, but inside with the doors closed the rooms were black as night. I went about lighting candles, chunky church candles each in its own saucer. The effect of all the light gently flickering gave the space an ethereal, moody feel.

For dinner, I made a tuna salad baguette and sat at the table, my attention absorbed by the candle in front of me guttering and fizzing then settling into a steady flame.

Establishing a routine I considered sensible, I filled a beaker and readied my toothbrush and went outside, keen to brush my teeth before nightfall. Then I brought in the solar battery.

Dashing to the portaloo for a midnight pee held no appeal whatsoever. Neither did my solution. I took the plastic bucket I had been using to water the garden and found a broken piece of plywood on the rubbish pile to use as a lid. My chamber pot, and I revisited my campervan idea one more time as I set it down in the far corner of the dining room.

Shut in my chamber for the night I was alert to every sound. No one would know I was alone in these two rooms, although they might see my car parked by the barn. If an intruder did chance by, then they would be sure to open one or other of the doors into my makeshift home. Which left me no choice. Careful not to damage my newly sealed floor, I shunted an armchair hard up against the dining room door as a deterrent. In my bedroom, I propped a chair so that the backrest was under the handle, as I had seen done in films.

To obliterate the silence that crowded in on me, I paired my laptop to my new sound bar that I had purchased on one of my numerous shopping trips, plugged the sound bar into my new solar battery and played the Cocteau Twins' *Treasure*, softly at first, then realising the acoustics offered a new sensory experience, I turned the volume up a little louder, and a little louder still. There were too many flat surfaces for sound perfection, but as I listened I knew Elizabeth Fraser's soprano voice belonged in my house. Her vocalisations soared, the distinct tones came alive, and the mood of the guitars, with their dreamy, wistful tones, opened in me that familiar if inchoate yearning that quickly transformed into a wide-eyed melancholy.

It was a moment of imprudence and I knew I should turn it off, play something else. Instead, I sat on my bed and opened myself up to the music and as the second half of 'Donimo' kicked in I was filled with aching loneliness. Cut off from the world by the walls of the house, cut off from the island by my newness, cut off from my roots and my family, I was bereft of all that I once had and it was a peculiar feeling, poignant, an emptiness needing to be filled.

The Cocteau Twins were interior music, to be played in castles and cathedrals, contained spaces, not lost on the wind, although somehow the sounds mirrored the emptiness outside too. Yet the music was discordant, out of place, for it was another wilderness it spoke of, another wild, rugged landscape, a Scottish one. Here, if I was to truly belong here, I needed to engage with the local music, maybe something akin to the Cocteau Twins, some musical group who would open up in me, the listener, the same longing.

Treasure came to an end and I put on *Heaven or Las Vegas*. All thought evaporated when Elizabeth sang the first verse of 'Iceblink Luck'. I hadn't anticipated what the music would summon in me to fill the hollowness I had succumbed to despite my, or maybe because of my heightened state. One sort of loss was a conduit for another and I began to ache for my mother. My throat constricted as though a heavy lump was lodged there and hot tears burst from my eyes and formed rivers down my cheeks. I was locked in to every vocal rise and fall as though the agony of losing my mother swayed along in synchronicity. What was happening to me? As if in answer, the void in me soon filled with memory.

A memory of a number 13 bus.

A bus that ploughed through a pedestrian crossing. The driver too slow to react.

She had fallen on her face directly in front of the passenger-side wheel. The bus served as a municipal steam roller. Her shopping bag, filled with overripe tomatoes, fell under the front wheel along with her, creating a god-awful mess of tomato juice and bits of vegetable skin and pip, all mixed in with mum's blood and skin and flesh. The combination of vegetable matter and my mother seemed thicker and much more obvious on the white stripes on the zebra crossing.

A horrific scene for onlookers and particularly for one onlooker, me.

Having seen the bus, I was still on the kerb. I had felt unsure the bus would stop. I was seven years old and I had more of a sixth sense than my mother. To be precise, I was exactly seven years old because the Number 13 bus hit my mother at thirteen minutes past one in the afternoon of the thirteen of July, which just happened to be my birthday. My mum had bought the tomatoes to make Gazpacho soup. My favourite.

The remembering was all too much, as was the guilt. My mother set off that day to buy the ingredients for her only daughter's favourite soup, a woman so lost in the music she listened to she failed to turn her head and see that great lump of metal hurtling towards her.

I had blocked out the horror of that day, the congealing mass of red on the white stripes of the zebra crossing.

The only vestige of the trauma I was aware of was I never cared to celebrate my birthday. My father and Aunt Clarissa had tried to lure me with cake and candles, and brightly wrapped gifts and trips to the seaside, but I retreated inside myself, stuck on a smile and laboured through the hours, numb.

I had always fought against the memory of that horrific day, my birthday, but it was there, I was there, forcing my way now through 'Pearly Dewdrops' Drops' as though my ears were my mother's and I was inside her head as the shock of that bus shattered all that she was.

I stood up, I walked around the room with its huge shuttered window and carved wooden door and beams, and it was as though inside this chamber I had summoned the grief, hot grief, and finally granted it permission to exit.

The crying went on and on.

I hugged my arms around me and paced the room, caving and crouching every so often. When I thought it was finally waning, some poignant melody would kick in and trigger more tears. Yet I couldn't replace the Cocteau Twins with anything else. It would have been disloyal to a memory.

Eventually, I put on *Victorialand.* The tempo, slower and gentler, allowed my feelings to settle and be still. Before long, the battery ran out of charge and the music came to a sudden halt. I was thrust into silence.

Tears of grieving locked away for over thirty years had to end sometime, and after three whole albums of music, I was spent. My eyes burned. There was a small mountain of soggy tissues by my bed. I moistened a clean tissue and dabbed at my tear-stained face and my hot puffy eyes. There I sat, shocked by the outpouring as reason took control.

I told myself I had spent too long almost entirely alone, under considerable strain and uncertainty, and enduring some significant set-backs. That it was natural that so much stress had triggered the memory I had been repressing for so long. That I needed to practice self-care and not allow myself to reach such a peak when triggers would set off an avalanche of pain. I found a sorry-looking block of dark chocolate in my bag and ate the whole lot.

There was nothing else to do except read. I opened the Olivia Stone, which already had pride of place on my bedside table, and started at the beginning of her journey to the eastern Canary Islands, sinking into her easy style as she described the day she disembarked at Las Palmas, steering my eyes back to her words when my mind drifted elsewhere.

She made the same kinds of observations as she had of Fuerteventura, only her point of entry onto Gran Canaria was not that of a tiny fishing village but of an established town with a small port, roads and houses. Upon her arrival in 1883 there were no hotels in the capital, but tourism already had a foothold and the Stones were far from the only English couple to appreciate the island. Hotels were poised to open or be built. Unlike the single-room fishing huts of Corralejo, Olivia described established streets flanked by grand, three-storey buildings. John Stone had sketched a fountain in one.

The descriptions were vivid. Hers was a travel diary to get lost in, and in two pages I had almost forgotten my grief. Two pages more and I was drifting to sleep.

I put down the book and went about blowing out the candles, saving the one by my bed until last. I had one last look around, blew out the flame and settled beneath the covers thinking a good long sleep was in order.

It wasn't to be. The moment the light had gone I was hypersensitive to sound. The town was as quiet as death. All I could hear was the wind whistling where it could. There was no barking dog. I heard a car engine, faint in the distance. I thought I caught the crackle and pop of fireworks as Tuineje enjoyed its celebrations. The sense of others out in the streets a few miles away did nothing to calm my unease. I had never before suffered from night terrors, but alone in the dark I felt nervous. I reached for my phone and opened the toolbox for the torch, ready to turn it on if need be. There was little else I could do. I lay on my back and drifted.

I must have fallen into a deep sleep for when I awoke daylight was squeezing through the cracks in the window shutters. A sense of wellbeing infused me. I had spent my first night in my new home, never mind it was a building site and never mind I had cried my eyes out. I lit a candle and lay still for a while, pondering the day ahead.

When I sat up and looked around, fear jolted through me, a sensation quickly followed by anger.

The chair that I had propped under the door handle was lying on its side on the floor. I got out of bed and picked up the chair, setting it down on its four legs against the wall.

I went into the dining room and found the armchair I had rammed up hard against that door, pushed away at an angle. The dining room door was ajar. Why hadn't the sounds of all that moving furniture woken me?

Someone had been on site, there could be no doubt about it. That someone had entered my bedroom as I slept. A reveller from the festival, perhaps? One of the workmen? A prankster? How many of them had there been and why had I not woken?

As the full realisation sunk in that I had lain vulnerable in my slumber while an intruder had crept into my room, a sickening dread seeped into my awareness. I was too unnerved to even wash. After scanning about to find nothing stolen or disturbed, I dressed quickly, downed a glass of water and pocketed an apple. Clearly my efforts at security hadn't worked. There was only one solution I could think of. Bolts. I would go to the hardware store in Puerto del Rosario and buy bolts for the top and bottom of both doors and for the window. Barrel bolts. Big ones. I grabbed my keys and purse and headed off.

It was Saturday and the store was busy with handymen. I explained my needs to the same assistant who had sold me the paint, and arrived back at the house kitted with bolts and a cordless drill. I managed to partially charge the battery before losing patience and setting to work.

I would not be defeated by that joker.

Bad Luck

A squeeze of the power drill and I had the last screw in place at the bottom of the dining room door. Pleased with my efforts, I packed the drill in its plastic carry case. Mario would no doubt be dismayed by the holes I had drilled into that ancient wood but my personal safety was paramount.

I went and stood in the doorway to the vestibule. It was not going to be pleasant camping at the house, even during the day, even on a weekend when I had the place to myself. What I had previously taken in at a glance now I absorbed in detail, the overwhelming scale of the restoration affecting every corner of the building. I had no idea how long it would take but even with an army of men on the job—minus Cliff—I couldn't see the project completed in six months. They had been at work about two months and in that time, despite having two habitable rooms, the rest looked a long way from finished.

The door to the vestibule was centred in a two-foot thickness of wall, on my side freshly painted white, on the other, old render and stone. The double front door was being restored offsite and the cavity remained boarded up. The wall facing me across the once prettily tiled floor was in a poor state, with large patches of crumbling render. The beams had been replaced in the ceiling but no floorboards had been laid and I could see up to the roof, itself in disrepair. At the patio end of the vestibule would be a door with transom window above. It was a low priority, but it would complete the house, creating an airlock between the patio and the street.

I went back inside and shut the door and fastened the bolts top and bottom, two satisfying clunks of security. Reassured I would be safe, I unfastened them, fetched the battery and went and hooked it back up to the solar, then grabbed my laptop and charger and walked to the café. Halfway up the street I spotted a stray dog in a field, watching me. The same dog? This one looked bigger, stronger, healthier. Probably not a stray. It didn't approach.

In the café, I felt adventurous and ordered an array of tapas, along with grilled fish and chips and a glass of orange juice, no doubt pleasing Gloria with my order, who sprang into action as I walked away. There were a few diners in and others having coffees, but fortunately the table I was after was free. I spotted it the other day. There was a power point close by. Since the solar battery would not work with the laptop battery – something that had almost stopped me buying the solar kit – I had no choice but to find other options. I went and asked Gloria if it was okay to charge my laptop and she nodded agreement from behind the counter.

There was a message from my father wishing me well and hoping the restoration was getting along. Clarissa sent her apologies for not having time for the Olivia Stone research as yet. She was busy attending to the arrangements for the funeral of another friend who had passed away suddenly and had no family to speak of. At least, none that cared terribly much. Her and her friends at the Spiritualist church had given poor old Dorothea a proper send off. Not one relative made an appearance. Astonishing. But yes, she said, ghosts do travel. Why do I ask?

I tucked away that last piece of information in a mental file marked doubtful. My money was still on Cejas.

Leaving my laptop to charge, I tucked into the tapas Gloria had set down at my elbow, enjoying the bursts of vinegary fish, the garlicky mushrooms, the sweet tang of tomatoes. As I ate I tuned into the conversation at the next table that had suddenly risen in volume and I was alerted to the word 'curse'. I couldn't make out what they were discussing as their Spanish accent was different and they spoke so fast. One of the party shot me a sideways stare and I had to look down at my plate to avoid meeting it. Were they talking about my house? Surely not, Surely, they were talking about something else.

Gloria came with my fish and took away the tapas. I was uncommonly hungry, which I put down to the catharsis of the night before and the lack of a proper breakfast. That, and the food was well cooked and the chips, of course, moreish. By the end of the meal I was feeling too full to drink my juice. I extracted my notebook and wrote down a few impressions about building dry-stone walls and the strength of the sun and some minor observations of the build. I refused to log my own emotions or the strange goings on. I wanted my notebook to report nothing other than the nuts and bolts of the restoration and how good it was to have two rooms already completed.

The laptop was sitting at about fifty per cent charged. I sat back and waited. Before long, the café emptied and Gloria cleared the tables around me and came back to wipe them down. When she looked finished I beckoned her over, thinking to use that conversation I overheard to raise the topic of the curse on my house.

She laughed. 'They couldn't have been. They were from La Gomera. They were discussing a local legend. The Curse of Lauringea.'

'Lauringea? Who was he?' I asked, watching her fiddle with the cloth in her hand.

'She. It's an ancient curse and it has nothing to do with your house.'

'Do you know it? I'd love to hear it, if you have time.'

She glanced at the door. Seeing no one was about to enter, she put down the cloth, drew up a chair and said, 'Alright, I will tell you. Legend has it Lauringea was an indigenous farmer's wife who was seduced when she was young by the ruler of Fuerteventura, Don Pedro Fernandez of Saavedra. A right womaniser, he was and she ended up having his illegitimate child. One of many, I should imagine.'

'He sounds like a real creep.'

'He was,' she said with a quick glance at the door. 'Then one day when Lauringea's son was a man, he tried to defend the honour of a young maiden who was being seduced against her will. The seducer was none other than one of Don Pedro's legitimate sons.'

'Must be genetic,' I said. 'You know, womanising.'

She laughed. 'I don't know, maybe it is.'

There was a pause and I realised she may have lost her thread.

'Sorry, I interrupted. Please, go on.'

She took a breath. 'Well, of course right then Don Pedro appeared. Seeing what was going on he killed the man who was trying to defend the poor maiden's virtue. Lauringea was horrified. She cried out to Don Pedro that he had killed his own son. I have no idea what he made of that.'

'What happened?'

'She was grief-stricken and also furious. She called on the Guanche gods and placed a curse on the whole of Fuerteventura for being under the rule of such a man as Don Pedro. An east wind blew and brought the calima and the flowers shrivelled and all the grasses dried to a crisp.'

'That truly is fascinating.' I meant it.

'That curse is five hundred years old,' she said, now all talkative. 'The curse on your house is different. It isn't really a curse but people see it that way. That is what they believe and, I promise you, with good reason.'

'But why?'

'For the last hundred and fifty years, ever since the Barasos lived and died in your house, something bad has happened to those who have tried to live there.'

'Like what?' I said, sceptical.

'I know of three examples. There was the Rivas family who had five children who all died of influenza in the one season.'

'That's sad.'

'Then there was the gentleman farmer, Juan Perera, who lived there with his family. They had to move after he lost his fortune due to a bad harvest.'

'That could happen to anyone,' I said, knowing I should have held my tongue.

'Not in a year of good rain when everyone else was enjoying abundance.'

'Fair enough,' I said, although I was not convinced.

'Then there was Concha Delgado, a mother of two, who died in childbirth.'

'Sorry to question, but wouldn't that have happened anyway?'

She stood up and made light finger stabs on the table.

'Perhaps, but every single person who has lived in that house has had bad luck. Over the years, people stopped wanting to have anything to do with the place. They don't like the feeling there.'

'What feeling?' I said, looking up at her, genuinely puzzled. I had never felt any kind of 'feeling'.

She picked up her cloth and proceeded to fold it into squares. Her manner had become a touch agitated. She held my gaze. 'An unpleasant one. I have been told one of the maids who worked there heard voices.'

'Voices!'

'Ghosts. And things moved.' She looked away and I sensed she regretted that last comment. A look of concern came into her face. 'I wasn't going to tell you. I'm not sure I believe all of it but that is what I was told. Things moved.'

The door opened and an elderly couple in shorts and sunhats strolled in. Gloria rushed away, leaving me to absorb what she had said. Her last comment reverberated in my mind. *Things moved.* But it was gossip, all of it, no one had lived there for over a century. The witnesses were long dead. What remained was hearsay and tittle tattle.

Once my lap top and phone had charged, I left the café and wandered up the street and bought supplies from the supermarket. A different assistant served me. I introduced myself but he already seemed to know who I was.

With a bag of groceries in each hand and my laptop weighing down my shoulder bag, I trudged back to the building site, the vigorous sun determined to scald whatever bare skin it could find.

There was still a long way until sunset. I toyed with spending time repairing the dry-stone wall, but thought better of it. I was spending too much time out in the sun, far more than was healthy for my fair skin. Instead, I put away the shopping and went for a drive to Ajuy on the west coast, where the ocean breeze would be strong.

Thirty minutes, I had joined the holidaymakers enjoying the beach, the surf and the outdoor dining of a tiny fishing village given over to restaurants. I sat in the shade and whiled away a few hours with Olivia Stone and an iced coffee.

It was close to six when I parked behind the barn. The air felt no cooler, the sun no kinder, but it was surely weakening. I changed into gardening clothes and ferried water over to quench the thirst of all those plants in my garden that were looking worn out from the day. Then I attacked the wall. I knew my skills were abysmal but at least the rocks were where they belonged and not strewn along the back perimeter of my block where I planned to create a border of small trees and shrubs.

Ideas for a garden were growing in my mind. I would close in the garden with a high wall running beside the pavement, leaving space on the other side of the house for a driveway and, eventually, a garage. I fancied a pergola outside the south-facing windows. I would grow wind tolerant plants in exposed areas and in sheltered spots, vegetables and tender plants. I had been reading up about gardening on the island, and observed the choices of others by peering into any gardens I passed whenever the opportunity arose. A lot could be done with the fertile soil, that was obvious.

As the sun disappeared behind the mountains, I fetched the battery and went inside. Not wanting to drain what little power the battery held—I already knew I had been sold a lemon—I lit the candles, poured a glass of wine and continued reading. Before daylight disappeared altogether, I took my first bucket shower, cleaned my teeth and brought in the chamber pot. Then, I bolted myself in for the night and returned to Olivia Stone and her travels in Gran Canaria.

I was enjoying the narrative more and more. Her observations were informative and practical, from the day's weather to the condition of the soil and the plants that grew. When she described the preponderance of superstitious beliefs and practices amongst the locals, even in the larger towns and the capital, Las Palmas, she did so with much scepticism, clearly incredulous that in the age of science such beliefs were still adhered to. Although she was at pains to mention that the same sorts of superstitious beliefs abounded in England. I had found an ally in Olivia Stone. She was a true rationalist, a woman who did not believe in ghosts, the supernatural or the evil eye. In the company of that intrepid explorer I felt comfortable, settled and contented. At ten, I blew out the candles and went to sleep.

She was reaching for me. I couldn't see her but I knew who she was. Her hand was smeared with fresh blood. I hesitated, watching. I wanted to reach out and touch that blood-smeared hand and pull it towards me, but I was repulsed by it all at once. Around us, all was thick black. I held out my hand. Hers protruded further out of the black, clawing for me, parting the darkness that began to fade around her. Then a light went on and she was staring at me with eyes that held no life. Her head hung back. The rest of her was mangled.

I awoke, startled, sweating, immersed in a slick of fear. The room was black, the same black as the dream. I fumbled for my phone. It was almost morning. I lit a candle and sat up in bed, dazed. The first rational thought I had was I needed a proper window, not those wooden shutters that let in no light. That may have been the tradition but I needed some glass. The dining room had no window at all.

I would talk to Mario.

I sat for a while in my own pool of light. The dream was still with me, a haunting. I had never dreamed of my mother before, and never in such vivid horror. I couldn't recall ever having a nightmare. It was as though moving to Fuerteventura had stirred up in me inner demons that had been lying dormant, waiting for their chance to unfurl.

I threw off the covers and put on a loose bathrobe. I went around lighting the other candles, something that felt like a ritual all of its own.

As I went over to the chest of drawers, fresh terror shot through me, a single drum beat.

The bolts were slid back.

Sometime in the night someone had entered my room and opened those bolts.

The dining room bolts were the same.

Not only were the bolts slid back but the door was ajar.

It wasn't possible. There was no natural explanation. I felt for a single moment like Jonathon Creek trying to figure out how the trickery might have been achieved.

I couldn't face the possibility of a supernatural force in my house.

A poltergeist?

Who?

My mother? She was certainly now haunting my dreams.

Olivia Stone? She didn't seem the type to haunt.

The Baraso family? But why? They had died of yellow fever. A tragedy, true, but that wouldn't explain a motive for haunting.

Aunt Clarissa always maintained ghosts were trapped on the earthly plane through intense emotions. Through trauma. Sudden death, suicide, that sort of thing.

What about Gloria's comment about the maid who claimed things in Casa Baraso moved? Should I take that seriously? If true, then the culprit could not have been my mother unless she was trying to frighten me into leaving the house well alone in order to protect me from other spirits.

What about the rock in my apartment that had moved twice? Was that my mother warning me too? Was I meant to draw comfort from that? Why didn't she, they, whoever it was want me to live in Casa Baraso?

What about that image of the woman in the patio that Paco had captured on film. She was not my mother. Could she be Olivia Stone? Maybe she was worried I knew her true whereabouts after she disappeared and she didn't want to be discovered, even in death.

No.

It was all rubbish, codswallop, cock and bull and I would not entertain one single element of any of it.

Someone must have got in through the window.

El Cotillo

Dawn brought fresh fear.

I threw open both doors to let in all the light there was to be had. Candlelight flickered in the moving air. The light inside remained dim, the dining room entrance shielded by the scaffolding. Steeling myself, I took a candle to the solitary window and placed it on the curved seat. An examination of the window shutters revealed what I already suspected. The bolts were drawn shut and there was no sign of a forced entry. Whoever had entered was clever, skilled, an expert. They had managed with considerable stealth to slide the bolts open, enter my bedroom, close the bolts, throw open the door bolts and exit through the dining room door all without waking me and for no other reason than to scare me out of my wits.

Cejas? Had to be. No one else had a motive. Although the culprit could be any prankster wanting to intimidate an Englishwoman bent on restoring a ruin. Some kind of activism perhaps. Someone with a deranged attachment to the ruin and a hatred of foreigners. Someone mentally unstable, rabid, paranoid, insane. How far would they go? It occurred to me that the perpetrator had been inside my room in my absence, seen the progress, studied the window fastenings and figured out a silent way of gaining access. They knew I was living on site and that I had installed bolts. They were watching, closely. It had to be a neighbour, someone nearby, someone who saw me return from the hardware store with the bolts. What about that assistant. I had told her what I wanted them for. That might have provoked gossip and speculation. Fallen on the wrong ears. It all seemed convoluted and outlandish, but my reasoning was a lot less outlandish than the alternative. A ghost.

I grabbed a towel and my toiletries, shuffled my feet in flip flops and went outside. My eyes were everywhere. For all I knew my stalker was right there in the building. Filled with reluctance I poked my head through the hole in the partition wall. There was no one with their back pressed against the wall, no one I could see in any of the downstairs rooms, although I didn't have a line of sight to every nook and cranny. I forced myself through the hole and walked over to peer into each of the south facing rooms. Empty, as anticipated. I went back through the hole and headed on outside, glancing in the kitchen on my way by. No one was there.

Needing to make absolutely certain I had no company, I placed my towel and toiletries on a large rock and returned to the patio to climb the ladder at the end of the interior scaffolding. Walking along the makeshift balcony and entering the upstairs rooms, an inexplicable sadness washed through me. I thought of my mother as I looked around for triggers, wondering if something I had seen had set me off. The vaulted ceiling? The vast windows looking out over the volcano? The decorative paintwork on the patches of old wall? None of it reminded me of my mother. The rooms along the north side were all empty and there was no evidence of an intruder that I could see. Not that I would have been able to pick the difference with so much activity on site.

I stood for a while looking down at the patio with its curious partition that destroyed the magnificence of the building. From that elevation, I could take in the state of the ruin in a single sweep. The house was gargantuan, the work involved in rebuilding the southern side enormous. What have I taken on? In one spot I was able to see past my house and down the street. A critical scan of the surrounding properties with their shuttered windows and absent inhabitants yielded nothing, and it was with a mix of frustration and defiance that I went downstairs, collected my things and made my way to my makeshift shower.

Crouching in the plastic bowl drizzling cold water tentatively over first one patch of naked flesh then another, shivering, I hurried through the motions as fast as I was able. Intruder or no intruder, I doubted I would get used to al fresco, bucket and bowl showers and made a mental note to tell Mario to prioritize the plumbing.

I ate fruit for breakfast. Seated in the dining room, I tried to imagine what it would be like when the patio was filled with plants and how pleasant it would be to sit inside a dark room away from the glare and the harshness of the summer sun. It was no use. My sensibilities would not adjust to the experience of a windowless room. No room should be a cave. I latched on to the matter, which was fast becoming a bug bear and the sooner glass panes were inserted in what was currently my bedroom, the better.

Even with a proper window, neither of those rooms I would occupy once the house was fully restored. They were too gloomy. I could see myself enjoying the south side where the windows I had included in the plans would look out over my garden.

The workmen would not be on site until the following day. While the morning was still cool I inspected my plants. The drago trees and aloe veras were standing proud and strong, the grasses seemed happy and the ground covers and succulents determined to thrive. I pulled out a few weeds then went and put a few more rocks on my wall. The view of the volcano and the mountains drew me as ever it did, the yellow and red ochres, the near total absence of green. Beholding the desert-like setting, it was hard to imagine the events of the previous nights, impossible to believe that anything could disturb the magnificent energy of the island.

Out in the open away from the house, I was prepared to contemplate the supernatural explanation, if provisionally and if only to dismiss it altogether. For surely that tenacious wind that blew and blew would sweep the spirits away? The sun blazed brilliantly, withering all but the most robust beneath its glare. Didn't ghosts lurk in dark, secluded places? Were they not the stuff of dank castles and ivy-festooned mansions deep in the woods? Places where the air was still and the energies trapped. Ponds and swamps and wells. Not here on Fuerteventura. Or was I buying into stereotypes, making assumptions based on gothic novels and haunted house films. There was no rationalising away the possibility along those lines. Besides, I had those two gloomy rooms in there. Yet I refused to entertain the idea of a spirit world that interfered with the real world. What I did know was I had no idea how I would sleep every night not knowing what next would occur.

The empty street, the closed-up houses, the lack of any living neighbour or a passer-by added to my misgivings. Not even the emaciated dog had returned. The absence of life down my street was little short of weird. Were the villagers hiding from me? Was that it? Too scared to interact in case the curse of Casa Baraso fell on them. Were folk still that superstitious? Perhaps they were. After all, Mario couldn't hire locals from anywhere on the island to work on my house. Instead of curious or nosy neighbours, I had fearful ones keeping their distance as though I had the plague.

I heard the rumble of a car engine in the distance and paused, listening. The sound drew nearer and to my relief and delight, Paco pulled up in his dusty old bomb. I waved and hurried over and we met by the southern wall of the house.

He leaned down and kissed my cheeks.

'I didn't expect to see you so early on a Sunday morning,' I said, smiling into his face, overjoyed to see him, knowing my exuberance mingled with relief.

'I wanted to catch you before you headed off somewhere.'

'I thought you would be working,' I said, my mind too slow for the pace of the conversation.

'Even a photographer gets a day off. It's Sunday. Come with me to the beach.'

'You like the beach?'

'What self-respecting majo doesn't like the beach?'

'It did occur to me to go for a swim,' I lied, delighted by the suggestion, 'but Morro Jable will be full of tourists. I thought of Gran Tarajal but that will be the same. Corralejo even worse.'

'Why go east? It will be too hot. I'm going to El Cotillo. Fewer tourists and it catches the ocean breeze. Claire, today is going to be very hot. I have come to rescue you from Tiscamanita.'

A dart of something I didn't recognise whizzed through me. 'El Cotillo. Yes, of course.' I paused, hesitant. 'Come inside for a minute.'

'That's okay.' He raised his camera that was an extension of his arm. 'I'll wait here for you.'

'Please, I have something to show you.'

He followed me around the back.

'Much cooler in here,' he remarked as we entered the dining room. 'Make sure you shut it up and it will trap the cool and be nice when you get home.' As he drew the door to, his gaze drifted to the bolts.

'That's what I wanted to show you.'

He inspected them more closely.

'You put these on?'

'I did.'

'Good job. But why bolts? You are locking yourself in?'

'I felt I had to. I woke up yesterday to find someone had opened the doors while I slept. Or I should say pushed open.'

'Pushed?'

I felt embarrassed admitting my fear but went on. 'I couldn't sleep for thinking about a possible intruder so I half barricaded myself in with chairs. When I woke one chair was lying on its side, the other was pushed away and the dining room door was ajar. I thought if I put bolts on the doors then that would prevent a recurrence.'

'Did it?'

'I wish. This morning the bolts were drawn and the dining room door was open. And don't say Olivia Stone. Please. I think someone got in through the window and let themselves out.'

'Possible.' He went over to inspect the window. I remained where I was, taking in my unmade bed, the clothes lying around.

'How could someone get in here?' he said, opening the shutter and closing it and drawing the bolt. 'You had locked the window, right?'

'I thought I had.' I hesitated, my memory hazy. Perhaps that was it; I had forgotten to lock the window. I didn't know whether to feel relieved I definitely didn't have a ghost or alarmed I definitely had an intruder. 'I don't know,' I said. 'Maybe I hadn't. Maybe they got in anyway, found a way to slide the bolt across.'

'That would have to be some magic trick. Maybe your intruder is an escapologist.'

'I know.' I cringed. 'I was thinking there might be someone like that around here. A prankster.'

'Unlikely.'

'Not as unlikely as a ghost.'

'Why do you deny it? I told you the house is haunted.'

'By the Barasos.'

He let out a soft grunt. 'By Olivia Stone.'

'You can't know that.'

'A photograph does not lie. And you saw it yourself. A woman sitting in the patio.'

I gave up. There was no point arguing with him. When it came to Olivia Stone, he was intractable. I stuffed bathers, a towel, a sunhat, sunscreen and a water bottle in my beach bag, along with a cotton sundress. 'Shall we take my car?' I asked, thinking he had already driven up from Puerto del Rosario, and besides, my air con was fierce.

'Sure.'

I closed both doors and he followed me to the back of the barn.

'Wow,' he said, seeing my Hyundai for the first time. 'Is it new?'

'I needed something to ferry building supplies.'

He laughed. 'My car would be better for that.'

I resisted offering my agreement.

Seated behind the wheel, inhaling the brand-new car smell, I felt my confidence returning. There was something about being behind the wheel of a large and brand-new car that made me feel grander, stronger, more confident somehow. I manoeuvred off the block and headed off.

El Cotillo was situated on the north-western tip of the island, accessed on the back roads past Tefía and on through La Oliva and Lajares. An hour's drive and we had covered half the length of the island and I was crawling down the village streets until I found a place to park.

Paco was happy for me to take charge. He seemed amused that I knew the area so well. I told him I had booked a holiday here one time and enjoyed it so much, I scarcely left the village to venture elsewhere. I must have eaten in every restaurant from El Cotillo to Lajaras.

I slipped into an indulgent mood, treating us both to an iced coffee in a café overlooking the harbour, using the opportunity to change into my sundress, with bathers beneath, in the facilities. Paco was all happy banter. I found him entertaining. He had a ready supply of amusing tales and a storehouse of knowledge about the islands.

Not wanting to miss the opportunity of the high tide we saw on our way into the village, we went back to the car and I took us up to my favourite beach, one of several where the reef protects swimmers from the force of the ocean.

With the creamy sand between our toes, we slipped out of our outer apparel like two excited children and dumped it all where we stood and ran to the shoreline, entering the cool, shallow water. Feeling the gentle push and pull, inhaling the salty ocean air, I emitted a pleasurable sigh. Paco splashed me, teasing. I splashed him back and we laughed, momentarily drawing the attention of the others in the water. Then, mindful of the rocks, we swam together the length and breadth of the enclosed bay, not stopping until we were both too exhausted to swim another stroke.

Never in my whole life had I enjoyed a swim at the beach more than that time with Paco. We fell into the pleasure of the experience as though we had been doing it all our lives, together, as friends or siblings, or as lovers. My thinking took me no further.

We dried off in the freshening wind and strolled back to my car. I drove into the village and took Paco to my favourite restaurant for lunch, tucked down a narrow lane away from the main drag.

Over tapas and grilled fish washed down with cooling beer, our senses mellow from the exercise, we chatted some more about the island and what it meant to locals and holidaymakers alike.

'I think the main thing is it's safe here,' I said, summing up. 'The average Brit or German or Swede gets the sunshine of North Africa without the ferocity of the climate and the hassles that come with interacting with markedly different cultures. Most holidaymakers who come here want nothing more than the beach.'

'Yet here I am, a photographer, a farmer's son, working in a restaurant. I embody the entire paradox of tourism.'

'And here am I, a bank teller made rich by chance and all I want to do is make things better. Is that so bad?'

We locked gazes.

'Most rich people don't care. They are selfish.'

'I'm not.'

'You are not used to it.'

He was right. I wasn't. I hadn't a clue. I was running on passion and dreams.

'Tell me about your family,' he said, changing the subject.

'My family? Nothing to tell.'

'There is. You know all about mine. Maybe you will meet them some day. I will take you to Caleta de Fuste and you can meet Ana and Julio.'

There was that feeling again as though there was something in the air between us. Was this friendship, or something more? I popped another chip in my mouth, stalling.

Paco persisted. 'Your father, what does he do?'

I cringed inwardly. 'Property developer.'

He didn't show a reaction.

'Is he rich?'

'No, not really. He hasn't been that lucky and he doesn't have the backing of big money.'

'What's he like? Are you close to him?'

'He isn't that kind of guy. Growing up, I hardly saw him. He was either working or out playing golf.'

'Who brought you up?'

'Aunt Clarissa. She is my mother's older sister. A psychologist.'

'Interesting.'

'You would like her. I think you share similar interests. She believes in ghosts and that sort of thing.'

'I am liking her already.'

I related her latest ghost-tour tale and he laughed.

'She's very down-to-earth otherwise,' I said. 'Practical.'

'And your mother? Was she practical?'

Something in me froze. It had been a very long time since anyone had asked me about my mother. I ignored the feeling and offered him an answer. 'Not that I recall. She was a dreamer. Clarissa and Ingrid come from a long line of occultists. Clarissa has traced the trait back through many generations.' I paused to look out the window at the ocean, the sky, the people. 'I think Ingrid didn't belong in the real world. She didn't make much of an impression, at least not on me. I hardly remember her.'

'When did you lose her?'

'I was seven.'

'Seven.'

'Yes.'

'Then you would have a lot of memories of before then. But you have forgotten them. You wanted to erase the memory of your mother. It would have been easier that way.'

He stared at me, expectantly. Under that interested and compassionate gaze I couldn't hold back. What was the point of holding back? Better to let things flow. I gave him a full account of the accident. I told him in a clinical, blow by blow fashion. When I got to the part about the squashed tomatoes he inhaled and reached forward to touch my arm.

An electric current shot through me as though in answer to my earlier puzzlement. This man invited me here because he wanted more than friendship. How could I not have spotted his intentions before? Am I so dim-witted, so inexperienced not to know when a man has designs on me? I let him hold my hand across the table. He gave it a squeeze before leaning back to attract the attention of a nearby waiter.

'We need ice cream,' he said to me. 'What flavour? Chocolate? Caramel? Vanilla? We'll have all three.' He looked up at the waiter. 'And two brandies, doubles, and two espressos.'

'I have to drive.'

'We must stay for the sunset.'

'The sunset?' But that was hours away. I didn't say it.

He grinned. 'Plenty of time to relax and enjoy the day. Besides, the ice cream is better with brandy.'

He was right. We poured the alcohol and the coffee on the ice cream and luxuriated in his version of an affogato. Neither of us was in a hurry to leave. We spooned our intoxicating desserts slowly and caught each other's gazes and offered shy smiles. The conversation meandered, covering what books we liked, what films, and what we thought of the world. Neither of us mentioned Olivia Stone. After a while we slipped into companionable silence.

'There's an exhibition at the tower,' Paco said eventually.

'That sounds marvellous.'

I stood on the pretext of needing the loo and paid at the bar. When I returned, Paco was scrolling through photos on his camera. Seeing me, he stood and we walked outside, squinting into the glare.

'You needn't have paid.'

'I wanted to.'

'Well, thank you.'

The breeze had strengthened, cooling the temperature of an otherwise scorching day. I imagined back in Tiscamanita it was forty degrees.

Torre de El Tostón was a short walk away and it was pleasant to stroll down the promenade, past the little harbour with its restaurants brimming with patrons, the hubbub of Sunday dining, and on across flat, gritty land to the low promontory on which stood a stout, stone edifice constructed to defend the island from attack. We walked up a short flight of stone steps and across a gangplank and entered the fort.

Hanging from the bare rock walls of the small, bunker-style interior were a series of landscapes. Expecting traditional works geared for the tourist trade, I didn't anticipate the vibrancy and originality of the pieces. My impulse was to buy one but I didn't want to embarrass Paco with my wealth. I chose instead to take note of the artist's name. Buying paintings represented a whole new level of shopping, one I had no experience in. It occurred to me Paco would make the ideal companion and advisor and I made a mental note to remember that.

We wandered over to the edge of the promontory to take in the view, watching as others scrambled down to the rocky ledge below. To the south, the creamy sand of the surf beach met the low cliffs, with the Betancuria massif in the distance. The setting was sublime and we stood together in appreciation as the wind pressed our clothes to our skin.

As we strolled back to the village, crunching our way over the gravely terrain, Paco took my hand. It was the most romantic gesture in the most idyllic of settings and I savoured the sensation of his flesh, hot and firm, against mine. Any stray thoughts lingering on the fringes of my mind of the build and the strange disturbances evaporated.

We went down to the harbour wall to admire the little fishing boats. Then we found another café and had a second iced coffee.

Deciding we were again too hot, we took ourselves off for another swim, and then lay on the beach in the late afternoon sun. One more swim and we were ready to visit a fourth café to share a paella. Never, had I enjoyed the company of a man so much. I didn't want the day to end.

By the time the sun sank low on the horizon and the sky glowed crimson, we were standing alone on the beach and Paco had his arm around my shoulder, and as the colours faded and the sky to the east deepened to indigo, we kissed.

An Interlude

Calle Manuel Velázquez Cabrera was as desolate as ever. No people. No cars. It was as though life in the village ended at the intersection, the last street light marking the end of civilisation. When I reached my block, I mounted the kerb and parked behind the barn.

After our deliciously pleasant day in El Cotillo, the arrival was a let-down. As I unbuckled my seat belt, I wasn't sure what to do next, invite Paco in or thank him for the day and bid him farewell.

He walked me to the house and we stopped beneath the scaffolding. The night was warm, all that stone radiating the heat of the day. The wind, blowing from the northeast, wrapped itself around the building, moaning, whistling through cracks. Plastic flapped, a plank somewhere above thumped lightly then stopped. Then the wind pulled back, leaving the building alone for a moment and all was quiet. Deciding I was not ready to face the night on my own I invited him in.

We used our phone torches to light the way, Paco pausing by the hole in the partition to shine his light into the other half of the patio, then standing back and shining the light at the hole itself, presumably at where he had taken the photo that had captured the image of a woman crouching.

Both doors to my rooms were closed. The air was cooler inside, if stuffy. I went in and lit the candles. Everything was as I had left it, bed unmade, a few dirty plates and cups piled on the makeshift bench.

Paco came up behind me. I turned and gestured at the table and invited him to sit and offered him wine.

'A nightcap.'

I poured two glasses of a Lanzarote red and joined him.

'Will you be okay sleeping here tonight?' he said, taking his glass.

'I have the Cocteau Twins for company.'

'Who?'

'Here.' I reached for my laptop and headphones and played him 'Iceblink Luck'. The expression on his face changed from curiosity to wonder. I waited for the track to end before speaking.

'What do you think?'

'Astonishing.'

'You like them?'

'Where are they from?'

'Scotland. Now I'm here, I think I need to find some local music to listen to.'

'You would like Luis Morera. He's from La Palma. He's the islands' greatest musical talent.'

I made a note of the name, not quite believing I would. Or was that prejudiced of me? He returned the headphones to his ears. He appeared to enjoy the next track. Listening to the spill, I felt excluded from the pleasure. I waited. I took a sip of my wine. It was piquant, robust. I thought of rioja, of tempranillo, of how Spanish wine travelled, finding its way on the supermarket shelves the world over. I reached and tapped his arm. He slid the headphones down to wrap around his neck.

'Have you ever been overseas?' I asked.

'I've just got back.'

'I meant, beyond the islands.'

'Barcelona, that's all.'

'And you?'

'Only here.'

'You would like Barcelona.'

'I'm sure.'

He smiled and returned my headphones to his ears and continued listening. The expression on his face was one of wondrous pleasure. Either he was determined to enjoy the music, putting on a good show to keep himself in my good books, or he really liked it.

Just then, I wanted to show him Colchester. He might like it there. Feeling the desire, I realised I had become closer to him than I might have found comfortable in other circumstances, this quirky photographer with a passion for Olivia Stone.

What was it with him and his fixation? Perhaps he was taken by her image, she might be attractive to a man like him, but that was unfair and belittling. A man like Paco didn't harbour a fetish for a dead woman. I was being absurd. Besides, I could see she reflected back to the islands a version of themselves now lost. That was justification enough for his admiration. So successful was her book that after its publication, tourism, on Tenerife at least, began in earnest among the wealthier classes. More steam ships were put on. Hotels opened. And on it went.

I drank more of my wine and kept watching him listening to my music. Now and then he would look at me and smile before his gaze slid away and he lost himself to the sound.

Through Paco, through Olivia Stone, I was receiving an unexpected education, a sort of induction into the ancient way of life of the islanders, in much greater detail than a museum could provide. Olivia Stone's narrative was lived experience. She was showing me how distinct the islands were from the land of their Spanish colonialists. I had never seen the islands that way before. I had always considered them a geographically convenient outpost of Spain, with year-round perfect weather and stunning landscapes. Somehow, when Paco was around, I ended up dwelling on Olivia Stone. I supposed she was my point of entry into the truth about the island.

The album was nearing its end. I didn't want Paco to leave but I had no clear idea how to make him stay. I replenished our glasses and sat back. He removed my headphones and took a slow sip. He was the one who brought up the haunting.

'You might need to do an exorcism. I know of a priest who does that sort of thing.'

'An exorcism?'

He nodded. 'You would be doing Olivia a favour. Setting her free.'

Why did he have to ruin the moment with this rubbish? I wanted to say don't be ridiculous. Instead, I kept sipping my wine.

He glanced around, his gaze lingering in the corners. 'This place has a definite vibe. Can't you feel it?'

'You are imagining things,' I said quickly, recalling Gloria mentioning the same. 'The place feels strange because it's a building site. That's all.'

'If you say so.'

I struggled to suppress a yawn that rose from nowhere, concerned it would give the wrong impression.

He looked uncertain for a moment. Then, as though making up his mind, he drained his glass. 'I better go. You need your sleep. Will you be all right on your own?'

'I should be fine. I'll lock myself in.'

'That didn't work last time.'

Part of me wanted to plead with him to stay but I resisted, not wanting to complicate what was developing between us out of fear. He was making to stand when the living-room door opened and slammed shut of its own volition. Startled, I let out a small yelp. He grabbed the table and leaned forward.

'That, whatever that was, well, it wasn't possible, was it?'

'The wind,' I said helplessly.

He stood and headed for the door.

'Paco, don't go.'

He came back and put a hand on my shoulder. 'I'm not going to. Don't worry.'

'Thank you.'

'I just need to …' He trailed off.

'Me, too.'

I took a beaker of water and my toothbrush and went out into the dark, lighting my way with my phone. I didn't bother bringing back the battery. When I returned, Paco went and did the same, using the new toothbrush I proffered. It was still in its packet.

While he was gone I straightened the bed and pulled off my dress. I hesitated, not sure what else to take off and what to put on, when he re-entered the room. He took one glance at me in my underwear, and went and bolted both doors, checked the window shutters and blew out all the candles save the ones beside the bed. Then he came around to where I was standing.

'Come,' he said, and we lay down together on top of the covers.

My skin was warm from a day in the sun, and salty too. I thought I would need to make a trip to a launderette before long. What a stupid topic to enter my head, given the situation.

My domestic musings were interrupted by the softest touch as his hand reached for mine.

I responded in kind and he turned on his side and brushed my hair from my face.

'You are very beautiful,' he said. 'May I?' And he leaned and reached for my mouth with his.

I yielded, tingling with anticipation and sudden yearning, opening up to him as he caressed the skin of my arm. He was tentative, slow, as was I as I touched him, although I was soon aflame, eager to sate a hunger for too long buried. Our kisses grew passionate, our flesh soon naked, and we wrapped our limbs up in each other, pressed together our torsos, our heat combining. Before long, we were a furnace, hot, wet and panting.

When at last we both lay back in the afterglow, breathless, I laughed.

'What's funny?'

'Not funny. Blissful.'

'Good.'

He blew out his candle and I mine and we lay in the darkness, holding hands. A million questions passed through my mind. Who was Paco, really? A good man? Bad? Was he sincere with his affections, or was he a womaniser and I another conquest, a chalk line on his doorframe filled with chalk lines? What did he want from me? My love? My wealth?

I only knew one thing. I had been seduced. Two things, because it had felt delicious.

Señor Baraso

The warmth of Paco's body beside me and the steady breath of his slumber put a seal on my decision to restore the ruin. It was as though out tryst signified some sort of deeper approval of my being here. I had no idea if he would form part of my future life on the island, if what was happening between us had any future to it at all, or if it was an interlude. In many ways, I would have preferred the companionship of female friends who would have filled out my life without any danger of a romantic complication. In a curious fashion, for the present, Paco reinforced my isolation.

It was still night. My bladder nagged to be emptied. I knew he was asleep but I wasn't about to pee in a bucket, not even at the far end of the other room. I grabbed my phone, fumbled about for my bathrobe and flip flops, and unbolted the dining room door as softly as I could.

He didn't stir.

Heading out through the patio, passing the hole in the partition wall that had come to symbolise the haunting, I felt more confident, knowing I had another living presence, a benevolent one, nearby. Yet my unease remained. Out in the backyard, I shone the torch around as I walked. Amid the chaos of the build I felt only an inkling of ownership of the land I trod. I was yet to make the place my own. More than anything, I felt like an intruder. Maybe Cejas was right and the ruin should have been demolished. Or maybe I should have taken Mario's advice and built a new house out of the old.

Exiting the portaloo, I paused to take in the night. The wind had dropped. The moon, a crescent of milky light, hovered about the volcano. Stars were visible in the firmament beyond its reach. I stared into the heavens, impressed by the magnitude of stars, their patterns, their brilliance. In Colchester, I could have been forgiven for not knowing they existed. I could scarcely recall ever seeing the evening star. Perhaps I hadn't been paying attention.

Feeling the strain in my neck I returned my gaze to ground level and took in the building, reluctant to enter despite, or perhaps because Paco was there.

I glanced at the outbuildings and then behind me at the volcano. As I turned back a flash of light caught my eye. I pinned my gaze to where it had come from and saw, emerging as if from nowhere, a brilliant dot of red light hovering above the patio. I watched it rise up suddenly, dart back down and up again, then make a frenzied, erratic dance like a crazed fly. The light shot up into the sky and disappeared. Had to be an insect, really, it did. Or maybe I was hallucinating and going slowly mad. Whatever the cause, it was weird and I hurried back inside, closed and bolted the door and slid into bed.

Paco stirred but didn't wake. I lay in the dark, eyes closed, mind racing. I refused to believe in the supernatural. Haunted houses do not exist. There is no such thing as ghosts. I thought if I sat up, if I stayed awake, I would discover who was opening those bolts. A better idea occurred to me and I slipped out of bed, grabbed a broom, a chair and some plastic containers and quietly made an arrangement of obstacles in front of the shutters. If anyone did manage to open that particular bolt, they would make a racket getting in and we would be certain to wake up. Satisfied, I slid back into bed, assured of more sleep.

I awoke to a gentle stroking sensation on my cheek. I slowly emerged from slumber realising it was Paco. The room was dark but a chink of light was visible under the door.

'You were busy in the night,' Paco laughed, shining his phone light at the window and pointing to my little fortifications.

I saw they were still as I had left them, as best as I could recall. I gave Paco a brief account of my nocturnal interlude, excluding the strange darting light. I didn't want to give him yet more fuel for his supernatural theories.

'And when you came back in, you bolted the dining room door?'

'I did.'

'Are you sure?'

'Certain.' Why would he doubt me?

'Well, it's open now.'

'That's impossible,' I said, diving out of bed to take a look.

He laughed. His laugh had me wondering if he was the one who had opened that door. I only had his word for it. Surely, he wouldn't be so cruel? Maybe not cruel, but capable of taking action, any action to prove his point.

As though to reinforce my suspicion, he said, 'I told you, Olivia Stone doesn't want her true whereabouts discovered and will stop at nothing to keep you from telling the world where she went when she abandoned her family.'

We locked gazes. I was naked, acutely aware of the fall of my breasts, the curve of my belly, my bushy mons. He was already fully clothed.

'If it's her,' I said, snatching my bathrobe off the floor in a moment of coyness.

'It's her. That photo proves it.'

'That could be anyone.'

'If you insist. But you do need to banish her if you want to live here.'

'Or live with her tricks, as my aunt Clarissa would say. Get to know what she really wants.'

He smiled at me and planted a kiss on my cheek.

'Wise woman, your aunt. Now, I need to go do some things. You'll be alright on your own?'

'Of course.'

Despite my irritation, I wanted to ask when I would see him again but it seemed possessive. I had to fight back a gnawing desperation watching him head out the door, not sure if he would give me the protection I suddenly craved.

Seeing the time—it was six—I grabbed my toiletries and a towel and rushed to my provisional shower. Once clean and dressed, I went and packed away the solar panels and battery, storing them under a plastic tarpaulin in the third outbuilding, planning to leave them there until I decided whether they would ever be any use. Then I bundled up towels, sheets, clothes and bathers into a large bag to take to the laundromat, grabbed my laptop and charger and set off on my way to the café for breakfast. As I drove off the block, the first of the workmen were arriving.

Other than washing my clothes, I had no idea how I would spend the day, or any day Monday to Friday with the build in progress, but I would just have to make it up as I went along.

I parked outside the café and marched inside with my laptop and chargers, determined this time to get a full answer from Gloria to the question of Casa Baraso. She had been holding something back each time we had spoken. I was sure of it.

There was a flurry of custom soon after I arrived and patrons hovered behind me. I ordered coffee and orange juice and toast and scrambled eggs and sat at my preferred table, the one with the power point. The moment I sat down I put my laptop on charge. With nothing to do but wait for Gloria, I checked my emails on my phone and watched the clientele come and go.

By the time she brought my coffee, the café had returned to its usual lull and I asked her who lived in the vicinity of my house. She said the houses opposite were bank repossessions, the stone building beside me was a holiday home that was mostly empty, and closest to me on the north side lived an old couple who were almost totally deaf. Further up my street most of the houses were either holiday lets or holiday homes left empty by their Spanish owners. Two or three were deceased estates. Altogether, that explained why I felt so alone in my street.

She rushed away to see to my eggs. Before long I heard the grind of the juicer. When she came with both, she said, 'I added some cheese. I hope you don't mind.'

I smiled up at her. 'I prefer them with cheese.'

Satisfied, she left me to eat.

I took my time over my breakfast. The laptop had charged by the time I had finished the toast. I plugged in my phone and ordered another coffee, awaiting another moment when the café was empty.

When Gloria came to clear a nearby table, I broached the topic without any preface. 'Did you know I am having to sleep at the house now?'

'Yes.' She put down the plates she was holding and came over. 'How are you finding it?'

'Strange. Comfortable enough in the two rooms, but strange.'

'Are doors opening by themselves?' she asked tentatively.

'How did you know?'

A worried look appeared in her face.

'Tell me, please. What are people saying?'

'You want to know what really happened at Casa Baraso?'

At last! I nodded, all ears.

'Then I will tell you. But you won't like it. Baraso was not a good man. He was brutal. He brought his wife and four daughters from Tenerife so he could terrorise them, hidden away in that house.'

'How do you know this?'

'My great grandmother was born in 1890, and her grandmother was twenty-three when the Baraso family died. She was their maid. She said they did not die of yellow fever. The truth was covered up. She saw the blood, the knife, the stab wounds. He'd smothered the girls in their beds, killed his wife and then himself.'

I gasped. 'But how did all that get covered up?'

'He was from an important family. They were well-connected. They paid my relative to keep quiet. And eight years later the house was sold. In fact, it took a whole eight years to sell it. Cejas didn't know a thing, being from the mainland, and it sold for cheap. No one has been able to live there since. Not for a hundred and fifty years. People have stayed there, but they have never stayed long and they always suffer some misfortune or other. I am afraid the same will happen to you.'

I took in her words, stunned by the awful revelation. A brutal murder suicide, *in my home*. I felt queasy and a little faint. Perhaps the Cejas who sold me the house had heard the rumour, discovered its veracity and wanted to demolish the house to erase the memory. Is it possible demolition would have solved the problem? Or would the spirits of those listless dead haunt the very ground where the house had stood? I caught myself as my thoughts strayed into realms I staunchly refused to give any credence. Ghosts! Yet dismissing the idea of a haunted house did not eradicate the bare truth, four girls and their mother were murdered there. I was not sure I wanted to set foot on my own property ever again.

Seeing the expression on my face, Gloria said, 'I should not have told you.'

'I would have found out, eventually.'

'Maybe. Just be careful, Claire. Very careful.'

I told her I would. As she walked away to serve a customer, I replayed her words, picturing the scene, wondering which of the bedrooms each of them had slept in. Four daughters and a wife meant probably all of them. A murder in every upstairs room. Images of that brutal attack ran through my mind like photos of a crime scene. I unplugged the charger and packed up my things. When Gloria came over to my table, I gave her a twenty euro note and told her to keep the change. I couldn't get out of Tiscamanita fast enough.

Escalation

I drove to Puerto del Rosario with Blur playing loud through the car speakers, refusing to give in to thoughts of the Baraso family and the horrors that had taken place in my house. At the laundromat in Avenida Juan de Bethencourt, I sat and waited for the wash cycle and then the dry cycle. I could have wandered up the street or crossed the road to visit the café opposite for a coffee, but instead, I tuned in to the steady drone of the machines, the heavy scent of washing powder and the brightly lit, industrial vibe. I lost myself to a shop full of appliances. There was something soothing about the normalcy, the domesticity, the basic humanity of washing clothes that I latched onto. Anything, so as not to have to think through Gloria's divulgences.

With my clothes and sheets folded and smelling like a field of flowers, I drove up the coast to the tiny village of Puerto Lajas and parked beside the little chapel at the end of the main street. The beach was sheltered but lacked the creamy sands of El Cotillo or Morro Jable. Here, the sand was basalt-brown and pebble strewn, the locale less developed, and there were less holidaymakers about as a result. Although it was clear they were missing out on an inviting location. A reef protected the bay and although the waters were deeper than the lagoons of El Cotillo, they looked safe to swim in. Small fishing boats, anchored offshore, bobbed about in the protected waters. I went over to the waterline and stared into the blurred horizon, comparing the azure of the sky to the azure of the ocean, listening to the gentle slap of the waves, the cries of fun and laughter carried on the wind.

What had I come to this island for? To live a hermit's life in a house disturbed by its own past? To be a pleasure seeker, tanning and swimming and eating in restaurants? Provide free holiday accommodation for my supposed friends? Or had I come here to be seduced by a local? I needed an occupation, that much was becoming clear, and plans for my house once it was restored, but I could think about neither. Maybe the Spanish course due to start in a couple of months would at least result in some friends and possibly even a fresh sense of purpose.

I was listless again, and troubled. The sun burned my skin and even in the brilliant light I couldn't shake a sinister, creeping sensation oozing through me as my thoughts settled on Baraso, who had murdered his four children and his wife and then killed himself. Gloria had been adamant and I had no reason not to believe her. It was hard to process. The heinous crime was ancient but that didn't change the knowledge that it had happened. I doubted it would have made much difference if it had taken place only last year. The fact remained that people, children had been slaughtered in my house. I found that hard to assimilate. The chances had always been high that deaths had occurred inside those walls over the centuries but a death from illness or ageing was part of the normal flow of life. Murder was different. It was brutal, sudden, shocking and I was disturbed by it. I couldn't recall ever being as disturbed by a sudden death, other than my mother's. I supposed that was why I was reacting strongly to the Baraso killings. I had intimate knowledge of the trauma of violent death, after having witnessed my mother's accident. Had I inadvertently been attracted to, obsessed by and then consequently driven to purchase Casa Baraso due to my own unconscious trauma? Did life work like that? Or was it all coincidental?

Maybe Olivia Stone had been drawn to the house for the same reason. The energy would have resonated. Only, she had escaped one bad domestic situation to land in the echoes of another, exemplifying what could have happened to her had she stayed with her husband. If Paco's version of reality was true.

It was nearing lunchtime and the smells wafting from the beachside restaurant were appetising. I wandered over and as I entered I was ushered by a friendly waiter to a vacant table halfway along a wall decorated with guitars. The interior had a homely feel with a green-painted floor. The lower portion of the walls were painted the same shade of green, meeting yellow ochre at waist height. Rustic, and the colours leant an earthy feel to the interior, the colour of green always a welcome touch on an island bereft of it. The tables were covered with brown and white check table cloths. I had taken the chair with my back to the kitchen and I looked out at the al fresco seating, the palm trees, the beach and ocean beyond. I ordered a coffee and soaked up the atmosphere. Paradise. It was unequivocal. As other diners wandered in for lunch, I hailed the waiter and ordered tapas of quartered tomatoes, seasoned with oil and herbs and slices of garlic, followed by paella. Pure indulgence, and since I was in a position to eat out on a daily basis, perhaps I would continue to do so. My way of supporting the local economy.

Over the last months, I had become accustomed to my own company but seeing couples all around me, my thoughts drifted to Paco and I wondered even if I would ever see him again, let alone be with him as his girlfriend or partner. They were painful doubts and my recent discoveries about the house made me want him to be with me always. I cautioned myself not to rush into a relationship with someone I hardly knew based on my fear. I cautioned myself not to want him simply because I was idle, bored, impatient and desirous of distractions. If I wanted to be with him, it needed to be for a solid reason, and that reason would be because I loved and admired him.

If all I wanted was a companion and a protector I should get a dog.

I arrived back at the build as the men were packing up. I left my car in the street, scanned for progress but saw none and headed round the back and into the patio. Mario was standing by the hole in the partition wall, talking to Helmud. He waved when he saw me and beckoned me over.

'I'm glad you're here,' he said in a serious tone. 'We need to talk.'

'Oh, yes?'

He hesitated. It was Helmud who broke the news. 'The partition wall needs to come down.'

'Wow! Already?'

'Progress is fast when you have this many men. Today, the kitchen windows went in. That lintel,' he pointed over my right shoulder, 'and the upstairs rooms on the north side are ready for the plasterers.'

'That's excellent news.'

'Only, we need to start work on the balcony. And we can't do that until the wall is down.'

'I'll be glad when that's gone,' I said, already imagining the sense of space. 'It's an eyesore, and it means the aljibe can be fixed.'

'All that, and much more. But...'

'There's a but?'

The two men exchanged glances and then both looked at me at once.

'It will make it very difficult for you being here,' Mario said.

'It won't be possible,' Helmud reinforced.

'Because of the dust.'

They were beginning to sound like Tweedledum and Tweedledee.

'A lot of dust,' Helmud went on. 'There will be rubble and rocks everywhere. The works on the balcony will be taking place right outside the doors to your rooms.'

'And you can't enter through the front door yet, as those doors are still being made.'

'We'll seal up the doors to protect your things, but you won't have access.'

'Is there anywhere you can stay?' Mario said.

They both looked at me expectantly. Then Helmud said to Mario, 'Maybe she can visit another island. Gran Canaria or Tenerife.'

'True. If she can get a flight.'

They started walking away in the direction of the back doorway. I followed, listening.

'There'll be flights, surely?' said Helmud. 'She's only one person.'

'For tomorrow? Maybe.'

Tomorrow?

'Well, she has to go somewhere, and as she says, there is no accommodation on the island.'

'A tent?'

'That is possible.'

'For how long?' I said, interrupting, preferring to be included in the conversation and not referred to as a 'she'.

'Until Friday,' Mario said.

Helmud looked doubtful. 'At least.'

'They should have the worst of the mess cleared up by then.'

'But what about the balcony? She'll need a hard hat just to go to her portaloo.'

'This is true.'

'I'll pack up and be gone by tomorrow morning.'

'Thank you, Claire,' said Mario, visibly relieved.

'No problem.'

Although it was a problem. A big one. It felt like being ousted. I had only been living on site one weekend and I wished they had told me before. Helmud must have known. All that work preparing those two rooms and I got to sleep in them for just three nights. My mind raced over my options. I pictured myself sleeping at the airport awaiting the first available flight off the island, bound for anywhere.

I was about to head inside when I caught sight of Paco's old bomb pulling up in front of Mario's clean blue Renault. Relieved, I went over and met him on the pavement. My concern showed on my face, in my manner altogether.

'What's up?' he said, kissing my cheeks.

'You won't believe it,' I muttered, leading him around the front of the building and down the north side, away from Mario and Helmud who were still talking as they ambled to their cars. 'I have to move out, or at least not sleep here for at least a week.' I explained about the partition wall.

'It will be good to see it gone.'

'They were suggesting I fly somewhere, or buy a tent.'

'A tent! You will not buy a tent. And you will not fly somewhere.'

'Then what will I do?' I asked, a little peeved at being told what to do again.

'You will live with me.'

'I couldn't,' I whispered. I was stunned, a little thrilled and extremely apprehensive all at once.

'Why not?' He sounded offended.

I hesitated. Would there be room for me in his flat in Puerto del Rosario which was bound to be small, very small? I wanted to ask how many bedrooms he had, although the question instantly felt ridiculous after yesterday.

'If you're sure.'

'Why would I not be sure?' He looked at me intently. 'It will be safer.'

'Yes, it will be safer.' I thought of telling him Gloria's version of what happened to the Baraso family, but I did not want to add any weight to his ghost theories.

Paco watered the plants while I packed. In under two hours I was back in Puerto del Rosario, this time in Calle Canalejas, in an apartment above an empty shop.

The apartment was two streets back from the promenade and the beach and a bunch of restaurants. The locale was lively, noisy, more vibrant than Calle Barcelona. Inside, a spacious, open-plan living area led through to a single bedroom. I saw at a glance Paco kept the place tidy. Had we not already shared my bed I would have eyed the deep and comfy-looking sofa with relief and plotted my next move, no doubt leaving the island on the first available flight. As I watched Paco deposit my suitcase at the end of his bed, I shrank inwardly in resignation. I had been catapulted into a domestic situation I was not ready for. Paco, in contrast, appeared fine with the arrangement, more than fine. Satisfied.

Five days turned into five weeks as the men demolished the partition and worked on the balcony and aljibe. When Paco was working, I whiled away the days wandering around the harbour, swimming or walking on the little beach, dining out, and dining in when Paco chose to cook. He was a good cook. He seemed to enjoy sharing his space with me, too, forever keeping me entertained. He even took me out on his photographic trips and introduced me to his parents and other family members – all who looked much the same as Paco – as his companion, the English woman restoring Casa Baraso. They all, each and every one of them, eyed me with real interest, and a hint of expectation. What else had he told them about me?

One evening we talked about my idea for a booklet and sat together selecting suitable photos out of the scores he had taken. I had never written anything like it in my life, but I thought I would mimic something similar I had found in a bookshop. It shouldn't prove too difficult, I thought, since I had no intention of getting it published. He was the one who suggested I should include a small chapter on Olivia Stone. I thought the idea absurd since there was no evidence she even stepped foot in my house, but I humoured him.

The next day he took me to another house she had stayed in, situated on the corner of Calle Ruiz de Alda and Calle Leon y Castille, close to the port and only a block down from the plaza surrounded by the town hall and government buildings. It was a house I had passed many times on my way down to the port and never noticed.

We went down the side street and stood together on an opposite corner. Paco told me the house had been owned by José Galán Sánchez and his wife, Benigna Pérez Alonso, who ran it as a small hotel. Olivia Stone offers a full paragraph description of its curious layout and windowless rooms. I took my copy of her book with me and compared what she wrote with what I could see from various angles and it was surely the right house. Only, it stood in complete disrepair, another ruin, this time right in the heart of the island's capital. For a horrible moment, I thought I had bought the wrong house. Then again, I would not have enjoyed living so close to the thick of things. Yet the dwelling was not alone in having been left to ruin. There were many ancient buildings dotted around, dating back well over a hundred years and probably closer to two hundred years old. The former hotel would have made a good café or small arts centre and could even be transformed into a small museum commemorating that auspicious visit of Olivia Stone.

'I wish I could save all these old buildings, Paco.'

'It's not your responsibility.'

'True.'

'But it is a nice thought, Claire.'

On the way back to his apartment, taking the circuitous route along the promenade, we linked arms and enjoyed the breeze coming off the ocean. In no hurry to return to the confines of the apartment, I suggested we go for a coffee somewhere.

We went to our usual and sat outside. As we watched the world of Puerto del Rosario go by, a funny little man sporting an I Love Fuerteventura t-shirt sat down at the next table with his wife – who was wearing an identical t-shirt – and assorted bags. He had a loud voice and spoke in a thick brummy accent.

'I don't know, Fred,' the woman said, 'the one on the corner looked cleaner.'

'Did you see their prices? I think we made a mistake coming this far south. Should have stuck to Corralejo.'

'But it was you who wanted to see Casa Winter, not me.'

'Worth it though.' The man called Fred chuckled. 'And who would have thought we would bump into Richard!'

'Richard Parry does tend to pop up everywhere we go, I've noticed.'

'Not everywhere, Margaret. Don't exaggerate.'

'He said he was researching another book.'

'I'm still struggling through his last.'

'Are you going off him, then?'

'Oh, no. But every author has their off moment. And I didn't quite understand his last…'

And so it went on. Holiday banter between an old married couple. After rummaging through their bags for a few moments, they left, having evidently changed their minds. I watched them walk away then saw they'd left behind a bookmark. Curious, I went and picked it up.

It was a novel called La Mareta by Richard H Parry. I put the bookmark in my bag, thinking I'd look him up sometime.

Back at the flat, Paco edited some photos at the dining table and I lounged on the sofa and read Olivia Stone. I could find nothing wrong with our cohabiting, we seemed to have fallen in with each other's routines with ease, yet watching him work I knew it couldn't last. Not least, with me in the flat, there was an acute lack of space. I sensed, too, that the situation was unnatural and somehow wrong. Yet, returning to the build felt like splitting up and I had to censure my heart.

In the days that followed I told myself over and again I couldn't stay.

One morning over breakfast, I finally summoned my courage and told Paco leaping into living together so soon was the wrong way to go about starting a relationship, even though it felt natural and harmonious and fine, and that if we as a couple was what we both wanted, the future would tell. I had taken all that talk from a film I had seen.

Paco was visibly disappointed.

I reached for his hand.

'I need to spend tonight alone. Please try to understand. I need to live in my house alone and not be terrified. Otherwise, I will never live there, or I will want you to live there, only because I am too scared to be there by myself.'

It made logical sense even though it felt awful and I knew Paco took it as a rejection.

On that day of my return, I pulled up at four in the afternoon to find all hell had broken loose on the building site.

The water truck was leaving, but an ambulance was pulling up in its stead.

Helmud saw me and came over.

'It's a carpenter. He's been injured.'

'Is it serious?' I asked, rushing to where the carpenter was lying on the ground of the internal patio, writhing and groaning.

Helmud followed. 'Could be. He was up a ladder when that short length of rafter swung away from the wall and hit him on the back of the head. He fell and cracked his arm on a rock. He's lucky to be alive.'

The offending rafter, which had sat in situ for hundreds of years, was situated on the south side of the partition, the last remaining rafter of the balcony hanging from the east wall about halfway along. The way Helmud described the accident, the rafter had taken a swipe at the poor carpenter. How was that even possible?

Everyone was wondering the same, and the men were clearly spooked. They shifted about, heads low, muttering under their breath to each other. I ferried in my things, not looking forward to when they all went home.

When they did, I was able to properly look around.

In five weeks, the men had cleared almost all of the rocks in the patio and built the balcony on the north and west side. It was deeper than I had imagined, with stairs running up beside the west wall, accessed at ground level near the vestibule leading to the front door. The men had re-rendered the aljibe, too, and upstairs on the north side, the plastering was finished and the bedrooms were ready for the painters. The front door was in, and work had begun on concreting the stretches of patio beneath the balcony, leaving the centre to be paved. I had a clear, rubble free run to the back door. The kitchen and laundry remained grey, empty shells.

On the south side, the walls were complete and beams tied them together at the start of the first storey. Some of the roof rafters were in place. Casa Baraso was soon to be Casa Bennett and I allowed myself feelings of pride. When all was said and done, nothing could detract from the magnificence of the house and I wasn't going to let ghosts spoil things for me. That was my resolve and I hoped I could maintain it.

I went through all the rituals I had established the last time I slept on site. I walked over to my little garden and examined my plants. I took in the view I loved. As the sun dipped below the jagged mountain ridge, I had a bucket shower to wash off the salt from my last swim at the beach in Puerto del Rosario, brushed my teeth and organised my portable latrine before locking myself in for the night. I put on the Cocteau Twins' *The Moon and The Melodies*, dined on canned tuna and a mixed salad, and settled back to read a Stephen King in Spanish. I was missing Paco, but I refused to give in to sentimentality. Above all, I refused to be dependent on a man.

It was only when I blew out the last candle that the knowledge of the violent deaths of the Baraso family came tumbling back to the forefront of my mind. Alone in the house at night, it was hard to shake off the belief that the place was haunted. The gruesome scene of the murder suicide replayed itself over and again and it took me a long time to fall asleep.

I awoke to the sound of whimpering. It was coming from the other room. I thought it was a dog at first, but as I listened I realised it sounded more like a child. Unnerved, I turned over and lit the bedside candle and looked at my phone. It was two o'clock. I wanted to use the phone torch but I discovered my battery was almost out of charge. I'd forgotten to charge it at Paco's. Instead, I took the candle and headed in the direction of the sound.

It was hard to place. I wandered around in the dining room and whenever I thought I was close, the sound seemed to come from somewhere else, as though the source was determined to remain forever out of reach. After a complete tour of the room, I knew there was nothing to see and no one was there. The sound must be coming from outside.

I went to the door to check the bolts. They were drawn closed. As I stood, pondering my next move, trying to decide if I felt brave enough to go out to the patio, the air grew preternaturally cold, so cold, it felt as though I had stepped into a freezer. I shivered. In that moment, the whimpering stopped. Then the candle sputtered and went out.

Terrified, I stepped backwards. The room was instantly warm again. It dawned on me, standing there in nothing but my panties, that I had to find my way back to bed in the dark. As I took slow, tentative steps, I vowed from then on, I would never let my phone run out of charge.

I couldn't sleep. For the rest of the night, I lay on my back, rigid with fear, thinking of sleeping in my car but unable to act on the impulse. For the first time, I faced the sickening realisation that Paco and Clarissa and Gloria were right, there were such things as ghosts and my house was haunted.

Casa Coroneles

My head felt thick, fuzzy and dull from lack of sleep, yet still, I was on edge. A dog bark, a gust of wind, every creak and rustle sent a ripple of panic through me. One thought kept returning over and again. If the whimpering were a child, it must be one of Baraso's daughters. Not my mother, not Olivia Stone, but a Baraso and a child. Perhaps it was harmless but I was not reassured. I had no defences against a ghost.

It was the realisation that prompted me to get up, open the doors and let in some light. August, and the morning sun had already set in with determination. I went about my usual ablution routine, keen to leave the building site before the men arrived.

When I was washed and dressed, I wandered the site. The aljibe meant water, but with no power I would have to use a bucket on a rope. The access port was covered with a square of wood, held in place by a rock. I imagined Helmut had arranged for a proper hinged lid of some kind to be installed in the future.

Much of the focus was on the front rooms in the southern corner, where the upper level looked about ready to receive its floor. Outside, beneath the scaffolding the façade of the house had begun to take on its former glory, with the insertion of the downstairs windows. I was keen to inhabit more rooms, but Mario had already explained the kitchen and bathrooms would be fitted last, and that it was better to wait for the painters to do their job before moving into the upstairs.

I took my usual breakfast in the café, forking into Gloria's tortilla as I went back over the terror of the night before. In the harsh light of day, I could almost convince myself I had been dreaming, but I knew I hadn't. I couldn't help linking the whimpering and the ice cold to that rafter that had taken a swipe at the carpenter. A violent child seeking revenge on her awful father? It occurred to me living at Casa Baraso could prove not only spooky, but dangerous.

During a lull in the morning rush, Gloria came over and inquired if I was sleeping at the house again.

I set down my fork. 'I couldn't stay in Puerto del Rosario forever,' I said, offering nothing further. She might have known I had been staying with Paco but I wasn't about to confirm it. She didn't ask.

'How is the carpenter?' she said with concern.

'You know?'

'Word travels fast. I saw the ambulance.'

'I'll find out more today. It was an accident.'

She shook her head emphatically. 'No accident. This is why men won't work on your house.'

'But it was a ruin. No one has done any work there for about a hundred years.'

'That is not true. Cejas started work on the renovations about twenty years ago.'

'They didn't do much.'

'They didn't. But that is why there is a hole in the partition.'

Ah, so it was Cejas who did that. something awful must have happened. More than one incident. Enough to cause him to abandon the project and decide to demolish.

'Did you know the wall has come down?'

She seemed to shudder. 'The ghosts of Casa Baraso won't like that.'

'What do you mean?' I said, having had the same thought as she.

'No sooner had Cejas' men smashed through the wall, than one of them was hit on the head by a rock that no one threw. A length of timber fell on another as he walked under the balcony, and part of another wall fell as the third man was walking by.'

Then my theory was confirmed.

'All of those events *could* have physical explanations,' I said slowly.

We locked gazes. Neither of us believed they had.

'Those men were not superstitious,' she said. 'They had scorned the rumours. Then they experienced for themselves the power of the spirits that haunt Casa Baraso. You are lucky to be alive. That's what everyone is saying. That carpenter is also lucky to be alive.'

She wasn't exaggerating. I watched her walk away, deciding I needed to take action to protect myself. I needed to get rid of that belligerent ghost.

As I waited for my phone to charge, I checked my emails. There was a short note from my father and another email from Clarissa. She made no mention of Olivia Stone. Disappointed, I reminded her. Then I closed the lap top and considered my options for the day. Recalling Olivia Stone had passed by Casa Coroneles and noted the building in her travel diary, I thought I would visit. Perhaps I might glean ideas for décor. At least it was something to do on a hot day and inside should be cool.

Set back on a sweeping gravel concourse, Casa Coroneles observes La Oliva in the near distance and a few volcanoes to the north and, despite the massif behind and the perfect cone of a volcano to the east, the building dominates the landscape. Stout crenelated towers at the corners and the uniformity of design give off an air of authority and military dominance, the building essentially a fortress. In the façade, eight large windows—those on the first storey with Juliette balconies— are arranged one atop another to either side of a grand entrance. Shuttered windows in the side walls complete the look. The windows and doors are constructed of carved wood. A close inspection will reveal the detail.

The interior patio was much larger and grander than mine, with deep balconies overlooking a stand of palm trees. Inside, the deep salmon-pink tones of the walls set off the timbers of the vaulted ceilings, windows and floors. The rooms were given over to a museum-style display, with large portraits arranged beside printed explanations. Empty room by empty room the visitor was taken on a historical journey of the reign of the colonels in what amounted to a lot of reading. Much of the information was a repetition of the book I had skim read in the library in Puerto del Rosario, the day I was researching Casa Baraso. Even so, I read every word, at once repelled by the glorification of what amounted to a rule of terror.

The colonels were a dynasty known for their opulence and the museum reinforced that grandeur even as it educated. Just like all aristocracy, the dynasty married to accumulate wealth and property. Since the colonel oversaw military rule and also functioned as the island administrator, he had absolute power and could do whatever he wanted. The bishops were complicit, leaving ordinary people with nowhere to turn. In effect, Fuerteventura, a tiny island with

a miniscule population, endured one hundred and fifty years of ruthless dicta-
torship, endorsed by the throne of Spain. The rich fed off abundant harvests in
times of rain, harvests exported for profit. None of that profit was poured back
into the island to benefit the people.

I came away from Casa de los Coroneles unsettled. I knew the British were
no better when it came to dominating other cultures, but I was saddened that
Fuerteventura should have endured such oppression when as far as I knew the
other islands had not.

Since I was there, I went for lunch in a café in La Oliva. While I waited for my
order, I texted Paco, hoping he would reply straight away but he didn't. Was he
upset with me? Of course, he was. Ten minutes passed. When the waiter came
with my meal, my phone beeped. I swiped the screen. Paco said he was busy,
sorry, and he would see me on his next day off. Which was when? I chose not
to answer. He was definitely hurt, then. I was hurting, too. More than anything,
I had put myself in a position of defenceless vulnerability. I wasn't sure I could
spend another night alone in my house, only I had to, or I would never live
there.

I recalled Clarissa talking about banishing spells. What had seemed ludicrous
nonsense now took on the appearance of sanity and necessity. I searched online and upon various instructions I went and bought two kilos of salt from a
supermarket and then drove to Lajares, where I knew of a new-age shop, for a
bunch of dried sage. I still had a few hours to while away. I wandered around
Lajares and went back to La Oliva, lingering in shops and in the church where it
was cool. At about four, I headed back to Tiscamanita, calling in at the garden
centre in Tefía for a browse.

Back at the house, when the last of the workmen had left, I set about my
ritual. I poured salt in the corners and entryways of my rooms. I lit the sage
and waved it around as I walked the perimeter of the space. I created my own
mantra, politely asking the ghost to leave. Finding myself engaging in banishing spells, I scoffed at myself, even as I knew the seriousness of living in a
haunted house with a grumpy ghost.

Satisfied I had done what I could, when it came time to sleep, I blew out the
last candle with a small measure of assurance that all would be well.

I awoke in the thick black of night to the sound of something scraping across
the floor. My breath caught in my throat. At first, I thought the sound was
coming from one of my rooms, but I soon realised the scraping was right above

my head. My heart was pounding. A few mores scrapes, a sudden bang, then all went quiet. Who was up there? And what could they possibly be dragging across the floor?

I struck a match with trembling hands. The sound seemed deafening. I lit a candle and then another. I murmured my mantra and lit the sage. The smell was pungent, but better that than the presence of an unwelcome spirit. How long till daylight? I checked my phone. Two hours. Two hours sitting up in bed, hugging my knees, too scared to move, waiting, hearing acute. As if the ghost was satisfied now I was awake and terrified, it made no further sound.

My rational mind slowly kicked in and made my situation even worse. In this instance, I didn't know for sure if it was a ghost. If it wasn't, then I had a prowler. Which was worse? I had bolted the doors. I was sure I had bolted the doors. Were they still bolted? I forced a look. Yes, they were. Then the prowler couldn't get in. If it was a prowler. The ghost would have no problem opening those bolts. Around and around my mind went until I was made dizzy and nauseous. I found myself wishing one of those brutal colonels were around to dispose of the torment.

Strong Emotions

By sunrise, I was angry. Angry that my one grand venture, my big statement in the world, such as it was, had been marred by the supernatural. I drew back the bolts and threw open the doors and let the light shine in. I donned a shift and some flip flops and went out to the patio. Before I lost my nerve, I marched up the balcony stairs and entered the room above my bed. The floorboards were rough and the walls unpainted. Some of the original paintwork had been saved on patches of old render. The vaulted ceiling was magnificent and reminded me of Casa Coroneles. I momentarily lost myself to its potential before my anger at my supernatural intruder rose up in me again. No one and nothing was going to scare me into leaving that splendour.

In the room were two saw horses and a step ladder and nothing else. I had no idea if one of the saw horses had been moved but I was relieved to find objects that could account for the sound I heard in the night. I might have thought I had a living human intruder, but that idea no longer tallied with other events no matter how much my rational mind wanted it too, not since the whimpering and the pool of cold air. I had to face facts even if they were metaphysical. I had a poltergeist, a child, and an angry one at that.

I showered and dressed and readied for the day, packing my bathers and a towel and making sure I left before the workmen arrived. In the café, I placed my usual order of coffee and tortilla to a nonplussed Gloria who no doubt saw the fatigue and irritation in my eyes, and received from me a gruff and harried demeanour, which was not like me at all.

I sat at my usual table and plugged in my laptop. Gloria came over with my order and I made a space for the plate and cup in front of me without looking up or thanking her.

'Is everything alright?'

She sounded tentative, and her question alerted me to my rudeness.

'Gloria,' I sighed, at last meeting her gaze, 'That ghost is persistent. I'll give it that.'

I told her I was woken by the sound of scraping on the floor above me and had spent the rest of the night awake.

She reached for my arm. 'You be careful, Claire.' She seemed about to say more when some of the workmen from my build came in the café. I gave them a courteous nod as they walked by. Gloria went back behind the counter.

I took a bite of the tortilla and slurped my coffee. When I opened my emails, I was surprised to find one from Clarissa. Seeing its length, I relished in the possibility of a distraction. She had at last found time to research Olivia Stone. Scanning her email, I saw she had been thorough, too. I read with interest, grateful for something to occupy my mind.

She said Olivia Stone was born Olivia Mary Hartrick in 1857, one of five children of Reverend Edward John Hartrick and Mary Macauley Dobbs. She couldn't find out anything about the Dobbs, but she said the Hartricks were descended from German Palatines, those Protestant refugees from neighbouring Germanic states who had escaped to Palatinate to rebuild their lives, only to again flee from persecution, this time sent to Ireland by Queen Anne in the early 1700s. They would have been on their way to America, Clarissa said, but Queen Anne's coffers ran dry. I had no idea who the Palatines were and I was not sure it mattered much, not to me, except that I was impressed by Clarissa's efforts and it was interesting to have a little context.

I read on, hungry for the information that mattered: Olivia's death.

Olivia married John Frederic Matthias Stone (b 1853, Bath) in 1878 and they had three sons. I knew that already, from the article Paco put me on to. Clarissa went on to provide more detail. John Stone was a barrister who participated in the social life of the moment, founding The Camera Club in 1885 and The Caravan Club in 1907. It was easy to see who was the driving force behind the couple's travels. Although it was Olivia who had a talent with words. She was one of several notable travel writers of her day, having penned the highly regarded *Norway in June* which was published in 1882.

Clarissa said the Stones had a great affection for the Canary Islands, not only embarking on a thorough six-month tour in 1883, but returning in 1889 and 1891 to conduct research for future editions of the book. Again, these were facts I already knew and I read with mounting impatience, unsure if I was about to be told anything significant.

They had lived in London, then moved to or had a second residence in St Margaret's at Cliffe near Dover, in a house they named 'Lanzarote'. She had highlighted the word in yellow.

Lanzarote? I paused. Not 'Fuerteventura'?

Paco told me she had named her home after his island. He had gleaned that information from that article he talked of, the article I had painstakingly translated for Clarissa. I kept reading. Clarissa had been thorough in her fact checking. She said the house was probably situated right beside the beach in St Margaret's Bay, since a hotel of the same name had been bombed in WWII, and the local historical society commented that the hotel had been created out of two adjoining private villas. Noel Coward had a residence further along the beach. Sounded like somewhere the Stones would live. It had to be their home. There would not have been two homes called 'Lanzarote' in St Margaret's.

When John Stone re-married in 1900 to Lillie Wellbeloved, he was listed as a widower. Discovering this, led Clarissa on the hunt for Olivia's death. She said she found it after several attempts, the location somewhat of a surprise since there was no connection to the county of Bedford that she could glean.

Olivia Stone died on 11 March 1897 in Priory Street in Bedford. The cause of death was a rupture of an aneurism of the aortic arch. She had died, Clarissa said, quite suddenly while taking a walk down a street in the heart of Bedford, very near St Paul's Church. Her husband did not appear on the death certificate. She was either walking alone, or with a companion, a Mrs Blanche Adams who was listed as present at her death. Her age was stated as 40. Clarissa went on to explain that her death would have been sudden and painless, and that it was unusual for a woman of her age to die of such a thing. She probably had an underlying condition, most likely genetic. That was the end of the email. Clarissa even provided copies of the relevant evidence.

I searched online for the misleading article that had caused Paco to make false assumptions and build a fantasy about his beloved Olivia Stone, and sat back gazing at that one photo of her. It was easy to see how Paco had conjured his story. She looked wan and wistful, almost ghostly in that loose fitting, short-sleeved dress fringed with tassels. A designer interpretation of a peasant dress of some kind. Her eyes were deep set and filled with longing and her hair, thick and wiry, was cut short and lacked style. In all, she looked like the sort of woman who would abscond and live a secret life on the island of her dreams. She also looked both determined and melancholic, even a touch sickly. Or perhaps my new knowledge was colouring my perception.

A mix of disappointment and outrage welled up in me. At first at Paco, who had insisted his erroneous facts were true and built up a ridiculous fantasy on their basis, but then at both the researcher and the author who had composed the article. How could they have got this crucial information wrong? Was it simply that the death certificate had not been entered into any online database from parish records? Or did the researcher not bother to look that hard? Surely they must have? Perhaps the language barrier had proven a research impediment. Whatever the reason, they had not found the death certificate and had hinted at the conclusion that Olivia may not have died in England. The arrival of a person by the name of Stone on the 'Wazzan' in 1895 was something of a red herring.

The second error was understandable, if annoying. I knew how easy it was to make a mistake when citing a record. A two can become a seven in a pen stroke. Although it was rather astonishing as I could see the census listing with my own eyes. I had a dozen excuses, for in every other respect, the researcher and the journalist who wrote the article had been meticulous. Yet the note that the house had been called 'Fuerteventura' plainly wasn't true.

The consequences for Paco were not pleasant. He had been deceived, basing his suppositions on false foundations. Out of all the islands, it was Lanzarote Olivia loved, not Fuerteventura. How sad, for him, and for the island.

At least now I knew without a doubt that Olivia Stone was not haunting Casa Baraso. She probably never even set foot in the house. She may not even have walked by.

I wondered how I would broach the matter to Paco. How would he react to the truth? Wanting to clear the air as soon as I could, I sent him a text. Told him I really needed to see him. It was urgent. He replied straight away saying his shift ended at five and he would come over.

I replied to Clarissa's email, thanking her for her findings and going on to describe the haunting of the past two nights. I mentioned the whimpering, the cold pools of air, the scraping, and the carpenter whacked on the head by a rafter. I told her I had resorted to banishing spells.

I ordered more coffee and by way of distraction I jotted down in my notebook the latest progress on the building site and then scrolled through websites looking at kitchen designs. As I was about to close the tabs I noticed another email had arrived in my inbox. It was from Clarissa. All she said was as long as the situation does not escalate, I should be able to deal with it using the methods I described. Escalate? Things were already violent enough. Whatever did she mean? I had no idea. What I did know was my mind was firmly back on the supernatural and I wanted to be as far from Tiscamanita as it was possible to be without leaving the island. I had two choices. I could drive to Corralejo, the island's tourist mecca, or head south.

Not fancying mingling with a throng of holidaymakers, I chose south and headed down to Jandia, all the way to the island's southern tip. The road turned to dirt not long after the resort town of Morro Jable, and wended its way some distance above the ocean along the rocky and barren mountainside. The going was slow, the views opening up along the way captivating. I was far from the only vehicle making the journey, and for a long stretch I was accompanied by those heading to or returning from Cofete and Casa Winter and the wild beaches below the Jandia massif. Past the turnoff, the traffic thinned to almost nothing. Empty beaches dotted along the coastline attracted the intrepid, those prepared to scramble down low cliffs. Beyond the massif the land flattened out, the landscape at the southern end of the island dominated by a single volcano. I headed for the lighthouse. Before it, before the land narrowed to form an elongated tongue, tucked beside a sheltered, tidal beach was a cluster of fishing huts with a campsite attached. A secluded resort for those preferring isolation, a real escape, somewhere for the locals to go perhaps, somewhere away from the hubbub elsewhere.

For the rest of us, the lighthouse was the main attraction. Situated on a paved concourse at the end of the tongue was a stout tower built of basalt, one of the oldest lighthouses in the Canary Islands. The tower had been built to form part of a formal building with a flat roof and tall arched windows: the keeper's cottage. What a life of solitude those keepers would have endured!

Beside the cottage was a smaller building, the same in style and given over to a small café. Some outdoor seating and even a windbreak in the form of a Perspex screen had been erected for the comfort of spectators. And people sat and gazed at the ocean, mesmerised.

Keen for a closer view, I went over to the edge of the low cliff, dodging a few others meandering about. What drew the sightseers to this end-of-earth spot was the meeting of the waters east and west. A strong current pressed against the southwestern side of the tongue and where it met the waters to the east, the waves rippled and I sensed the force of those mingling forces beneath the surface. Treacherous and for swimmers, deadly. I stood until I was tired of standing, then I sat until I was tired of sitting. I didn't tire of the view. There was something about being on the edge of things, something about setting, the rocky land where almost nothing grew, with the mountains of Jandia rising behind, and all that ocean. Like everyone else, I found it hard to pull myself away. For a whole hour, haunted houses did not enter my mind.

Not ready to leave, I went inside the main cottage that had been converted into a museum in the same fashion as Casa Coroneles, with a few artefacts and numerous information boards explaining the history. Each room was painted a different colour and portrayed a different theme. I meandered around the rooms not taking much in, and eventually went back to my car.

On the way back up the coast, I stopped at Morro Jable for a swim. It was good to be in the water despite the preponderance holidaymakers who were noisy and idiotic. I ate a pleasant lunch at my favoured beachside café and then I drove inland, crossing the island's narrow waist to La Pared – a town largely given over to surfers – then I tracked my way up to Pájara on a back-road through the mountains. A dawdle around the town and I was back in Tiscamanita close to five.

When Paco pulled up outside my property, I no longer had the heart to dis-abuse him of his Olivia Stone fantasy. The risk to our relationship, fragile as it was, was too great. Seeing him all tentative and concerned, I weakened. I needed him by my side. I could not face another night of terror alone in that house.

We hugged and kissed and I sensed his relief. 'What's happened?' he said in my ear.

I pulled back and recounted the events of the last two nights, the whimper-ing, the cold pool of air, the scraping sound of something being dragged across the floor above my head and then I described the carpenter's accident. Paco saw the salt on his way into my rooms, and he couldn't help but smell the sage.

'What *is* that?' he said, sniffing.

'I read somewhere that burning sage banishes ghosts and salt keeps them at bay.' I laughed to cover my embarrassment.

Paco looked serious. 'Olivia Stone would not wish to cause anyone harm. I could never imagine her trying to kill someone.'

'I think it might be someone else,' I said gently, biting back my urge to divulge all. Instead I recounted Gloria's testimony of the Baraso family, and how señor Baraso had murdered his entire family before killing himself.

As he listened, Paco shook his head. 'They died of yellow fever. That's what everyone says.'

'I think that was the story put about to cover the truth.'

He didn't speak. I hoped he wasn't going to be stubborn. I went on, needing him to believe me. 'Gloria has first-hand accounts handed down through her family, and I am convinced she's telling the truth.'

'First-hand?'

'Her grandmother's grandmother, no less, who used to work for the Barasos as their maid.'

'But *murder suicide*?' His mouth hung open a little. He looked shocked.

'It would explain a lot.'

I waited for him to process the information. A silence grew between us. He broke it with, 'I appreciate what you are trying to do, Claire. But you can't be here alone. Not until this is dealt with.'

I had no idea how I would ever deal with that ghost. If salt and sage and little mantras were not going to banish it, what would? Or should I be thinking of who? A priest?

All I knew for certain was we had returned to coupledom. Our togetherness was as natural as breathing, the rapport undeniable, and it felt right to be with Paco, even if we had been forced together by a ghost. Even for someone as cautious as me.

Seeing him there all concerned for my welfare, I realised I had been fighting against being with Paco not out of a sense of propriety in terms of how a relationship should unfold, but out of a deep-seated fear of entanglement. I could trace that fear all the way back to the zebra crossing and that awful moment when I witnessed my mother's death. It wasn't hard. There was little in between other than the monotony of my work at the bank, the predictable interactions with my father and aunt Clarissa, and a few failed attempts at having a boyfriend.

I had never lived with any of those men. I hadn't wanted to. They hadn't attracted me that way. None of them were right for me. Although perhaps I hadn't been right for them.

I found it hard to be open and emotionally available and I could not abide an emotionally needy man. Oddly, I had managed to attract that type over and again. Until now. Paco was different. He kept his reserve. He didn't have temper tantrums, displayed no jealousy or possessiveness and even handled rejection well. I suppose I had put him through his paces, inadvertently but still, testing him without realising that was what I was doing.

We shared a plate of canned tuna salad and a bottle of wine. I described my day down in Jandia and he said he'd take me to the other lighthouse near Gran Tarajal. I was about to say I had already visited but I caught myself in time. After all, I hadn't been there with him, and after our day in El Cotillo, I knew he brought something magical to my experiences of the island. I asked how he had spent his day, and he recounted a funny scene in the restaurant where he worked, involving a very loud and very drunk couple so sunburnt they looked like lobsters. The staff had a running joke at their expense in the kitchen out the back.

'The chef was saying he should find a large pot to boil them in and we were choosing ingredients. It was really very funny.'

I laughed and yawned all at once. He took my hand. We took turns in the bathroom, made love and slept curled in each other's arms. On the ghostly front, that night was quiet.

An Uneventful Month

For the rest of August and the whole of September, I stayed with Paco through the week and we spent weekends at mine. We settled into a routine of companionship.

As part of my campaign to forge a life with friends on the island, I attended the Spanish class I enrolled in back in April, held in a room at the local library and run by a native Spanish speaker who was fluent in English. Her name was Sofia. She had long black hair, warm eyes and an expressive mouth. I took to her immediately. As for the other students, they proved a prickly bunch of highly competitive expats. There was a lot of jostling for position both with regard to who spoke the best Spanish and who was closer to Sofia. I found the interactions, the asides and jibes and pointed if jocular barbs tedious. I was there to learn and after one session I had given up any wish I held of making friends. After finding I had nothing in common with any of the cohort, I had to quell my disappointment and force myself to attend.

My position was made even harder once the others discovered I was restoring Casa Baraso. Sofia was the one who told the class. In the introductions, I had simply announced I was renovating a ruin, for which I received many eye rolls and comments about local builders. It was during the second session that Sofia asked me, in Spanish, if I was the new owner of Casa Baraso. Honesty prevailed, there being no point in denying it, and one of the other students overheard and before long everyone was gasping and carrying on like there was no tomorrow. What was bothering all of them was that I was rich. Somehow, they all knew I had won the lottery. I could hardly believe it. Back in the apartment, I discussed the matter with Paco, and between us we managed to surmise that it was the estate agent who had spread the word that an Englishwoman who had won the lottery was restoring a ruin not even the local government were able to buy off the previous owner. Gossip. And my word, did it spread fast. I was famous without realising and without knowing barely a soul on the island. Incredible.

At least the classes gave Paco and I something else to talk about. We had taken to conversing in both our native tongues in rotation, a habit that benefited us both.

I tried hard not to mention Olivia Stone and if she came up, I changed the subject. The pressure of the withholding was hard, it felt like a betrayal, but I didn't know Paco well enough yet to calculate how he would react and I didn't want the truth to jeopardise what we had. It would most likely trigger our first row.

At Casa Bennett, I had begun to believe my banishing spells were working and the haunting was over.

Despite the heat the men continued to work hard. I suspected both Mario and Helmud were pushing them, anxious to complete works as fast as possible, in case there was another incident and the workmen downed tools and left.

All the windows were in, all the doors hung, and the painters had finished the upstairs of the north wing and the exterior walls of that half of the build. The floors were sanded and sealed. A week later, and the scaffolding came down on the northern external wall and sections of the east and west walls as well. Carpenters had erected the timbers for the balcony awning on that half of the patio. Corrugated iron would protect the balcony from rain and Helmud had suggested I insulate and sheet beneath to absorb the radiant heat. Having spent one entire summer on the island, that sounded like a good idea.

On the south side, the roof reconstruction was slow due to the vaulted ceiling, but the floors were laid and the downstairs walls rendered and the balcony was under construction.

The last week of September I received delivery of three four poster beds, along with wardrobes and tallboys, filling the rooms above the dining and living rooms and kitchen. I took the room over the kitchen as my own. It had an ensuite – or it would have – and a spectacular view of the volcano. I arranged for my possessions that had been in storage for months to be delivered and I was eager to make my home my own.

Mario and Helmud took my presence in their stride but I knew the workmen preferred me not to be around. Until then, I had obliged by leaving the site early every Monday with Paco and avoiding turning up through the week, but now

I was insisting on subverting the order of things by moving in my things and by having a kitchen and the plumbing installed, and there was a little friction and a few grumbles. I was not about to give in. Besides, it couldn't be helped. The two halves of the build, at distinct stages of restoration, with one almost complete and the other a work in progress, created an odd situation.

Mario relented and arranged for a plumber to install the ensuite and a downstairs toilet and connect the property to the mains sewage. In anticipation, I bought a pump for the aljibe.

Sewage coincided with the kitchen installation. I chose an ultra-modern, glossy white look with polished concrete bench tops. All the appliances were steel. The room was a large rectangle with the window centred in the longer wall facing east, which determined the location of the sink. On the shorter, north wall, were the stove and fridge. A breakfast bar formed the third arm of a U, leaving about half the room spare. I bought stools for the breakfast bar and an oval dining table and chairs, all in a polished ebony, allowing room for a matching wooden rocking chair in the near corner. Whoever sat there could observe the whole kitchen as well as a portion of the patio beneath the balcony.

Unpacking my crockery and putting appliances in cupboards and drawers had to be the most satisfying of feelings. My past, decades of it, had found its way into my future and I was pleased with the blending.

Life at Casa Bennett just kept getting better. The day the electrician came – a demure and petite man called Simon – I was singing inside. I took a keen interest as he connected the power and wired the power points on the usable side of the house. He put the kitchen on a separate circuit, the oven on one of its own, and all the lights and power points of the living and dining room along with the bedrooms above, on a third. He created another circuit for the laundry, a grey rendered shell, and the patio lighting. No more generator. It took Simon three days and I used that time to accumulate light shades and desk lamps and occasional tables to put them on.

The day the power was connected to the mains, I raced back to Puerto del Rosario bursting with delight to find Paco had news of his own. He had received another assignment, this time for a prestigious geographic magazine. He would be away three weeks and had to leave immediately. We went out to dinner to celebrate.

So full of joy at my own red-letter day, I didn't give his absence a second thought, other than I knew I would miss him. He wanted me to stay at his in his absence but I had much to occupy me on the build and the ghost appeared to have gone for good.

The first evening of power was heaven. I was overjoyed. I could read by a beside lamp, charge my phone and laptop, and go up and down the balcony stairs without a torch.

I stood at my bedroom window watching the sky darken behind the volcano as the sun set. The sense of space gifted by the view was exhilarating, expansive. Contemporary Fuerteventura shaded into an eighteenth century version beneath my gaze, to a time when the farms were going concerns, when Tiscamanita was a centre of activity. The mill, the wells and the simple lifestyle was an idyll. It was a time when superstition abounded. When I thought of all those churches in every little village, I was reminded of the division between rich and poor, the Spanish inquisition and the era of the colonels, throughout all of it the church was abiding towards those in power.

My house afforded a sense of dominance over the surroundings and I couldn't help remembering it represented the lives the nobility and the bourgeoisie enjoyed as they imposed themselves on an impoverished and compliant poor. After considering all of that, it was easier to gaze at the present, at the legacy, at the ruins dotted all around Tiscamanita. I wanted to resolve the past and the present but I couldn't. It wasn't my place.

I headed downstairs in the gloaming, flicking on the kitchen light as I entered the room. It was a defining moment, the brilliance of all the shiny white dazzling enough for sunglasses and I chuckled to myself. The room was a triumph. Modernity housed in ancient walls. It worked. I poured a glass of chilled white wine to celebrate and threw together a cold chicken salad. When I had chomped my way through the mountain of lettuce on my plate, I went and sat back in my rocking chair to listen to *Treasure* through my sound bar, enjoying the way the Cocteau Twins filled the space as though they, too, had been craving room to expand and breathe.

Following the rise and fall of the vocals, my head brimmed with joy in the knowledge that whatever I did with my life on the island, I was going to delight in my home.

When the album finished I sat in silence wondering what to play next. It was then that the air around me went suddenly incredibly cold. I shivered. I wanted to rub the bare skin on my arms but I dare not move. I stared straight ahead at my shiny white kitchen. Would this ghost child reveal herself to me? Is that what was about to happen? Could I handle it if she did? Maybe not.

I scarcely had time to inhale when the lights, my beloved lights that had only been burning for a few hours, went out. An outage? Temporary? The room was still freezing which meant the ghost was still around.

I couldn't sit in the dark. Plunged into blackness with no phone in reach I was disoriented. I needed light but I waited.

Nothing changed.

I stood and walked tentatively in the direction of the kitchen bench, feeling my way. Two steps and two more steps and when I thought I was about halfway something lunged at me from behind. I stumbled forwards and crashed my left hip into the bench. Terror rang through me. I groped about on the polished concrete bench for my phone. There was a bar stool at my side. I shunted to the left. I knew I had left it there somewhere.

As my hand found the phone, the cold dissipated and the lights came on. I looked around. There was no one in the room. I went out and switched on the patio light hoping to catch a figure scampering off, something corporeal, but there was no sign of anyone. I thought maybe I had been too slow. My rational mind seemed to me then pathetic, scrambling to explain the event away any way it could so I didn't have to feel the terror.

I knew I wouldn't sleep. I wanted to leave, get far away but the impulse made me angry. I was entitled to occupy my own house, my big and beautiful house. If that ghost was going to be territorial, well, so was I.

There were no bolts on my bedroom door, so I stayed downstairs, planning to bolt myself inside the living room which still contained my old bed. Leaving nothing to chance, I put obstacles under the window. I sprinkled another trail of salt around the whole perimeter of the room, repeating my banishing mantra as I went.

I left a light on in the dining room, carefully removed the plastic dust cover and got into the bed fully clothed, drawing the covers up to my chin. Despite my precautions, fear kept a hold and I knew I would be awake all night.

I found myself trying to think like a ghost. If I had scared my victim out of her wits, if I had made her freeze, deprived her of light and pushed her hard from behind, hard enough to make her tumble, what would I do next? Would I go and put my feet up somewhere, satisfied? Would I take pleasure in the terror I had invoked? Or would I plan my next move? Do ghosts think or do they act spontaneously? I soon found it wasn't possible to think like a ghost. All I knew was I had been physically assaulted, that this entity could not only blow out candles, turn off lights, make the temperature of a room plummet, slide bolts, open and close doors, move rocks, send timber flying and whimper, it could make *real physical contact.* This was a ghost with dogged intent, a ghost with malice in its heart, a ghost prepared to leave the place of its haunting to frighten the owner wherever she might be. This was one determined spirit and I had few defences.

At least the salt seemed to work. I spent hours sitting up hugging my knees, interspersed with periods lying down and tossing and turning. Nothing weird happened. There was no scraping of furniture, no doors slamming. Nothing. All I heard was some light rain. It didn't last long. The moment I saw daylight, I went and had a shower.

The roof tilers arrived as I was heading to the kitchen for strong coffee and breakfast. I heard vehicles pull up and conversations, then footsteps up the scaffolding outside. It was barely dawn. Then Helmud poked his head in the kitchen door and greeted me, saying there was more rain forecast and they wanted to get the roof on before it came.

I remained on site and spent the morning sorting out my things and cleaning rooms. I ignored the workmen and they ignored me. There were far fewer men on site; the stone masons were long gone, and the other tradesmen too. I didn't care to interact with the roof tilers who seemed to me a raucous bunch of larrikins.

In need of a change of atmosphere, after lunch and more coffee, I drove down to Gran Tarajal for a swim. Billowing cloud filled the sky but there was no rain in it as yet, as far as I could tell. I spent the whole afternoon doing laps in the ocean and walking on the sand.

The tilers were still there when I returned home at six. I spent an hour in the kitchen, reading. The slam of a car door and a few revving engines told me the men were knocking off. It was then seven. I watched the cloud thickening over the volcano as I prepared a salad and, not wanting to leave the kitchen after I had eaten, I settled in the rocking chair and streamed Dolores Claiborne on my laptop.

When the film ended and I was sitting in the quiet of the house contemplating whether I thought Dolores was justified in doing the things she had, I sensed my otherworldly companion would soon start its nocturnal activities. It was only a matter of time.

As though in tune with the thoughts running through my mind, my laptop screen went black. Then I realised it was the power saving kicked in. I was about to get up and close the lid when the kitchen lights flickered. A step ahead of my supernatural foe, I had my phone torch to the ready. When the lights went out I switched on the phone's sharp beam. It was a brief moment of triumph. I had outfoxed a ghost.

My smug satisfaction did not last long. The room turned to ice in an instant. I was alert, tense, waiting, listening.

Nothing could have prepared me for the cold hands that gripped my throat. The sensation was real, thumbs against my neck bones, fingers curling tight, pressing hard against my larynx. I gagged and gasped for breath. Alarm filled me, blinding. I was suffocating. I had an impulse to scream but I had no voice.

I struggled to get free. I lunged forward in my seat but it made no difference. I dropped my phone in my lap and reached to pull away the hands that were determined to lead me to my death – *but there were no hands. Only air.*

Panic bolted through me. I was being strangled. The pain was excruciating. I couldn't breathe in or out. Blood boomed in my head in synch with my racing heart.

I couldn't peel away those murderous fingers. I was surely at the point of death. In a final terror-fuelled effort, I jumped up off the rocking chair.

The hands slid away, as did my phone, falling face down on its torchlight. The room went black. The air remained ice cold. *It wasn't over.*

I panted, each intake of air laboured. I clutched my neck, disoriented. I wanted to run, flee the house, but I couldn't see. I had no idea which direction to take or where the next attack was coming from. *I can't just stand here.*

But the moment I took a step forward I was shoved from behind. I stumbled and regained my balance and was shoved again, harder this time. I lurched forward and stumbled to my knees. I heard a crack. Was that a kneecap?

Too vulnerable on the floor, I recovered my stance. I reached out and felt the wall and stood with my back to it. Then I screamed in a voice hoarse and rasping, and in that scream, I told that ghost to leave me the fuck alone.

All returned to normal in an instant. The room grew warm and the lights came on. My laptop sat on the table where I'd left it. The fridge whirred. The dishes were in the sink. It was almost as though nothing had happened. I saw my phone on the floor behind me. A chair was askew. That was all the evidence of the attack, that and my throbbing throat.

I picked my phone off the floor and used the camera as a mirror to see myself. The red marks around my neck was all the confirmation I needed that I had not imagined that attack. I knew in that moment that ghosts were capable of hands-on physical harm.

I was accommodating my new awareness and examining the finger marks on my neck, when the whimpering started. Not more haunting! The sound was coming from the patio. I had no intention of following that sound but I needed to get out of the house and there was only one way out of the kitchen, and that meant walking out to the patio and through the passageway to the back door.

The whimpering carried on, the sound moving, fading and then getting louder. For a while the sound came from the doorway and when it did the kitchen lights flickered. I thought of shutting myself in the kitchen but what would be the point? Ghosts could move through walls and there was just no telling if I would be attacked again.

As if to confirm my thinking, upstairs a door slammed. I jumped, startled. That was all the motivation I needed. I grabbed my purse, phone and car keys, waited for the whimpering to fade and ran out the kitchen with my heart hammering in my chest. I didn't stop to look around. I went straight through to the back door, scrambling for the handle.

I didn't close the door behind me. I just ran. I ran holding my phone up to light my way. I ran straight to my car, pressed the remote and fumbled my way into the driver's seat.

I was shaking so hard my teeth were chattering. I inserted the key in the ignition but I had nowhere to go other than Paco's, and knew I was in no state to drive. Instead, I locked myself in. Surely, out in the open I would be safer. Surely the ghost won't attack me out here?

The sky had cleared. I sat for a long time staring at the stars, watching the moon rise up over the volcano. I gradually grew calmer.

I must have dozed. Sometime in the night I awoke. It was teeming with rain.

Before I opened my eyes, I knew I wasn't alone. Call it a sixth sense. I didn't want to look. I wanted to keep my eyes shut and will whatever it was away. But I did open them and I saw, outside my window, a face. It was a woman's face and she was staring at me. At first, I thought she was my mother. Then I saw her long black dress and I knew who it was. Señora Baraso. Had to be. She looked pale, desperate, terrified. Yet no part of her was wet.

She pressed her bone-dry hands against the glass. I shook my head. I mouthed to her, no. She seemed crestfallen. She hurried off, into the outbuilding where I used to take my showers.

After that, I didn't sleep. I began to wonder if I had dreamed that face as I scrambled to regain a sense of normality, but I hadn't. All I knew was I had two ghosts, a child and its mother. Which one had strangled me?

It was with sickening certainty that I realised it was neither.

Hunting for Graves

With daylight came a tormented calm, a head fuzzy from lack of sleep and a body stiff in places it shouldn't be: neck, hip, small of back and one ankle.

I shifted and sat up straight. The windscreen was fogged. Using my arm, I swiped away the mist on the side window. The rain had gone, the ground was damp and there were small puddles here and there. Before I got out of the car, I studied my neck in the rear vision mirror. The bruising was plain to see.

My first thought was that I would pack up and stay at Paco's. But that would mean defeat. Whoever those ghosts were they had no right to occupy my home. I held on to the practicalities and a strong impulse to protect my home, taking umbrage at the potential damage to my person and my property that a bad-tempered ghost could achieve. I had been pushed from behind and strangled. What next? Would, could a ghost really kill me?

I extricated myself from the car and marched into my house and on upstairs for a shower. It was easy to be defiant and territorial in daylight. Once clean and dressed, I straightened out my rooms and closed all the doors, leaving through the back door as the workmen were arriving. Heading behind the barn, I could only hope I had become the only target of the spooky shenanigans and none of those men would come to harm.

I drove up the street and parked opposite the café beneath a shade tree. The village was quiet. The church, the centrepiece of the village with its high white walls, its lack of windows, looked inwards, at itself and its god, warding off evil forces, a fortress of faith. I had no faith. I no longer had much confidence in banishing rituals either. I did the only thing that constituted faith. I called Clarissa.

'How are you, my dear?' Her voice alone brought peace.

'I'm not interrupting?'

'Not at all. The funeral was yesterday.'

A jolt passed through me. Whose funeral? I didn't like to ask. 'Did it go okay?' was all I could think to say.

'Low key. Dear old thing was ninety-five, so not too many tears.'

I hesitated. But this was not a time for chit chat. 'I wanted to ask. I'm having more trouble at the house.' I filled her in on the latest happenings. 'I had no idea ghosts could cause humans physical harm in a hands-on way. I thought they would pass right through us, so to speak. Things are getting out of hand.'

'I did wonder if things would escalate. They usually do when violence is involved.'

'It tried to strangle me,' I said, my voice wavering as I relived the horror.

'He,' Claire. 'That would have been Baraso himself.'

'You think Gloria's version of what happened there is true?' I had related the full story to Clarissa in an email.

'These latest events prove it. As in life, so in death.'

'What about the whimpering child? The woman Paco photographed?'

'Sounds like you have at least three spirits trapped there.'

'*Three.*'

'At least. Could be the whole family.'

'I need them gone,' I said with an air of desperation.

'Difficult.'

'There must be something I can do. The banishing spells are not working.'

'You can try the ten tips of Madame Boulanger.' She sounded doubtful.

'I'll try anything.'

'On second thoughts, you are already employing the basics. Exorcism is a last resort.'

'Exorcism!' I glanced at the church. My mind reeled with images of priests and strange rituals.

'It isn't as dramatic as you think. I've witnessed several. Poltergeists don't only inhabit ancient ruins, Claire. Even your regular two up, two down can contain a cantankerous ghost or two. They seem to attach themselves to teenage girls or others experiencing turbulent emotions of their own.'

I didn't speak. We both knew the grief I had harboured in me.

'Where are they buried?' Clarissa asked.

'I have no idea.'

'Ah, then you should find their graves.'

'What will that achieve?'

'Claire, usually with these things, people just want to be heard and understood. Acknowledged is some way. Laid to rest, so to speak.'

A grave hunt? It couldn't hurt and at least gave me a strategy, even a possible solution. I thanked her and said my goodbyes.

Gloria beamed a smile at me as I entered the café, and gestured for me to sit down. I wondered what could be making her so pleased to see me as I took up my preferred table, although I no longer had need of the power point. She brought over my usual coffee and tortilla. After setting down my cutlery she took a step back, hovering.

'Another lovely sunny day,' I said, beaming up at her, a smile behind which all I could think of were cemeteries. 'The rain was good, too.'

'It was.' She hesitated and inhaled to say more. 'Tell me, Claire, what do you plan on doing with your big house?'

It was the same question, every time, and I was surprised she hadn't asked before.

'I don't know yet,' I said, which was the truth.

'You should come to Maria's computer class in Tuineje,' she blurted and I realised that despite her forthright manner, deep down she was shy. Or maybe wary, of me, of what I represented. I hesitated, holding her gaze with interest. There she stood, all expectant and enthusiastic and unsure in her neat and clean apron protecting her blouse and skirt. 'It's for mature, rural women,' she went on, pointing at my laptop. 'We need to learn all this technology or we will be left behind.'

'I already know how to use it, though.' Even as I spoke I wished I could have come up with something appreciative to say instead. Fortunately, she wasn't about to be deterred.

'This is why I ask. There are ten of us. You will make many friends.' She told me they met every Saturday morning at eleven o'clock at the library. 'Will you come?'

'I would be delighted. Thank you.' I made a note in my phone calendar as she stood over me. I held up my entry for her to see. 'There you are, my phone won't let me forget.'

We both laughed. A door had unexpectedly opened, the welcome mat displayed. I had gained entry into the everyday life of local rural women. The invitation marked a turning point. No more Spanish classes. An opportunity to participate in the local community? Nothing could have brought me greater joy. I knew it was rare and it felt almost like a reward for my loyalty to her business.

When Gloria went to serve another customer, I opened my laptop and searched for all the cemeteries in the area. I targeted Tuineje and Gran Tarajal to the south, and to the north, Casillas del Ángel, Tetir, the old cemetery in La Oliva and two in Puerto del Rosario.

When the café emptied, Gloria rushed over, a look of concern on her face.

'I have to ask. What is wrong with your neck? And your voice? You sound husky.' She made a rasping sound of her own, in case I didn't understand.

I didn't want to tell her. I knew once I did the news would spread around the village. Yet the evidence was there and how else would I explain the marks.

'Something strangled me last night. I think it was trying to kill me.'

'You mean, a ghost!'

'I managed to get free,' I said, trying to downplay the drama. 'And thankfully, I'm alive.'

'I told you it is not safe to stay in that house.' Gloria looked frantic.

'You are right. But I have to. I can't let those ghosts win.'

'Don't sleep there again, Claire.' She reached for my hand. 'Please.'

'I'll be fine, Gloria. Really.'

She released her grip and I took back my hand thinking I should have worn a scarf and pretended I was sick with a cold.

I paid my bill and set off to spend the day wandering inside walled cemeteries reading headstones. To begin with, I headed to Gran Tarajal and on to Tuineje. In each cemetery, there were a far larger number of niche stones, typically arranged in rows four high flanking lanes filled with flowers. Niche upon niche, headstone upon headstone, and nowhere yielded a single Baraso. Most of the cemeteries contained recent burials and I wished I had been more thorough back at the café, and narrowed my search to only those cemeteries containing old graves. I wasn't to know and besides, I wanted to be certain and see for myself. Relying on the internet was not always advisable.

Entering the cemetery in Casillas del Ángel I felt more optimistic. At least I was surrounded by old graves, many dating back to the nineteenth century. Niches lined the perimeter wall and other, internal walls. Paths meandered around graves set in pink gravel. The dead, as always, were sheltered from the wind and away from the gawping gazes of the living.

The cemetery at La Oliva was old, too, and contained the grave of the last of the colonels, Cristóbal Manrique de Lara Cabrera, replete with a large statue of an angel, looking down as though to bless where he lay. The locals, I presumed, would have been glad to see the back of him.

I saved the cemetery near the port in Puerto del Rosario for last. The cemetery was close to Paco's apartment and situated on what was essentially a roundabout that adjoined another, making for a noisy and frenetic environment for those old souls buried there. A wander around the graves yielded nothing. There were no Barasos buried there. If the family had been buried in unmarked graves I had little to no chance of finding them, other than by searching local archives. Disheartened and exhausted, I called into a café Paco and I frequented and ate a late lunch.

While I forked a paella, I did a quick internet search for information on the old cemeteries. The first arresting piece of information I discovered was that the graves in the cemetery I had visited last had been desecrated, skulls removed for satanic rituals held in some abandoned houses near Caleta de Fuste. What was it with people? Had any of those skulls belonged to a Baraso? I dearly hoped not, for I feared walking into that dark terrain.

Upon further research, I discovered that the older graves might also be found within church walls. Intramural graves were only for the rich and powerful, people of honour, although Señor Baraso, while undoubtedly a wealthy man, had not been a local dignitary, rendering intramural burial unlikely. Besides, in the late eighteenth century new legislation required the creation of municipal cemeteries within which to bury the dead, in an attempt to stamp out the medieval practice of intramural burials, not least due to the stench of decomposing corpses in shallow graves and concerns for the health of the living.

I thought of visiting all the churches in the vicinity of Tiscamanita, but decided to leave it for another day. Perhaps the remains of Baraso and his family had been returned to Tenerife for burial there. Defeated, I went back to Tiscamanita and called in to ask Gloria what she knew. Thankfully, the café was empty when I walked in, and I made my inquiry without any preface.

A shadow passed across her face.

'I really couldn't say.'

'I've looked in the cemeteries all over the island and there is no sign of any Baraso. I am thinking their corpses were taken back to Tenerife. Did that sort of thing happen?'

'I really don't know. No one said.'

Was she holding back on me? Or merely worried for my safety? I left thinking maybe that is all the family wanted, after all. To be found.

I returned home as the workmen were leaving. I should have gone to Paco's as I had earlier thought to do, but courage and defiance quelled my misgivings. I tended my garden, added a few stones to the back wall and wandered around the block.

A strange peace descended. At sunset, the sky blazed red. I felt the wind. It was warm and coming from the east. A calima was on its way. I went inside and threw together some dinner out of some cheese and the raggedy salad vegetables in the fridge and I struggled through it while I watched an episode of Black Books.

It wasn't until night fell that I began to feel that all too familiar fear. To assuage it before it claimed me, I doused the perimeter of my upstairs bedroom with salt. I did the same with the kitchen. I put a bead of salt across each of the doorways. I walked from room to room, repeating my mantra over and again. I smudged the entire building, even venturing up the scaffolding to smudge the rooms that remained bare stone. I resolved that the instant anything happened, I would yell at the ghost to leave me alone. It was my last defence and it had seemed to work before. It would be a battle of wills and I had better win.

All I could do was hope. Worn out from the day, I took myself upstairs to bed, choosing to leave the light on in the ensuite, for the sense of safety it afforded. I lay in the semi-darkness and slowly drifted to sleep.

A Case of Influenza

I awoke disoriented after a full night of sleep. Emerging out of slumber, I found I was heavy and weak and my throat burned. Maybe I was dehydrated after yesterday's cemetery tour, or I was still hoarse and my throat inflamed from the strangulation. Whatever the cause, I felt terrible.

The room was dim. Threads of grey broke through the blinds and I noticed a strip of light under the ensuite door. I sat up, ignoring the head spin. I had left that door open. I know I did. Now, it was closed. Fear bounded in, my unwanted companion.

Alert to every sound, I switched on the bedside lamp and scrutinised the room. Nothing had been disturbed. The door to the balcony was closed. I got up and flung open the enuite door and examined the room. All appeared normal.

I slipped on a bathrobe and a pair of mules and went and stood on the balcony, scanning the patio below. Two wheelbarrows were propped against the southern wall just as the workmen had left them. I went down to the kitchen, scanning for signs of change but there was no evidence of things having moved about in the night. Other than that ensuite door, my banishing efforts must have worked, at least for now.

Dawn broke in long red streaks, silhouetting the volcano. The calima had arrived. Perhaps it was just the dust irritating my throat, compounding the strangulation. But then, why did I feel so awful?

It was Saturday. At least there would be no workmen to interrupt me. I made tea and took it with me as I wandered around the building. I had asked the painters to re-create the decorative frieze in the front corner room downstairs. Standing in the doorway, I stopped thinking about ghosts and imagined my furniture arranged in the space, the light flooding in through the south-facing windows. My home would be splendid, fit to feature in one of those glossy magazines. Paco could take the photos. I would sit, first here, then there, describing how it felt to have restored an ancient home and brought it back to its glory days.

I hummed to myself as I made breakfast of fruit and yogurt. I took a shower and, without thinking, I donned an old t-shirt and slacks, and went to tend my garden. I was on my knees putting a rock on the back wall, aware of its weight, when I became overly aware of my arm muscles aching from the strain. I then grew aware of the heat and the dust. What was I doing out here? When my phone sprang to life, I yelped.

It was Paco. He said had taken some terrific shots of Alegranza.

'I miss you.'

'And I miss you,' I replied huskily.

'What's with your throat?'

'I think I'm getting sick,' I said, at last admitting to myself that all my aches and pains were symptoms of a bad cold.

'You know what to do. Plenty of fluids. Stay warm. Rest. There's a pharmacist two blocks from the apartment, in Calle Dr. Fleming.'

'I'm at home.'

There was a long pause as he assimilated the news. Then, 'Claire, what are you doing there? You must go and stay in the apartment. I don't like to think of you at Casa Baraso all alone. What if something happens?'

'I'll be okay. I slept well last night. Things were uneventful.'

'That might not always be the case. You know from before. That ghost is unpredictable. There's no telling what it might do next. Promise me.'

'I promise.'

'You do not sound much like someone who is promising.'

'Paco, please. I don't have the energy.'

'Which is why you must drive to Puerto del Rosario where there are people who can look after you. Where you will be safe. Where…'

The line dropped out. I tried returning his call but the reception had gone. I took my weary body inside, made myself some more tea and checked my emails.

I had received an unexpected email from my father. He wanted to know when I was coming home for a visit. I replied, asking him when he planned on coming to the island to see what I have been up to. Touché.

As if our wavelengths were in synch, an email arrived from Clarissa saying she was booking a flight to Fuerteventura for Christmas. I answered straight away saying I couldn't wait. Her visit gave me a date to work towards. I wanted her to see my home restored, scaffolding-free, and fully painted.

I changed out of my gardening clothes and readied to wander up to the café before realising I had no need to leave the house. Although by mid-morning, my throat was raging and I knew the weakness, the aching, the touch of fever and the sore throat were signs of influenza. Wasting no time, I drove to the pharmacist in Tuineje for various cold and flu remedies, tissues and pain killers. I visited the supermarket next door, stocking up on fresh produce, yogurt, custard, ready-made soups, whatever would slip down easily. Eyeing the others pushing their trolleys, I thought back to who I might have come into contact with in the last few days, someone who had coughed or sneezed in my proximity. Someone from Australia or New Zealand or Chile or Argentina who had brought the virus with them from their winter. It was impossible to know. I had passed by scores of tourists on my travels.

By lunchtime my throat was so sore I could barely swallow. All I could do was try to stay comfortable and ride the virus out.

For a while, I sat in the rocking chair and tried to read. Outside, the wind blew and blew. I got up and looked out the kitchen window. The air was thick with dust. I shut the kitchen door and carried on reading. When turning the pages became too hard I made a cup of soup and took myself, my phone, the meds and a pitcher of water upstairs to my bedroom. And that was where I planned to stay.

The virus proved vicious. I spent the rest of the weekend with my chest on fire, aching from head to toe. I was hot and cold all at once. For long periods, I sank into semi-delirium, half awake, half asleep, too ill to move a muscle, burning up and shivering.

In my delirium, I called out for my mother. I experienced memories, not of the accident, but dim memories of birthdays and beaches. The memories were hazy, just fragments – a pretty dress, a sunny day, laughter, a hug – but they were mine and I held onto them for solace and I tried to replay them, keen to recall them, keen for more.

I hugged myself and cried. Paco was right; I should be in Puerto del Rosario, but I had left it too late. I was incapable of going anywhere.

Now and then, I dragged myself to the bathroom, and once or twice I made it downstairs for food and water. Most of time, I had no idea of the time, or even if it was day or night.

I saw each of the children first. Ghostly apparitions of girls of varying ages dressed in dated frocks. I thought I might have been hallucinating. I was too ill to feel scared of them. Standing by my bed, they looked forlorn, haunted, withdrawn, heads bowed. The eldest three avoided my gaze. They seemed shy. But not that shy since they wanted me to see them.

The youngest was more confident. She locked gazes with me as she sucked her thumb and whimpered. She brought chill air with her. Yet I didn't feel frightened in her presence either. I was consumed by sadness. Nothing more.

The mother had a cowering, imploring look about her. I recognised her as the woman in the photo Paco had taken of the patio, the same woman who had appeared at my car window. She seemed to want to communicate. She reached out to me, as though to pull my hand, but I couldn't get up.

Seeing I wasn't moving she grew agitated, wringing her hands. A door slammed somewhere in the house and then I heard footsteps, heavy and slow, climbing the stairs.

The woman vanished. The next instant the ghost of Señor Baraso stood over me, staring into my face, his own riven with anger. He had an intimidating look about him. As he hovered I took in the set to his jaw, his moustache and unkempt hair. The temperature of the room dropped dramatically. Only then did I react, pulling the covers up under my chin, shifting my body to the other side of the bed.

A piercing scream echoed around the house. Baraso turned away and disappeared. I didn't imagine he would be gone for long.

Footsteps clomped down the stairs. There was a long pause in which I sat up in bed, wondering what I should do. I coughed, violently, over and again, then sneezed and groaned.

More screams, childlike and high-ptiched screams that went on and on. I ought to have issued a scream of my own but when I tried I found I had no voice.

The screams turned into yells and a commotion of activity started, involving running, lots of running between rooms.

Was I imagining all this?

The bedside lamp did not come on when I pressed the switch. I groped around among tissues and bottles and blister packs for my phone. When my hand touched the cool glass screen, I exhaled in relief. In its torchlight, I swung out of bed and slipped on my bathrobe and mules.

Outside my room, the commotion was escalating. There were bonks that made the floorboards tremble. The clatter of china as a tray was carried by someone with an unsteady hand. I opened the door, thinking I would be better off in another part of the house.

I went and stood on the balcony and shone the torch around. The patio was empty. The ghosts were not making themselves visible. Then the woman appeared right beside me. I jumped, startled. She stepped forward and tugged at my arm. I resisted, pulling away. She gave up and leaned against the railing pointing down at a spot in the patio, then she looked back over at me and our eyes met. I shone the torch at her face. She didn't squint. She was trying to communicate something with those eyes.

She then walked away. I followed her with my torchlight. I heard footsteps on the stairs. Shining the light at the patio, I watched her cross. She stopped in the centre near where the hole in the partition wall had been, and where the ground had been left thus far untouched. She pointed at the ground at her feet and then looked up at me, her demeanour changing from anguish to purposeful intent.

I saw it then, the reason for the distress, and I knew without needing an explanation what I had to do to bring the haunting to an end. The youngest child had started her whimpering. The sound was coming from the top of the balcony stairs. I walked towards the sound, shivering as the air grew cold. I sensed her sisters nearby. I could feel their distress. Would any of them try to stop me? I wasn't sure. Perhaps there wasn't a consensus amongst them. Maybe some wanted me to follow their mother's wishes and others did not, preferring another hundred years of haunting.

My feet felt leaden and I was burning up, but I kept walking. Gripping the rail and taking it a tread at a time, I descended the stairs. I expected a shove but none came. Not one of my paranormal companions stopped me heading outside to the barn and returning with a garden fork and shovel.

Where had Señor Baraso got to?

I had little strength but a frantic will consumed me. I was sick, yes very sick, but I was even more tired of the haunting. I ought to have been terrified but I wasn't. I tried the lights and found the power was back on. Making the most of the illumination, I switched on all the patio lights. Then I went to the spot

Señora Baraso had indicated and I plunged the fork into the ground with all the strength I had.

A few hard stabs and the surface soil was loose enough to shovel. I used the fork to loosen some more. I forked and I shovelled, aiming for a hole about a yard wide. Any larger, and I would run out of stamina.

The going was hard but I persisted, alternating between tools. Every two shovels I had to break for a short rest. Now and then I had to stop for a good long cough. I was aching and feverish but determination had a hold of me and I was not going to stop.

The going became easier once I had shovelled down about two feet and I found I was removing not subsoil but topsoil. Someone had been here before me.

My digging became more urgent. At one point, my fork stabbed something hard. I shovelled around and found there was a large boulder situated at the edge near the aljibe. I avoided the boulder as I dug.

Down and down I dug. Before long, I had to step into the hole and shovel the dirt out from the centre. Then I attacked the sides. Eventually, after digging and resting and digging and resting the spade hit something soft.

I put down the shovel and knelt down on both knees, brushing away the soil with my bare hands.

My fingers touched cloth. I leaned down further and used both hands to pull at the fabric. A few firm tugs and it gave way.

The cloth served as wrapping. Gingerly, I unfolded it. I sensed by the weight and feel what it was and when at last the cloth fell away, I gazed, horrified and satisfied all at once. It was a skull. A small skull. The skull of a child. My hands were shaking. I quickly wrapped it back up and placed it down carefully beside the hole. My own bones ached as I stood.

I stepped out of the hole. I needed to think things through and act, act fast, but I was caught up in a strange mix of immobilising terror and morbid fascination. My head swam. I felt faint and unsteady. I was burning up.

I needed to phone someone. Paco? The police? I looked around for my phone. I saw it beside the fork on the other side of the hole. I was about to go and grab it when all went black.

It took me a while to process that it was still night and the lights had gone out. I had unearthed the dead in the dark. Not the best plan. Maybe it would be daylight soon. Would that make a difference?

The air temperature plummeted. I knew in a flash that Baraso was back.

The next second I felt a thump on my shoulders and I lurched forwards. Another thump and I stumbled and fell into the hole of bones.

Dread sped through me. I scrambled to get out. Hearing the crunch and rattle of the bones beneath me I knew I had fallen on top of the grave, the grave with six bodies buried, and my first thought was I did not want to break any of those bones.

I manoeuvred myself with care, placing a hand here a foot there, hoping to avoid causing more damage. I was almost on all fours. Before I could get my body in a position from which to stand, I was kicked in the face from above.

Hard boot met with soft cheek, and then with ear and with chin, and I keeled to protect my face. My body took the form of a turtle. It was not the ideal position, I soon found, as the boot landed on my back in the area of my kidney, sending sharp pain right through me.

There was a long pause. I panted and cowered. I thought the attack might be over. If it was, I had to get out of the hole.

I rose slowly, cautious, and eased myself up. My head swam. I was sweating. I sat down heavily at the edge of the hole, thinking I should stand and leave the patio as fast as I was able. But I couldn't see. The darkness was thick. I desperately needed my phone. I started to scramble for it in the dirt around me. All I felt were small stones.

My heart was galloping but my body cooled enough for me to realise I was still in an icy pool of air.

There was a scream. A long, piercing scream and it sounded close. I wanted to leap up. I had to leap up. I had to at least try to get out of the house. As I drew my legs up and out of the hole, cold hands gripped my throat.

The pressure on my throat was strong. I reached up with my hands and clutched at nothing. I struggled to get free but he was too strong. I could scarcely breathe. My heart felt it was about to explode in my chest. My neck was on fire and throbbed all at once.

Desperation shaded into panic. He was going to kill me. I was dying and there was nothing I could do to stop it. I writhed but I had little strength.

I felt myself drifting, fading, slipping, falling.

I passed out.

Recovery

Alarm shot through me when I awoke to find another face hovering over me. Who was it this time? Slowly I saw that it was Paco gazing down at me, smiling, a look of relief in his eyes. He was holding my hand. He leaned down and kissed my cheek.

'Thank god,' he murmured.

Yes, I thought, thank god, the universe, whoever, but where was I?

I looked around at the sterile white of a modern hospital room, at the drip stand by my side. Why was I here?

Memories returned, gradual at first, then in a gush and I was back in the grave I had unearthed in my patio, a grave of old bones, a grave I had dug for myself. I remembered digging, falling, no, being pushed in. Strangled. Then, nothing. All was blank. Had I been lying in that grave all night?

I couldn't have been unconscious for long. The flu still had me in its grip. My throat felt like someone had gone at it with sandpaper. My neck throbbed. Swallowing was agony. I moved and winced.

'You broke an arm,' he said.

I did? How? I must have fallen on that boulder.

'I saw a ghost.' My voice croaked and was barely audible. 'So many ghosts.'

'Sh. Not now. You're safe. Olivia Stone was protecting you, I think.'

I groaned.

A look of concern appeared in his face. 'What is it?'

'Not Olivia Stone,' I rasped.

He seemed puzzled. We stayed together like that, with me lying on my back and him beside me, neither of us speaking. Eventually, I whispered, 'Who found me?'

'I did. The trip was shortened. I went to my apartment and found you weren't there so I drove to the house. It was before dawn, but I thought I would surprise you. Only, it was me who was surprised.'

Later, when I had gained some strength and felt able to sit up, I told Paco in short phrases the information I had been holding back for months. I owed him the truth. He listened with patience to my circuitous preamble, trying to make me stop for the sake of my throat, but I wouldn't. I told him it was important. Then, I came out with the first of my hard facts.

'Olivia Stone died in Bedford in 1897. I have a copy of the death certificate.'

A look of disbelief came into his face. Then he seemed confused.

'Then she was not a recluse living in Casa Baraso.'

'No, she wasn't.'

'That does not mean she didn't stay in that house.'

'There is no record of her ever having stayed there.'

'But the Stones returned to the islands twice on follow up research trips. They may have stayed at your house then. After all, they were friends with Marcial Cabrera of Tiscamanita and they called their home "Fuerteventura".'

I cringed. It was easier telling Paco about her death. 'They didn't. Paco, they called their house "Lanzarote". I should have told you when I found out. I can prove I am right. Aunt Clarissa did all the research.'

He looked crestfallen.

'Then that article was wrong,' he said slowly.

'I'm so sorry, but she never came to live here. She stayed in England with her husband and their three sons and she died at forty. Where's my phone?'

He passed it to me. A few swipes and taps and I showed him the Census entry and death certificate. It didn't take him long to assimilate the information. I thought he would have railed against the truth, but I had misjudged him. First, he scoffed at himself for believing the article and not fact checking. That was when I saw he wasn't as attached to his fantasy as I had imagined. The only elephant in the room was the one I had put there.

Then he laughed and said, 'It was fun while it lasted, I guess.'

'I don't follow,' I said coolly.

He cringed. 'I never really thought Olivia Stone had lived in your house. I just made it up to tease you.'

'You did what!' I coughed, wincing at the pain that shot through my throat.

'Take it easy,' he said. I settled back on my pillows and he went on. 'At first, I wanted to toy with you a little. Then I wanted to entice you. Without that story, you would not have bothered finding out about Olivia Stone, or her book. You bought into my theory and kept asking questions and I could hardly turn around and tell you I had made it all up. You would have thought I was nuts and I would have blown my ruse.'

'But you *did* have me thinking you were nuts.'

'The joke is on me, then. I didn't mean for it to get this far. After I took that photo of the woman in the partition, I had even started to wonder if I was right after all. I'm sorry, Claire, I never realised you were taking me as seriously as all this.' He gestured with my phone before putting it down on the bedside table.

'I am a serious person.'

'That I am discovering.' He smiled at me. 'And bull-headed.'

As a nurse entered the room, Paco kissed me goodbye and said he would be back to take me home.

The following afternoon, I returned to Casa Bennett, to a giant hole in the patio and a mountain of dirt beside it. There were men everywhere, packing up for the day. Seeing me arrive, Helmud came and told me the remains had been taken away for investigation and then they would be buried in Tenerife, where the family came from.

Paco already knew.

He had cut out all the press articles and I read them while he made chicken soup, glancing up now and then to watch him prepare it, marvelling at him marvelling at my kitchen. He was a delight to watch.

Later, Paco opened his laptop and paired it to my sound bar. He told me to listen as he put on a band called Taburiente. The music sounded as dated as the Cocteau Twins and I loved it. The vocals soared, the melodies were moving and evocative and I enjoyed knowing I was listening to local music for a change. The songs made me imagine the islands, the culture and traditions.

When the album ended I realised I hadn't told him the other news I had been holding back for months.

'I never did tell you about the weird lights I saw.'

He looked up. 'Lights?'

'That night when I came here to see if there was an intruder. After that guy, Cliff, had his tools relocated. I was about to leave when this weird light rose up out of the patio and started darting about. That one was red. Another light, blue this time, rose up out of the outbuilding I used for my rustic shower room. That light was crazy, zigzagging all over the place. It even bounced off my chest before zooming up to the sky.'

'That was months ago,' he said reproachfully. 'You were still renting that apartment. Why didn't you tell me?'

'It happened again. While you were asleep downstairs. Our first night together, it was.'

He looked at me with genuine regard. 'Astonishing.'

'What's astonishing?'

'That you, a foreigner, should have seen those lights.'

'What do you mean?' I said doubtfully.

'It's a local myth called The Light of Mafasca.'

'Another of your tall tales?'

'This one is real. Or at least, many say so. You can read up about it if you like.'

'Tell me.'

I waited while he gathered his thoughts.

'Legend has it, a group of shepherds were walking home after a long day in the mountains. Tired and hungry, they agreed to rest and make a fire and roast the ram they had killed that day. As they were collecting wood, one of the shepherds found a large wooden cross hidden behind a bush. He knew someone had died in that place.

'Now, firewood was hard to find, so as night fell, the shepherds decided to take advantage of the cross to feed their little fire, hoping to fill their bellies and get warm.

'When the flames had devoured most of the cross, a tiny light, little more than a spark, sprang from the fire and began to move among the shepherds. At first, they were puzzled. Then they were terrified. The light leapt around from one shepherd to another, as though it had a life of its own. And they realised it was the light of the soul of the person buried behind the bush. By taking the cross and setting it on fire, those men had disturbed that soul's slumber, destroying the only memory still linking the soul to the human world.'

'Are you saying those lights I saw were the lights of those ghosts?'

'Maybe. Or maybe they were the lights of an ancient soul buried on your property long before your house was built.'

'What happened to the shepherds?'

'They bolted in terror. Ever since, that restless soul, taking the form of this spark of light, appears to travellers passing through unpopulated areas around Antigua on dark and clear nights. Legend has it the light is bright and always has a strong colour – blue, yellow, green or red—and is similar to a cigarette alight in the dark. Sometimes, the light can reach a large size before returning to its usual small point. Everyone who has seen it says the light moves in an intelligent way as if it were conscious. It can stay still, or accelerate, all of a sudden.'

'So, it had nothing to do with the ghosts of the Baraso family.'

'No, other than that it might have been trying to warn you.'

I let it go. I wanted to allow Paco his metaphysical fantasies in the same way that I wanted Clarissa to have hers. After all, I could not quibble with them when I knew that the spirit world existed and if the terror of recent months had taught me anything, it was that.

Besides, I had made up my mind that I wanted Paco in my life as a fixture.

I was hesitant asking him to move in with me in case it dented his male ego, but a week later, when he told me the lease on his apartment would not be renewed, the owners preferring the temptation of the lucrative holiday let, I begged him to come and stay at mine. 'Until you find something else,' I said, but we both knew that was never going to happen.

Over breakfast the next day, we discussed the house and what I planned doing with it in the future. I still had no idea. 'Make use of as much of the space as you want,' I told him. To my ears, the remark sounded flippant.

He was tentative.

'Please,' I added.

'I can make use of your two dark rooms downstairs.'

'I thought photography was all digital these days.'

He laughed. 'I would love to have a dark room. And a studio.'

'Then consider those rooms yours.'

'Are you sure?'

'I cannot think of a better use for them.'

'That only leaves five vacant bedrooms.'

'I am not opening this house up to paying guests,' I said, all uppity and defiant. 'Besides, it will be good to have a couple of spare rooms for visitors.'

'Leaving three rooms spare.'

'A sewing room. A writing room. A painting room.'

'Are you serious?'

'Hell, I don't know. I don't see myself sewing or writing or painting but those are the sorts of things people do with rooms.'

'Or hold séances.'

'Séances! You are joking.'

'You are a medium. You just don't want to acknowledge it.'

I rebelled against the word, the concepts, the occult altogether. Yet he was right. Those ghosts had all communicated with me in the end. But I would not want to put myself at such risk and I certainly wasn't about to host ghost tours in my own home.

My arm was out of plaster when Clarissa arrived for Christmas. The broken radius was still giving me twinges, especially when I drove, but otherwise I was fine. The first thing she said when I met her at the airport was that I looked like a skeleton. I had lost two whole dress sizes since moving to Fuerteventura, but it took her a few moments to realise the implications of what she had said and we both laughed about it on the way to Tiscamanita.

She adored the house the moment I slowed to mount the kerb and pointed out the various features. By then, all the scaffolding had been removed, the building fully restored and painted and all that was left to do was erect a garage and work on the garden. Paco had finished repairing the wall at the back and we had begun marking out garden beds and planting up the areas around the house and barn. I had decided to leave the other two outbuildings for the time being, as relics of a long and disturbing history. They looked quaint now we were using them as infrastructure to shelter herbs and vegetables and fruit trees.

'I wasn't expecting it to be green,' she said, taking in the scenery as I showed her around.

'Sometimes it is. We've had some rain.'

'I can see why you wanted to come here. This is magnificent.'

'I'm glad you think so.'

We entered through the back door and, starting with the upstairs, I showed Clarissa around the house. She cooed as she entered each of the rooms, taking on all the details of the décor and furnishings.

'You have done a grand job, Claire, you really have.'

I swelled with pride.

'This room is yours,' I said. I'd installed her in the bedroom above the main living room. It was light-filled and looked out over the garden.

She swept her arms wide and said, 'So much space! You may have trouble getting your guests to leave if you put them in here.'

'You are welcome to be here for as long as you want.'

'That isn't what I was intimating, but I will surely be enticed to come back.'

It was a remark that made me glow inside. I led her downstairs.

'What's in here?' she said, approaching the original dining room.

'Paco's studio.'

'Better not enter, then,' she said with a chuckle. I took her through to the south-facing living room and as we sat down, Paco sung out from the patio.

'We're in here,' I called.

Clarissa stood and faced the door, her demeanour filled with anticipation. I watched them both closely as they greeted each other and I was relieved to see sparkling eyes and looks of real appreciation. Paco came over and kissed me as well.

'Wine?'

He withdrew from the room, appearing moments later with two glasses and a bottle of Lanzarote white.

'Are you not joining us?' Clarissa said, looking into his face as she took the glass he proffered.

'There are the groceries to unpack and the food to prepare.'

She shot me a look of amused surprise and I met it with a grin.

'You have him well trained, then,' Clarissa said once we were alone.

'He just does it.'

We sat back in our seats and soaked in the festive atmosphere. I'd bought a small Christmas tree and created a festive centrepiece for the marble coffee table. Garbed in a rich red skirt suit with matching scarf, Clarissa added to the sense of yuletide cheer. She ran her hand down the arm of her chair, admiring the fabric – it was a gold damask. She asked me how I was spending my days now the ruin was restored and I told her of my Saturdays at the library in Tuineje, where I sat chatting with ten others about computers and smart phones and other technology in a class designed to help rural women get to grips with the modern age.

'You could probably run the course,' Clarissa said.

'But I wouldn't want to. I'm having far too much fun getting to know everyone.'

We exchanged smiles. I had formed an especially close bond with Gloria, who enjoyed showing me off as the woman who had banished the Barasos. I was something of a local celebrity, although I had done nothing other than almost get myself killed.

The conversation drifted to my father, who we both agreed would never change, and on to my account of the tribulations of restoring a ruin, finally halting at the inevitable topic of the haunting.

'The thing that I ask myself is, why me? Why was I drawn to this house and why did all those ghosts appear to me?'

'That is a lot of whys and requires unpacking. To start with, you brought with you the anguish over the loss of your mother.'

'I never knew how much her loss affected me,' I said quietly.

'It was how you lost her.'

'I know.'

'And your unresolved grief connected you, made you a conduit for the anguish of the spirits.'

It made sense. Even my own reason couldn't argue with her remark. I didn't have a reply. I now had few memories of my childhood when my mother was alive. I could only hope more would return, one day.

She took a sip of her wine and gave me a sideways stare. Her face darkened.

'I did try to warn you when I read the astrocartography.'

'You never mentioned a thing about the spirit world.'

'I didn't want to scare you. And besides, you wouldn't have believed me.'

'I believe you now.'

She nodded sagely. 'You are a natural. I always knew it.'

'Paco says the same.'

'He's a good man.'

'You've only just met him.'

'I can tell.'

She probably could.

'We're producing a booklet on the story of this house,' I volunteered, explaining that it would be a keepsake, nothing more.

'It would interest a lot of people,' she said. 'You should think about a print run.'

Typical Clarissa. I supposed she thought I would include the details of the ghosts. She would be telling me to host ghost tours next. Thankfully, there were no ghosts in Casa Bennett, not any more, not since the bones had been relocated.

I wondered which one of the Barasos had moved my rocky memento, from the shelf to the floor, and from the kitchen cupboard to the front door. The mother, had to be. She had been trying to warn me, even protect me.

What about my own mother? Where was she – earthbound, or free?

The setting sun threw shafts of warm light into the room. I topped up our glasses and we sipped our wine and sat quietly in admiration. When it was dark enough, I went and switched on the lights. Clarissa changed the mood by getting up unexpectedly and walking out the door. Curious, I followed.

When I got to the doorway she was creeping across the patio.

Paco came out from the kitchen and we exchanged glances. I shrugged and followed her. He joined me.

By the time we reached the vestibule she had pushed open the living-room door. Paco was about to follow but I put out an arm.

Before long, she exited and stood at the bottom of the stairs. Her face wore a curious expression, part wonder, part astonishment.

'Those are the two rooms you inhabited when you first moved on site?' she asked me.

'Yes,' I said slowly. 'Why do you ask?'

She gave us both a devilish grin and said, 'We've got company.'

Dear reader,

We hope you enjoyed reading *Clarissa's Warning*. Please take a moment to leave a review in Amazon, even if it's a short one. Your opinion is important to us.

Discover more books by Isobel Blackthorn at https://www.nextchapter.pub/authors/isobel-blackthorn-mystery-thriller-author

Want to know when one of our books is free or discounted for Kindle? Join the newsletter at http://eepurl.com/bqqB3H

Best regards,

Isobel Blackthorn and the Next Chapter Team

Acknowledgements

I am enormously grateful to J F Olivares, a photographer and artist indigenous to Fuerteventura who I became friends with when I was first researching this novel and whose photos, links and stories of his island, along with our mutual affection for travel writer, Olivia Stone, proved a major source of inspiration. I share with Juan an enduring passion for the precious island of Fuerteventura, where long ago I almost lived. Through Juan's generosity and enthusiasm, I have been able to reclaim lost memories and capture something of the essence of an island that is too often known only for its idyllic beaches.

My sincere thanks to Miika Hannila and the team at Next Chapter publishing for having faith in my writing and nurturing its progress through to publication.

In my Canary Island series, I write from the perspective of tourists and British migrants (expats) but I always include a local character or two and I do my best within the confines of fiction to help raise awareness of the islands' special history, culture and environment.

Some historical notes: I would like to thank Susan Middleton and the 1841-1939 Beyond Genealogy Discussion Group of Facebook for helping me research Victorian travel writer Olivia Mary Stone. I am also grateful to Daniel García Pulido for his biographical article of Olivia Stone in La Prensa del Domingo, El Día, which can be accessed here - http://eldia.es/laprensa/wp-content/uploads/2015/02/20150215laprensa.pdf

There is a rule of thumb in fiction, it goes like this – If you want there to be a bakery between the butcher and the greengrocer, put one there. I've transplanted a magnificent building in La Oliva, Casa del Inglés, changed its dimensions and situated it in Tiscamanita. I kept the dividing wall, as it proved a major source of inspiration. The wall was built to separate the building in half as part of an inheritance. I also borrowed the fact that the owner of Casa del Inglés was reluctant to sell the ruin to local government.

About the Author

A Londoner originally, Isobel Blackthorn has chalked up over seventy addresses to date, in various locations in England, Australia, Spain and the Canary Islands. Elements of her extraordinary life have a habit of finding their way into her fiction, providing her with a ready supply of inspiration.

Isobel grew up in and around Adelaide, South Australia as a ten-pound Pom. It was in 1973 and she had just turned eleven when she discovered she wanted to dedicate her life to writing fiction. That was the year her parents owned a roadhouse with a pool table, a juke box and a pinball machine. The year she hand-reared a lamb and spent weekends on her best friend's farm. Isobel may have pursued her dream right then, but life had other plans.

Isobel returned with her family to spend her teenage years back in London, where she attended the infamous Eltham Green Comprehensive in the year below Boy George. Her creative passion was crushed in an instant and she endured years of relentless bullying.

When her family returned to Australia once more, Isobel stayed behind. By then she was a rebellious nineteen, and she went on to live wild and free through the 1980s. She first moved to Norwich, where she satisfied her creative impulses writing maudlin song lyrics inspired by Joy Division, and little bits of poetry. Her desire to write novels never went away but she lacked the confidence, the skills and that all too crucial guidance.

She soon moved to Oxford where she became a political activist in the Campaign for Nuclear Disarmament, often protesting at Greenham Common. She lived for a time in Barcelona, teaching English as a Second Language. After another spell in Oxford, she moved to a squat near Brixton in London's south.

From there she moved to Lanzarote, where she renovated an old stone ruin, taught English and mingled with the locals.

She never planned leaving the island of her dreams, but she fell wildly in love with a man who swept her away to Bali. When it slowly dawned on her that her life might be at risk, she hightailed it to Australia on a holiday visa and reunited with her family.

During all this time, Isobel was studying for her undergraduate degree with the Open University. She graduated with First Class Honours and not a clue what to do with it.

After that reckless decade, life took a sobering turn. Isobel became the mother of twin girls, and trained and worked as a high school teacher. Deciding teaching was not for her, she then undertook a doctorate. She received her PhD in 2006 for her research on the works of Theosophist Alice A. Bailey. After an interlude as a back-to-earther and a brief spell as personal assistant to a literary agent, Isobel arrived at writing in her forties. By then, her creativity was ready to explode.

Isobel's stories are as diverse as her life has been. She speaks and performs her literary works at events in a range of settings, gives workshops in creative writing, and writes book reviews. Her reviews have appeared in Shiny New Books, Newtown Review of Books and Trip Fiction. She talks frequently about books and writing on radio, in Australia, and in the USA, UK and the Canary Islands.

Isobel now lives with her little white cat not far from Melbourne on Australia's wild southern coast. In her free time, she enjoys gardening, learning Spanish, visiting family and friends and travelling overseas, especially to her beloved Lanzarote, an island that has captured her heart.

An avid storyteller with much to say, the author's professional ambition is to keep writing suspenseful novels set on the Canary Islands, interspersed with other works of fiction.

Books by the Author

A Matter of Latitude (Canary Islands Mysteries Book 1)
Clarissa's Warning (Canary Islands Mysteries Book 2)
A Prison in the Sun (Canary Islands Mysteries Book 3)
The Unlikely Occultist

You might also like:

A Prison in the Sun by Isobel Blackthorn

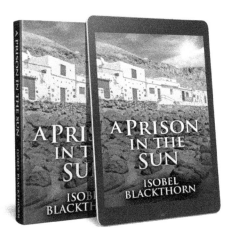

To read first chapter for free, head to:
https://www.nextchapter.pub/books/prison-in-the-sun

9 781034 270072